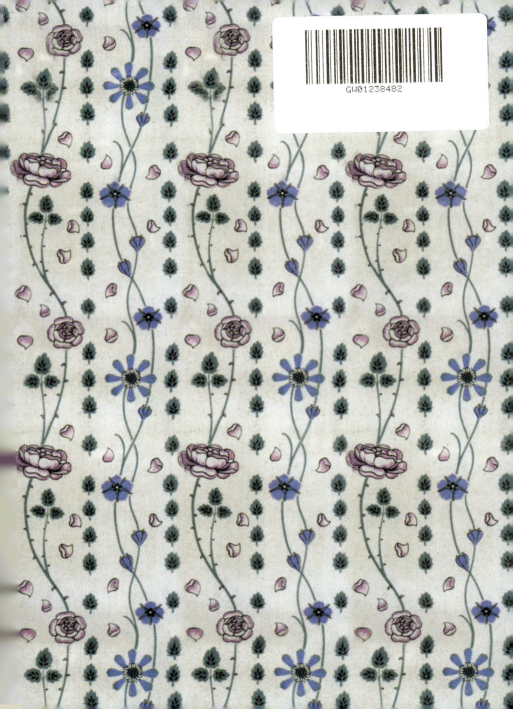

YOUNG ANNE

Persephone Book Nº 127
Published by Persephone Books Ltd 2018

© The Estate of Dorothy Whipple

Preface © Lucy Mangan

First published in 1927

Endpapers taken from a machine-woven silk and linen furnishing
fabric originally designed by Allan Walton in the 1890s and marketed
in 1925 as 'Summer Flowers' by Sundour. In a private collection

Typeset in ITC Baskerville by
Keystroke, Wolverhampton

Printed and bound in Germany by
GGP Media GmbH, Poessneck

978 191 0263 174

Persephone Books Ltd
59 Lamb's Conduit Street
London WC1N 3NB
020 7242 9292

www.persephonebooks.co.uk

YOUNG ANNE

by

DOROTHY WHIPPLE

with a new preface by

LUCY MANGAN

PERSEPHONE BOOKS
LONDON

PREFACE

It is an honour, but a bittersweet experience to be writing the foreword to the final novel by Dorothy Whipple to be published by Persephone.

No more – bar infinite re-readings of course – Dorothy Whipple! To reach the end of one of her books is bad enough. To be reaching the end of her work entire feels positively injurious to health. Even the most stoic among us, I'm sure, have spent too many wonderful hours with her to greet this news with perfect equanimity.

I have lived in *The Priory* with the Marwoods. I have been racked with worry *Because of the Lockwoods* and for all those who *Knew Mr Knight*. I have felt the joy of Jane's first pay packet and growing success in *High Wages*, while another part of me reveled just as delightedly in the perfectly-rendered details of a turn-of-the-century shop girl's life. And oh, the convulsive fear that gripped me throughout *They Were Sisters*, alongside awed admiration for the skill with which Whipple manages to evoke precisely the dread that stalks a household at the mercy of a violent man. The deep fires of hatred for Louise Lanier consumed me as ferociously as I consumed *Someone At a Distance*. They burn in me somewhere still.

And now we reach *Young Anne*. The first shall be last – this story of five-year-old Anne Pritchard growing to womanhood is Whipple's debut, originally published (after a chastening rejection by Heinemann) by Jonathan Cape in 1927, when the author was 34. 'This is the proudest day of my life!' she records in her diary. 'Mr Cape . . . showed me the Reader's reports. As I read about my extraordinary sense of humour and remarkable powers of characterisation, my face must have got imbecile in expression.'

As with most – all? – first novels, it is quite heavily autobiographical. Like Whipple, Anne is the youngest child of a respectable, middle-class Lancastrian family, sensitive yet unsentimental, and alert to the nuances of human behaviour, even if she struggles at times to understand their full meaning. Anne's impetuosity, leading to a variety of scrapes and quickenings of conscience, have near-exact counterparts in the early chapters of Whipple's autobiography *The Other Day*. Like Dorothy, Anne's first school is run by a pair of well-meaning unqualified sisters, the extent of whose desperate impoverishment is only discovered when – just as they did in real life – one sister dies of starvation and the other is removed to an asylum when her mind finally gives way under the strain of such chronic stress and suffering. Anne is then sent – although Protestant – to be educated at a convent school where the nuns find her more to be pitied than censured. All this is young Dorothy's story too.

In later parts of the story you hear echoes, perhaps, of

her own experience rather than direct depictions. She loses her first love, George, to circumstances, bad timing and their own immaturity rather than to the war as Whipple did her own fiancé, and marries an older man instead, as the author did (and seems to have been as happy with him as the suggestion is that Anne will be with her husband in the end).

The plot is slight – even for Whipple who was, as she herself said, always more interested in character than story, though of course the ability to limn a person's consciousness, and the careful truthfulness she brings to every situation they find themselves in, is exactly what makes her such a thumping good storyteller for all those readers who do not need a gunfight or explosion per page to keep them going. It is 'only' the story of a girl coming to womanhood, via very ordinary travails and the loss of innocence that growing up entails.

But because it is a Whipple, this is more than enough. Her craft might not be perfect in her debut – the pacing is maybe slightly off, and for me the ending does not quite convince, though I think this is more through underdevelopment rather than any wrongheadedness in the construction of her characters or events – but her art is all there.

From the tiny moments of perfect authorial character assassination – of Anne's querulous Aunt Orchard, 'she liked to destroy people's pet hopes, or at least scratch them a little in passing'– to the themes that arise in the telling of Anne's story: all that her fans (then and now) would come to know as Whipple hallmarks are satisfyingly present. Her anatomisation of class differences is already very precise, even – or especially – when filtered through the prism of little Mildred

Yates's understanding of the difference between her and her cousin George's 'social posishun' in Chapter Two, or funny; it's one of my favourite scenes in the book – not least because it also shows Whipple's dry wit, ending as it does with the note that 'Mildred was a very correct young person. She even ate jelly with a fork at tea.' Who cannot love an author prepared to assassinate small children as well as awful aged aunts?

In *Young Anne* Whipple also pays great attention to what would become the absolutely central concern to all her work: the differences, large and small, between male and female lives. Henry, Anne's father, is not monstrous in the way – say – Geoffrey is in *They Were Sisters* – but his (rarely improving or beneficial) presence and mood dominate the household as a matter of course. The lack of consideration given by her parents to Anne's desires (unlike her brothers, she is shipped off to stay with awful Aunt Orchard when her father falls ill) and her education is in marked contrast to the reverence with which George's mother treats 'the gift of a son', as she pays extra to have noted in the *Bowford Weekly News* at his birth. 'A gift to be paid for in sacrifice and denial of self. . . . How she would teach him! How nobly she would rear him!'

The dignity offered by work and the liberation of a personal pay packet is of course explored in far more depth in *High Wages*, but it has its first celebration here in Anne's delight at her first job – 'magic word to unemancipated femininity; the abracadabra, the open sesame!' Opening the inaugural monthly envelope, 'she felt a sudden unlocking and a letting in of air on her old unhappiness.' These are the Whipple moments I most love: the recording of women's experiences and reveling in their triumphs. As Anne peers in at her four pound notes I feel I am peering down the line of distaff history, connecting those first moments of independence (even when your dependence had previously been invisible to you) wherever women have found them, and finding a link through the ages. And the long-standing housemaid and pseudo-mother Emily lending her the money to do the secretarial course that has resulted in Anne's independence is an incidence of another of Whipple's more covert themes – the shadowy network of ways in which women help each other to bypass a system set up to oppress them and circumscribe their options. Gloriously satisfying stuff all round.

And naturally her unmistakeable voice is already there. The book that would start her on her career as a novelist (it got good reviews and sold well) is written with all the sense of command and restraint that her fans (then and now) would come to know and love so well. The temptation of the debut author is to overwrite – to show all that you can do, all at once and repeatedly, so that people Get The Message. We have all read them and been exhausted by them. But Whipple, from the off, keeps her ego and her insecurities in check. As in all her later, more experienced works, she is not a showman but a patient, disciplined archaeologist at a dig, gently but ceaselessly sweeping away sandy layers of human conventionality and self-deception, and on down to deeper pretences to get at the stubborn, jagged, enduring truths about us all beneath. The maddened fury of Vera – a beauty trapped in an unsatisfactory marriage and losing the looks that attracted flirtations and made life bearable – as she casts about for the best way of despoiling 'the cool youth of her cousin', and the brutality of the verbal blow she throws, is so brilliantly executed that you gasp when it lands. And there is a world of heartbreak evoked in Whipple's few neat lines of description of one of the young novices in Anne's convent – '"Come and talk to me," she called all the time. "Do come and talk to me!" She was like an affectionate young calf, ungainly, with great soft brown eyes. You felt she would suck your fingers if you'd let her.'

And, above all, the indescribable magic, the elusive alchemy all writers aim for but do not always secure, infuses the whole: it is, like all her books, not only a fine collection of cleanly-pared prose, deft portraits and exquisitely-rendered truths, but compulsively readable. It has been said many times of all her other books, be they novels, short stories, her autobiography or her diary *Random Commentary*; and it is as true for *Young Anne* as it is for any of them: once started, you simply cannot put a Whipple down. Most of us reading this will have proved this empirically for and to ourselves – but to anyone coming to *Young Anne* as their first DW, I will simply say: first, welcome! and second – learn from us. Clear an afternoon. Buy cake. Make tea. Declare yourself not at home to family or callers, settle down and enjoy.

However, if all this is true, we must turn once more to the vexed question of why our beloved Dorothy, wildly popular in her day (*High Wages*, her very next book, sold thousands of copies and ran to at least a dozen editions, and several of her others became Book Society Choices and/or were made into films, which also brought her fame across the pond) does not now sit in her rightful place with the greats. In calling her 'a novelist of true importance', Hugh Walpole evidently thought she would, and deserved to, endure. So why has she not? Why is she not as commonly known as John Galsworthy or John Buchan? Or if we stick only with female novelists, why has she never been (widely) rediscovered and rehabilitated like Elizabeths Bowen, Taylor and Jane Howard or Barbaras Comyns and Pym? It can't simply be a matter of having the wrong forename. . . .

There are a million overlapping filters that stand between an individual's work and its mass and enduring popularity. One is fashion. Possibly Dorothy Whipple's greatest strength is the fact that she is a born storyteller, with that aforementioned alchemical gift of making the reader simply have to turn the page, whatever the increasingly clamorous calls on her time. Possibly you are a better mother/wife/person than I am, but if I have misjudged how long a book is going to take me, children go unfed, calls unanswered and clothes un-ironed until I am DONE. And I include in that the time necessary for luxuriating in the afterglow of a good read.

But good storytelling – like plotting – has long been unfashionable, despite its being what first drew us out of the stone age shadows and round the firelight to share our knowledge, experiences, culture and – eventually – ourselves.

Narrative has been described by literary scholars and increasingly by those working in neuro- and cognitive science as 'a primary act of mind', meaning that it is a structure we instinctively impose on events. If we experienced them as the (mostly) random happenings they are, and appreciated their meaninglessness and our own insignificance (people are just more scattered data points across an uncaring universe), we would go mad. Stories save us. Links, causes, consequences – they matter because we are blind to the truth that most of them are essentially mythical. Stories keep us sane – they keep us going, they keep us motivated and, when written down, they keep us turning the page.

Why good, properly constructed ones have, then, begun to be looked down on over the last few decades is a mystery. Perhaps it derives from a misguided belief that it is easy to do, or a feeling that by this stage of our literary history we should have moved past all that primitive stuff. Or maybe it is another manifestation of the subtle but pervasive belief that 'proper' books – that literature– should be difficult enough to keep the riff-raff out.

This is not Whipple's ethos. She is endlessly accessible. You are drawn in, not kept out, and invited to linger over the rich feast she sets before you.

But alas, not only was Whipple foolish enough to be a brilliant storyteller, she was also foolish enough to be a woman. The biases against women novelists (you can take the word 'novelists' out of this sentence of course, but let us stay for reasons of time and practicality within these set confines here) within a male-dominated literary establishment (and you can take the word 'literary' out here. . . .) are too well-known to be repeated. Suffice it to say that although she had several contemporary male champions – Walpole, as noted, but also JB Priestley and HG Wells – she is one of many whom the bastion entire failed to embrace. No one thing is fatal to an author's longevity, but this will certainly affect your odds.

And then, counter-intuitively, there is the fact that she is a female author who doesn't write quite like readers (or The Bastion) expect a woman to write. Her central characters are female but the male ones are also fully-realised, not ciphers. And I wonder how many people have come to her over the years expecting a stereotypically feminine account of the emotional encounters and inner lives of characters – full-blooded, sprawling, a safe venting between covers of things inexpressible in real life – and been slightly discombobulated by Whipple's understatement and slight detachment from the proceedings she is conjuring into being? I wonder how many readers she lost through confused expectations? (Of course I wish to rise immediately to our heroine's defence and cry: 'Who needs readers like that, so easily confounded and put off! A plague on all their phonograph/DVD-filled houses according to era!' But sheer weight of readerly numbers affects one's chances of entering permanently into the collective consciousness and, obliquely, the canon. The odds are, once more, against her.)

Another handicap, perhaps, is the very source from which – I think – that understatement and detachment springs: her northernness. Whipple was Lancastrian born and bred. In *The Other Day* she describes the 'stern, steep, stone cottages . . . in a bleak row' along with a chapel, a shop and a school across the road. 'Man's mental and physical needs were recognised with his spiritual needs in the upper village, but, as they say in

Lancashire, "Obbut just". There was no excess.' 'Obbut just.' No excess. Either of these could be the Whipple writing motto.

Northerners (I speak as the offspring of two ex-pat Prestonians, though as I am reminded repeatedly at every family gathering, I myself have had the misfortune to have been born in London. I contend that this gives me a useful insight into both northern and southern camps. My family contends that it is saying exactly this kind of thing that proves I am a southern ponce. Anyway. On we go) are not needy, and Whipple is not a needy writer. Even in *Young Anne*, there is no sense of a young writer eager to please. She has written what she wanted as well as she could, and her side of the bargain is complete. She is content now to wait for the reader to fulfil his or her part of the contract, make the minor imaginative leaps required, and come to her.

The Bastion, of course, the Establishment, is southern. And as it is a self-perpetuating entity that habitually recruits in its own image, this is another barrier to Whipplonian entry.

Will Whipple ever get her due? There are reasons for both optimism and pessimism. On the one hand, in politics, in art, in entertainment, and in a culture increasingly dominated by online clickbait and so on – understatement, detachment, cool appraisal and anything that looks like a middle way is as unfashionable, if not more so, than it has ever been. Stoicism too is on the skids. On the other, there can be no doubt the fashions are fragmenting, and the old power-centres and their monopoly on the arbitration of quality and taste are becoming decentralised. It is becoming ever easier to spread the word and to find other people – around the world if need be – who share your passions. When niche authors' niches start to join up, it can quickly develop into rather a nice-sized mansion. A Saunbyesque Priory in which we can all live happily ever after would be nice.

But then there is the question of that thing Whipple over two and a half decades, from *Young Anne* to *Someone at a Distance,* delineates and dissects so beautifully: female experience. Moments like Anne's bitter comment as she climbs the stairs at her marital home before tea – 'I feel as wild as a Pendle witch. And I must sit by the drawing room fire and eat a poached egg on toast at a little table' (which has its mirror in *Random Commentary*'s comment by Whipple that 'I would have liked to hit him [husband Henry], but had to sit alongside smiling, as wives do') – still by and large pass unrecorded. Our lives, compared with the detailed, dedicated recording of men's, remain an under-explored, under-appreciated hinterland, one still too often dismissed by reviewers and those charged with documenting humanity's history. They are still too often of the sex that does not truly recognise the truth of that image of turmoil trammelled at a little table, and they cannot feel its power.

I would like to hope that the current wave of feminism we are riding will mean a renewed interest in those who have been charting women's lot in the past, so that we can fill in and take strength from our history, but we will have to see. Nevertheless, as the new feminist movement starts to take on a proper shape and to become a genuine force, so do my hopes for Whipple and other forgotten female novelists; because who better to sustain us than a woman who starts from a position of disbelief that 'the world of men is so different from the world of women. It is a wonder they speak the same language or even understand one another' and sets out to examine and make that difference comprehensible to all.

To read Whipple is to realise how much we as women, regardless of individual age or collective era, had and have in common, and to see how much and how little has changed over time. To read any of her accounts of the accommodations made in marriage, for example – whether arguably reasonable, like Anne's or Celia's in *They Knew Mr Knight*, or poisonous like Charlotte in *They Were Sisters*, or simply blindly reactive as in *Someone at a Distance* – enables you to look again at your own and others' and compare your modern lot. You may find yourself grateful or horrified by what you find, but it will be valuable – and fascinating – either way.

One last ground – albeit a rocky one – for optimism: Dorothy Whipple first found her audience in a time of upheaval, beginning with the Depression and on through the Second World War and its aftermath. Perhaps our volatile times will send us back to her and her ilk, with a renewed appreciation for the power and the importance of story and instead of an appetite for exotic tricks, one for clarity of expression, for a calm, searching intelligence that is never without compassion and for someone who despite her own clear moral precepts nevertheless seeks to delineate our inner lives and pose questions rather than impose answers.

Maybe this is, at last, her time.

Lucy Mangan,
London, 2017

YOUNG ANNE

CHAPTER ONE

§ 1

The Pritchards were in church, the church of St Jude. They
stood in their own pew, No. 14, looking rather like a gate; Mr
and Mrs Pritchard the posts at each end, joined together by
the little stakes between, which were Gerald and Philip and
Anne.

Nearest the painted pillar, which was like a stick of
chocolate at the base, and a roll of heaven, all blue and stars,
at the top, Henry Pritchard, very straight and thin, joined
with the Psalmist in cursing his enemies in a way only possible
on the Sabbath. He wore a grey suit, a wing collar and a black
tie, and looked what he was – a respectable dyspeptic solicitor.

Next to him, Gerald carefully rolled a pear drop in his
mouth, tucking it under his tongue now and again to raise
his clear pipe in case his father should suspect anything.

'Ah . . . ah . . . ah . . . ah,' he sang, the abundant juice of
the red and yellow delicacy not allowing him to articulate
further.

Philip eyed him in disgust. He thought him deceitful.

Mrs Henry Pritchard's prayer book sagged in her hands. She looked, though indifferently, at Mrs Bramwell's new hat in the pew in front.

Anne alone, not being able to read, was freed from any appearance of devotion. She stood with one foot forbiddenly on the other, both hands on the top of the pew over the toothmarks she made during prayers, and scrutinised the congregation with serious grey-blue eyes.

Anne at five was indescribably endearing. A small, sweet wild-rose thing. Her hair came diffidently out in tendrils of gold, curling outwards and inwards, this way and that, trying to make a softer thing of the stern sailor cap that proclaimed itself 'Indomitable' above her childish brow. Her folded mouth had, for the moment, the gravity of the very young.

She gazed at Aunt Orchard's pew under the pulpit. Aunt Orchard was her father's aunt, which made her seem very old. She had a face like a cat, complete even to whiskers. She looked like a cat mewing when she prayed; her lower jaw opened and closed. When she was pleased, Aunt Orchard narrowed her oblique eyes and stretched her long, thin mouth. She seemed to purr when she sat by clergymen at tea. Not beautiful Aunt Orchard, but much respected in the parish of St Jude; a great friend and admirer of the Reverend William Archibald, and the giver of the reredos, the East window and part of the pulpit in memory of her husband, Ephraim Orchard.

Anne did not linger over Aunt Orchard. She was not good to look at like her niece, Vera Bowden, who was over on a visit from Birmingham with her new husband. Vera Bowden was a dream of beauty this Sunday morning in spring; dark lashes lowered over blue eyes, a red, red mouth, an exquisite lace frock, gold bangles and pearls and a wide hat with a nodding pink rose. She raised the dark lashes slowly and smiled across at Charlie Brookhouse, to whom she had once been engaged. Charlie Brookhouse coloured furiously and turned away. Vera lowered her lashes again, but her smile lingered. She moved her hand, with its new wedding ring, along the pew-top until it was so close to her husband's that he covered it with his.

The thin little thing shrinking out of sight at the end of the pew was Jane, the maid. Aunt Orchard always took the maid to church on Sunday mornings. The maid didn't seem to like it much.

'What if we brought Emily,' thought Anne. 'Who'd cook the dinner?'

A sudden vision came upon her of the dinner Emily would now be cooking. Her small nose went up with an ecstatic sniff, but drew in disappointingly the characteristic church odour of pitch pine and hassocks.

For lack of something better, she gnawed the end of her glove finger until her father leaned forward and removed it from her teeth.

Her eyes wandered again. There was much to look at in church.

The Yateses, for instance. Henry Pritchard had remarked, only yesterday, that they were making a great deal of money out of cotton. They looked like it.

Mr James Yates was a small and highly-polished person. He had a neat, round stomach festooned with gold watch chain, which reminded Anne of the looped railings round the bandstand in the Park.

Mrs Yates was a fine figure of a woman, with bust and hips encased in an expensive silk dress. She wore a feather boa and tight white kid gloves.

Between them was their one ewe lamb, their adored daughter Mildred, of Anne's age, elaborately dressed in pink silk. She had bobbing dark curls, and wide-awake brown eyes. Her behaviour was decorous in the extreme. She made believe to sing out of a prayer book like a grown-up person. Anne caught her out when she was rounding her mouth to make a word that was not there, the psalm having ceased. Anne smiled. But young Mildred Yates did not smile back. She did not think it was the thing.

At the end of the Yateses' pew was a boy, some years older than the girl. He did not seem to be of the Yates family, yet in some way connected with it. Anne felt something different and aloof about him. She did not know it was his celluloid collar, his ill-made suit, the way his hair had been shaved behind and left long in front in the manner of cheap barbers that set him apart. Anne was vaguely sorry for him, though he was not attractive, with a bony, hooked nose, incongruous in his child's face, and a short, scornful upper lip.

Like a covey of birds settling to ground, the congregation knelt to pray. Anne hurried to join them, and to indulge in her favourite occupation of digging her teeth into the soft wood of the pew-top. A paternal hand reached across the boys and gave her a stern squeeze on the shoulder. Startled, Anne applied herself to the service.

She thought the Vicar and the people were very polite to each other.

'The Lord be with *you*,' said the Vicar.

'And with *Thy* spirit,' replied the people.

Then they were not so polite. In fact, to Anne's mind, they indulged in an unseemly struggle for the attention of God.

'Endue Thy *Ministers* with righteousness,' said the Vicar for himself.

So the people cried for themselves:

'And make Thy chosen *people* joyful.'

Then they came back to polite ways.

'Oh, Lord, save thy *people*,' said the Vicar kindly.

And the people, equally kindly:

'And bless thine inheritance.' Which evidently referred to the Vicar, Aunt Orchard's friend.

The service went on. The loud voice of the Reverend William Archibald in the pulpit did not interfere with Anne's musings on Vera Bowden, Mildred Yates, the queer boy, angels in the windows, recurrent visions of dinner.

At last she slid to her feet for the final hymn. To her delight, she knew it by heart. Emily Barnes had taught it to her.

'There is a green hill far away
Without a city wall.'

She didn't know why a green hill should be expected to have a city wall. But she sang it so heartily and so sublimely oblivious of time or tune, that again the paternal hand

reached out and restrained her. She fell abruptly from the
pinnacle of joyous abandon into shame and silence. She
threw her hair forward to hide her face. From under it, she
looked to see if Mildred Yates and the boy had seen the public
rebuke.

She cooled her cheeks in her kid gloves for the last prayer,
then, lost in the skirts of the congregation, moved out of the
church.

Outside in the blowy, fresh air, Henry Pritchard turned his
sallow face on his wife.

'Olive,' he said, 'Anne behaved very badly in church. It is
quite time she had sense enough not to bite the top of the pew.'

'Well, I can't help it,' returned Olive.

Henry Pritchard was doubly annoyed. With Anne. With
Olive. Really, women! . . . Even when young.

He stalked with stiff, long legs, his lips drawn into creases
of disapproval. Anne, running a little to keep up with him,
looked anxiously into his face now and again.

At the garden gate, Olive Pritchard paused.

'There's an hour before dinner. I think I shall go on to the
Broad Walk.'

'Very well, Olive,' said her husband, still with pinched lips.
'But Anne cannot go.'

'Oh, well,' said Mrs Pritchard, moving off with rustles. 'She
can set the table for Emily.'

Anne, her head low, followed her father along the asphalt
path and the house swallowed her up.

Emily Barnes, extremely red in the face, was bustling
about the kitchen.

'What's to do as y'aven't gone with your mother?' she inquired.

'I bit the pew,' confessed Anne, with reluctance.

'Wot – again? Deary me, ther'll be no church left soon,' said Emily cheerfully, rushing to retrieve a golden tart from the oven. 'Eh, by gum! But that's 'ot. Take your 'at and coat off. No. Not on that chair, thank you. Take them upstairs. When 'ull I ever learn you to be tidy?'

'Father's cross with me,' volunteered Anne.

'Never you mind, love. Put it down to them sausage 'e 'ad for breakfast. Poor thing, I wouldn't 'ave 'is stomach at a gift. Now run along, and get your pinafore and come and 'elp Emily. You can scrape the dish I made the cake in. I've saved it for you.'

'Oh, Emily,' Anne glowed. 'How lovely!'

'Better than pew, anyway,' said Emily, wiping her brow with her apron.

'Now get it done before Philip comes in,' she admonished Anne, who lingered over the licking of the wooden spoon, whereon the cake mixture clung in yellow deliciousness. 'I've 'ad enough with them pains of 'is. 'E eats too much, that's what's the matter with 'im.'

'That cupboard in his room's got gingerbread in it,' Anne said.

'Aye, and 'e takes all the cream off the milk when I'm not about to stop him.'

'Ooooh!' Anne put down the spoon at last. 'It was so good, Emily. Why do you have to cook cakes? I'd rather have them raw. I'm glad I bit the pew. I'd rather be here with you than on the Broad Walk.'

She clasped Emily's print knees.

'Bless me, you're going to 'ave me down!' cried Emily, 'Cupboard love, that's what it is, go on with you!'

'Emily, you won't ever leave, will you?' Anne besought earnestly.

This threat of Emily's, evoked by storms in the Pritchard household, was a bogy that returned to frighten Anne at intervals.

'Leave?' said Emily, freeing herself to baste the hissing roast of lamb. 'Nay, I don't know what to goodness would 'appen to this 'ouse if I left.'

She experienced a grim satisfaction at the idea of the house without her, but she had no intention of leaving it.

Emily Barnes, a small sturdy creature round about thirty years of age, with a chronic sniff that expressed in a remarkable way war and peace, scorn and sentiment, energy and lassitude as they occurred in turn in her life, Emily Barnes would have been lost, would not have stayed in a place where the mistress held the reins of the household in her own hands. Emily loved to 'manage'. It gave her a vicarious motherhood. She threw herself heart and soul into the Pritchard affairs. She had no real life away from them. She spent her nights out, rare and movable feasts, in looking round the shops, picking up a pan-scrubber here, a bit of streaky bacon there. Once a year, she took a week's holiday at Morecambe. Before she went, she talked a great deal about the grand time she was going to have stopping in bed in the mornings, and being free of the children, but she always came back with obvious relief, having, to all appearances, spent her time in collecting new recipes and tips for house-cleaning. Almost before she got her things off, she would wax lyrical about them.

'Eh, but I can't rest until I get that "Inamin" metal polish. It makes the taps shine that much, that when sun's out, you can't 'ardly bear to look at 'em. I went into Mrs Morton's kitchen yesterday and I was fair struck blind by her taps. They come at me like two sword blades. You just wait till I get a bit on mine!'

Or:

'Just a little 'armless-looking pad it is that you passes gentle-like over yer windows and before you can say Jack Robinson, all fog's gone – not a streak nor a smudge nowhere – and the windows looking as if there wasn't any glass in them at all. It's wonderful! I'm fair itchin' to 'ave a go at mine.'

And so she would talk while she unpacked the small Japanese basket hamper that contained all her worldly goods. She replaced on the dressing table the red plush box with a picture of Blackpool Tower and Wheel on the lid and the tin of camphor ice for her chapped hands, and with Anne hanging round to admire her strong, ribbed corsets and scalloped flannel petticoat, she changed into her 'black', and plunged again into her task of running the house, of keeping Gerald in his place, Anne out of scrapes, Philip from overeating, of coping with her mistress's indifference, her master's indigestion and his righteousness.

He passed through the kitchen now, and looking at the smoking tart on the table, inquired:

'I hope you didn't bake this today – Sunday – did you, Emily?'

'Oh no, only warmed up,' Emily lied cheerfully. Anything to please him.

'I wish I could have dinner with you in the kitchen,' said Anne. 'Why do we have to have dinner in the dining room and you have to have yours in the kitchen, Emily?'

'Bless my life, child, because you're gentry – better-end. . . . I don't know what, and I'm only a servant. But I wouldn't thank you to be in the dining room. I'd rather keep meself to meself in the kitchen, thank you.'

'I wish I could be in the kitchen with you and then Father wouldn't keep telling me not to frown, and I wouldn't have to eat fat. I wish I could be sick on the carpet like Philip did when Father made him eat vegetable marrow.'

'Now don't you be 'arbouring any such dirty notion,' cried Emily sternly. 'Giving me more work. Now, 'ere's your mother coming in. Just pop into the dining room with the mint-sauce, there's a love. Eh, it's Emily's grand little girl, isn't it?'

§ 2

The Pritchards' house was square and flat. It had no jut of door or window, and was like a face without features. The garden was square and flat too. Some sooty grass grew there, and a few rhododendron bushes rattled their stiff leaves. The air of cotton-spinning Bowford did not encourage flowers. Outside the low privet hedges, people were always hurrying to and fro, setting up a restlessness about the house. As early as five o'clock in the morning, Anne woke to hear the mill-folks clatter by in their clogs. In the winter when the street lamp was lighted, for some reason which she never understood, it threw their shadows in little on the bedroom wall, making a frieze of dwarf things hurrying round Anne's room. It rather frightened her.

Many things frightened her in this room. It was next to the bathroom, up a stair away from the rest of the house. All night long the water went 'drip, drip, drop' in the cistern. Sometimes she could not bear the small, ghostly sound. She got out of bed, then, and sat on the top of the stair. At first, she would not dare to go beyond that, because of her father. It was part of his omnipotence that he used to hear even her tiniest stirrings, and call out sternly:

'Anne, go back to bed at once!'

'But I'm frickened,' she whimpered, holding her cold toes in her hands to warm them.

'What on earth is there to be frightened of?' asked her father impatiently.

'There's all sorts of things looking at me,' she wailed. 'Weary Willie and Tired Tim and things.'

'Olive!' Henry Pritchard protested angrily to the recumbent figure of his wife, 'I absolutely forbid you to let the children have those vulgar comic papers.'

Anne, on her stair, wished this middle-of-the-night conversation could go on for ever. It was comforting to hear voices in the dark. But Henry Pritchard ended it by coming to carry Anne back to bed.

'Now, no more of this, do you understand? How do you think I can work if I'm disturbed every night like this?'

He put the little creature in her bed, covered her firmly and strode away – a grotesque figure in his long white nightshirt.

On the other side of the wall, the 'drip, drip, drop' began again. Sometimes Anne drifted off into sleep, sometimes she lay looking into the thick dark, full of moving things and creaks and breathings, until it became even more terrifying than her father. She then stole out of bed again. Holding her breath and her feet poised over each step, she crept to Emily's room, and found in the dark the friendly soapy smell and the friendly warmth that was Emily. Welcoming arms clasped the small cold body, and in them Anne curled up in happy sleep.

CHAPTER TWO

§ 1

The afternoon was long. Gerald and Philip were at school. Emily Barnes was busy turning out a bedroom. Anne wandered among the red plush of the dining room chairs, the red paint and green wallpaper. There was a faint smell of Father, a smell of cigars and tweed. Father was even in the air.

On the green chenille tablecloth stood a plant. It was new. It was exciting, with shining red berries and small pointed leaves. It meant, to Anne, that Christmas would soon be here. She looked long at it. Then she had an idea about it. One of her games was coming to her. The plant was a school, and the berries were rosy-cheeked children sitting on little green seats. She would be the schoolmistress. She flew to the bookcase, and picked, with care, the oldest book. She flew to the sideboard and found a bitten stump of pencil in the drawer. Chiding the children in a good imitation of her father's manner, she proceeded to pencil crosses with extreme earnestness and much licking from cover to cover of the old book. It had a musty smell, that book, and little brown spots in the paper.

The children on the green seats began to be troublesome. She smacked one offender smartly with her pencil. It rolled off its seat onto the tablecloth.

'You're so fat, Jenny Thistlethwaite,' said the teacher, 'that you bounce.'

'Now, Timothy Button, what are you doing?' She smacked him. He too rolled from his seat, and he, too, bounced.

'You naughty children!' cried the teacher. 'You naughty wicked things!'

Thwack, thwack! went the pencil, and pupils flew to right and left.

The dining room door opened, and Emily's hot face appeared.

'You're very quiet,' she said.

To Anne, kneeling on the table, pencil poised, the school with its red-cheeked scholars changed with terrible swiftness to the new plant completely denuded of its berries.

'Oh, my goodness me!' whispered Emily, her hand at her mouth.

They stared at each other. Anne's eyes appealed.

'Nay,' said Emily, 'I can't help you. Nay, you've done for yourself now. I can't do nothing.'

Anne, rather pale, climbed down from the table. The front door opened and closed. Her mother came into the room. She looked in her turn at the fallen berries – at Jenny Thistlethwaite and Timothy Button and the rest.

'Oh, you children!' she said in an exasperated voice, 'you ruin everything. Your father will be very angry. I haven't time to bother with you, you naughty girl.'

Anne stole up to her bedroom. She climbed into the wardrobe and shut the door. She liked to have the feeling of shutting herself into somewhere small. She sat in the dark, whispering to herself.

She heard the boys come in from school. She heard Emily call them to tea; rock buns and strawberry jam, they would be having. A few slow tears rolled down her cheeks. There was no handkerchief in the wardrobe, so she stretched out her tongue and licked them off. It was quiet and dark in her refuge, and by and by she forgot to be resentful and defiant, and slipped away into her favourite 'pretend'. She was a princess, though no one knew it. She had come to that house for a time, but soon she would go back to her father's kingdom. There she had a white horse with a red harness and a little baby so small that she could keep it in her pocket in a matchbox.

She was brought back to stern reality by her father's step in the hall. She waited with her heart banging against her drawn-up knees. There was an ominous silence downstairs. Then Gerald came clattering up, kicking the stair-rods as usual. He burst into her bedroom and called out, with cruel cheerfulness:

'Anne, come on! Father wants you, and you'd better hurry up, I can tell you!'

She clambered out of the wardrobe, and blinking like a little owl at the light, went down. She stood looking up at her father from between her tangled curls, her serious grey-blue eyes searching his face to see what was in store for her. He took her into the dining room and shut the door. He pointed to the stripped plant and to the old book, and asked her what she meant by it. Henry Pritchard was always strictly just. He allowed the culprit to state her case.

In a small, husky voice, she said she had been playing at school and hadn't 'membered it was a plant.

'You have ruined my most valuable book,' said her father sternly. 'You know I have forbidden you to touch my books. And you have spoilt your mother's new plant. You are a destructive, disobedient girl, and I shall have to whip you.'

She was chiefly conscious of the awful humiliation of the proceeding. It hurt her inside somewhere, she felt. Henry Pritchard was disconcerted as, fumbling with the door handle, she sent him a look startling in its revelation of her feelings. But he bolstered up his indignation by the sight of his book.

'My Boswell – ruined!'

He would have sworn, but for the fact that he never swore. He said, 'Upon my life,' or, on great provocation, 'Confound it!' but never 'Damn.'

§ 2

Anne was, unconsciously, working towards a climax. It came when Henry Pritchard sang in the drawing room. His wife played the piano, her fingers running up and down the keys, her eyes wandering away from the music. She was bored to extinction. By the fire sat Aunt Orchard, listening. She wore a green dress, and her long face took a green tinge from it.

Anne tiptoed into the room. She climbed on to a high chair, and tucking her feet under her, considered her father.

How funny he looked, standing there and letting such a noise out of his open mouth.

'Go – oo – ood night, love! Goo – oo – ood night, love. Oh, love, good night, goo – oo – ood ni-i-ight. D – e – e – e-er love, go – oo – ood night.'

Low down in herself, Anne felt a laugh beginning to bubble. She crossed her hands over it, and squeezed it in.

'Go – oo – ood night. Go – oo –'

Anne shook. Aunt Orchard turned to look at her solemnly. Like a pussy in specs, thought Anne. It encouraged her mirth.

'Go – oo – ood night –'

The laugh rose in her. She stuffed her pinafore into her mouth and doubled her legs tighter.

If he would only stop – just for one minute! She shrieked silently, rocking herself. She was done for now, abandoned, past all hope, carried off on such a gale of laughter as she had never known before.

'Tut-tut,' clicked Aunt Orchard.

Her father turned, and the song ceased suddenly.

'What's the meaning of this?' he demanded.

Anne, crimson in the face, could not answer.

'Leave the room,' thundered her father.

She uncrumpled and fled, still stifling her unseemly outburst in her pinafore.

Henry Pritchard was outraged. He was dumbfounded. The impertinence of the child to come in and laugh at his singing! To laugh at him!

Aunt Orchard looked up at him over her glasses. She hoped he would whip Anne with a good strap. Disappointingly, he stalked back to the piano. It would be undignified in him to be put off. He continued to bid the love good night, but it must be admitted that he was considerably shaken. Before the song came to an end, Anne's fate was decided. She must go to school.

§ 3

Anne was sent to a little school kept by two maiden ladies with no qualifications whatever. Boys were taught by Miss Janey upstairs, and girls by Miss Kate downstairs in a dark room overlooking a dismal backyard.

The big girls sat round the sides of the room doing nice things like stags and big and little dogs in charcoal, and embroidering table-centres. Anne, among the little girls, sagged on a bench in the middle of the room, and did straggling pot-hooks on a slate, and stitched in wool on cards. Sometimes she had to stand on a form and be called a dunce. She didn't mind much. It was better than doing sums, and people looked so different from a height.

Sometimes, monotony was broken by the arrival of Miss Janey from upstairs to say she couldn't manage Jack Baker, the biggest boy. Anne was intrigued by Miss Janey. Her teeth fell about so in her mouth, and she was so thin and flat, her skirts had to be pinned to her, back and front, to keep them from falling off. She had a stringy neck, and wisps of hair hanging down over her face. She looked as if she were on the point of bursting into tears.

Miss Kate was large and firm, and had a loud voice that

made Anne rumble inside when she spoke. The organ at St Jude's church did the same. When Miss Kate stalked upstairs, Jack Baker was soon subdued.

Anne did not like school much until, one morning, she found Mildred Yates had come to it. Mildred wore a sailor suit, too, but with a difference. Her skirt was pleated and flew out elegantly, showing a needlework petticoat beneath. Instead of the modest ribbon that tied Anne's blouse, Mildred wore a huge black satin bow, duplicated on one side of her bobbing brown curls. She wore white silk socks, four silver bangles on one wrist, two on another, and a gold ring with a blue stone on her finger. Anne thought her very fashionable.

Mildred looked very important as she frowned over her slate, counted on her fingers, rubbed out and put in, tossing her curls backwards and forwards. It was not for a long time that Anne discovered she was rather stupid at lessons.

Mildred's behaviour in school was correct in the extreme, but at break in the backyard, she showed she could jump about and play as well as anybody. Anne liked her.

'Will you come to tea on Saturday and bring your paint-box?' she asked.

'I don't know,' said young Mildred. 'P'r'aps if your mother wrote to my mother, I might be able to.'

Anne, instructed in etiquette, persuaded her mother to write, and Mildred went to tea. When they settled down to paint wonderful ladies with triangular skirts and round busts, Anne remembered a question she wanted to ask.

'Who's that boy that sits in your pew?'

Mildred blushed, and wriggled on her chair.

'It's my cousin,' she said reluctantly.

'What's his name?' pursued Anne.

'George.'

'George what?'

'George Yates, of course.'

'Does he live with you?'

'Oh, no!' Mildred was indignant.

'Has he got a father and mother?'

''Course he has.'

'Why don't they come to church?'

'I don't know. We don't see them much . . . only George.'

'Don't you like them?' persisted Anne.

'Well, you see . . .' Mildred was embarrassed. ''Course I'm only telling you because you're my friend. . . .'

Anne glowed.

'You see, they're very poor, and they live in King Street and they haven't got a maid or anything, and mother says they're not in the same so – social posishun' – she balked at the word – 'as us, and mother does wish George would get some better clothes to sit in our pew with. Isn't it awful for us?'

Anne stared. She had never heard of social position. Mildred, who was the daughter of her mother, had to explain.

'But he can't help it!' said Anne indignantly. 'How can he buy new clothes if he hasn't got any money?' she asked.

'Well,' said Mildred, rather sullenly, 'he shouldn't come and sit with us then.'

'But wouldn't you let me sit with you if I had old clothes on?' questioned Anne and hung breathlessly on the reply.

'Oh, you! It 'ud be different,' said Mildred.

Anne was relieved, but puzzled.

Mildred was a very correct young person. She even ate jelly with a fork at tea.

CHAPTER THREE

§ 1

Anne could read. She had a book of her own, an *Illustrated Child's Bible*, a present from Aunt Orchard. She went to bed with it and got up with it. She read it while she put on her socks, and when she went downstairs to be done up at the back by Emily, she kept on reading the *Child's Bible*. It was about her friend Jesus. Jesus had always been her great friend. She played with him. When her mother's callers asked her what she had been doing, she mostly answered:

'Oh, just playing with Jesus.'

'How *sweet*!' the scented ladies would exclaim, and kiss her.

She couldn't see anything sweet about it. Jesus was a private, invisible friend of hers, that's all. God was Jesus's father. Anne sympathised with Jesus. She knew what fathers were, and God and Henry Pritchard had much in common. They were everywhere at once, and all-powerful.

There was a great deal in the Child's Bible that Anne, try as she would, could not understand. There was, for instance, Faith. Jesus said that if you had Faith you could move mountains. But Anne stood at her bedroom window all one cold afternoon staring at the scarred and snowy summit of Pendle Hill, and had nearly burst with the effort of faithing it away. No matter how often she shut her eyes and told it to go, when she opened them, it was always still there.

She asked her mother about it. Olive Pritchard, looking up from her novel, said that she supposed it was because moving Pendle Hill couldn't do any good. Anyhow, she said, she didn't know, and would Anne go away and not bother her.

Anne considered the matter of faith again, and planned to do a miracle that would do good. On Saturday afternoon, when Emily went to market, she went, too. She impatiently went the round of the stalls piled with shining apples, glowing oranges, tight round cabbages, until she came to the place where the Blind Man stood against the wall, and held out his tin mug to the passers-by. She darted away from Emily.

'Oh, please, Blind Man, bend down and shut your eyes, and let me spit on them like Jesus did, and then you'll be able to see!' she implored breathlessly.

'What's that?' he asked in a gruff voice.

'Let me spit on your eyes, like Jesus did, and then you'll be able to see!' she repeated urgently.

''Ere,' said the Blind Man loudly. 'A copper'll do me more good than any spit, young miss – and I'll thank you to keep your spit to yerself.'

The disconcerted Anne felt herself seized in the rear.

'Eh, dear me!' cried Emily Barnes. 'Whatever are you up to now? I can't watch you. Beg this poor man's pardon, now, and give him your Saturday penny.'

'But I wanted to cure him, Emily . . . you don't understand. I wanted to work a miracle!' protested Anne, as she was dragged away.

In the crowded car, wedged low down among people's knees, she pondered on the bewildering mysteries of Faith.

§ 2

Anne woke early one May morning. She had been dreaming about a fish, a silver fish swimming in crystal water. An affection for fishes filled her heart. She lay in a flood of sunlight, musing.

'I wish I had a silver fish in a glass jar.'

The wish gathered force in a way her wishes had, and became a most imperative need. Her thoughts ran rapidly up hill and down dale, searching for a place where a fish might be. She came, mentally, to the Corporation Park. To the stream in it. She leaped out of bed, and tore off her nightgown.

Of course, it was forbidden to fish in the stream. It was forbidden even to walk on the grass round the stream. But she really couldn't bother about that just now.

She dressed hurriedly. Oh, the blessed independence of being able to manage, more or less, your own buttons and tapes! She stole downstairs, waiting with bated breath over the steps that creaked. She expected every second to hear the voice of her father from the front bedroom. But it did not come. She crept into the kitchen, which looked strange, waiting there to be occupied. She took a glass jar and a piece of string. She opened the back door cautiously and went out into the morning, inhaling freedom as she ran.

The houses still slept with closed eyes in rows along the road. In the Park, the hedges and the grass were slung with cobwebs, all bedewed. Anne thought these cobwebs were perhaps the hammocks the fairies had slept in and hadn't had time to take down yet. She ran on until she came to where the stream came tumbling out of the lake under the jagged rocks known as 'Jeannie Greenteeth'. Anne shivered at the name. It gave her a picture of a hideous old witch who did not use a toothbrush. The stream was too boisterous here for fish.

'They'd be banged to bits,' said Anne. 'I must go further down.'

She flashed a look round for matutinal park-men, and ran down the steep bank. No one about. She had the world to herself, and the pink-and-white hawthorn blossom was thick on the trees and the laburnum dangled tassels of gold. Here was a quiet pool under a tree. Just the place where a silver fish might be! She lay down on the grass and peered into the water. The ends of her hair slid into the pool, her breath ruffled its surface. What a strange world was there under the water, green moss spread in waving patterns, silver bubbles coming up from nowhere, and under the roots of the tree, dim caves. . . .

'Oh! Oh!' Anne almost fell in with excitement.

From under the roots of the tree he came, her fish, as silver as could be. With trembling hands, she lowered the jar into the water. She was as careful as possible, but he saw it and flashed back into the caves.

'Oh, Jesus!' breathed Anne, 'let him come out again.'

In a moment, he poked out his nose and investigated with adorable tiny red eyes. But the jar was a good jar; it lay in the water looking like water itself. Deceived, he came right out. More; he came right into it! Anne, speechless with delight, drew him carefully up. She had him! Her silver fish in a crystal jar! Here was a fairy tale come true. How beautiful he was! More beautiful than the fish in the dream, because he had a red stomach, a beautiful bright red stomach. He was a prince among fish.

She scrambled up the bank and ran home, her wet hair dripping down her frock. It wasn't often, as she had realised in her short life, that you got something you had wanted so much.

Smoke was hurrying upwards from the home chimneys.

'I do hope,' said Anne, 'that Father's not up.'

Emily was frying bacon in the kitchen. Anne tiptoed up to her and whispered about the fish.

'Well, I never!' said Emily. She never lost her faculty of wonder over Anne and her doings. 'Look at your frock! You'd better not let your father see that. Take that fish up to your bedroom? Well, I suppose so; better than cluttering up my kitchen.'

'Is Father anywhere about?' asked Anne apprehensively.

'I'll just see,' said Emily. She left the bacon, and went into the hall, humming loudly to prove her guilelessness. 'It's all right. Up you go, you young monkey!'

Anne scuttered up the stairs, making a storm in the jar. She gained the haven of her own room, and put the fish on the table by the open window. Round and round he swam in the sunlight. Anne doted on him until breakfast-time.

She was dreadfully startled to hear her father ask, in the middle of her porridge:

'What had you got in that jar you were bringing in this morning?'

She gulped.

'A – a fish,' she faltered.

'Where did you get it?' pursued the relentless voice.

The eyes of her mother, Gerald and Philip were on her. She was very uncomfortable.

'Out of the Park,' she murmured, shaking her damp hair forward to hide her face.

'The Park!' said her father, putting down his newspaper. 'But how? Where?'

'Out of the stream,' admitted Anne grudgingly.

'But do you know that is breaking the Law? Those notices telling you to keep off the grass and not to fish in the stream are there for a purpose. If every child in the town chose to go on the grass and fish in the stream, there would be no grass and no fish. Do you understand? The Park would not be worth going into. And you knew it was forbidden to take fish out of the stream, didn't you?' His stern eyes bored into her very soul.

'Yes,' said Anne miserably. 'But it's only a very little fish . . . I mean, it's not any good to anybody.'

She looked appealingly at her father.

'The size of the fish makes no difference at all. It is the principle of the thing that matters. She's quite old enough to understand these things, Olive,' Henry Pritchard explained reprovingly to his wife, who was reading her letters and taking no further notice of the affair. He turned to his daughter again.

'Therefore, Anne,' he concluded, 'you must go and put that fish back.'

Anne jumped up from her chair.

'Oh, I can't!' she cried. 'No, don't make me, Father – please! Please!'

'Stop that noise,' said Henry Pritchard sternly. 'Sit down at once. You will do as I tell you.'

'Oh, Father!' Her mouth turned down ominously at the corners.

'Not another word,' said her father.

She sat struggling with her tears.

'She looks like a frog,' remarked Philip with detachment. 'Doesn't she, Gerald?'

Gerald scrutinised his sister's grimacing face.

'Just,' he said.

Anne tried to drink her milk, but her lips trembled so that they shook the glass away. She slid from her chair and ran to cry in Emily's apron.

Later, looking, from weeping, for all the world as if she had the measles, and still hiccupping from sobs, she took the fish in his jar and made her bitter way to the Corporation Park. The High School girls stared at her, so did the Grammar School boys, the girls from the County School, the hordes of children going to St Jude's, St Mary's, St Martin's. She threaded her way through them, because it had to be done.

She reached the Park, and took the secluded path where the trees made a low canopy overhead and shut her away from an unkind world. She felt beaten quite flat with woe. Gazing her last on the adored fish, swimming so beautifully in the crystal water, she lifted her foot to step over the peaked stones on to the grass.

'Hullo! What's up?'

She turned. There in the middle of the path, like an apparition, was the boy out of church, George Yates, with his school books under his arm, and the ridiculous striped cap of the Grammar School on his head.

Anne looked at him out of her painful eyes.

'I've got to put this fish back,' she said hoarsely. 'I took it out of the pool this morning.'

'Why have you to put it back?' asked George. He was a big boy; quite eleven.

'My father says I have to.' An unexpected sob came up and hiccupped her again. She was annoyed. Her weeping was over and done with. It had no right to 'repeat' as Emily said about onions.

'I say, cheer up.' George Yates considered her with anxiety.

Anne's face puckered again.

'But I do like this fish,' she gulped, holding up the jar, and gazing at it with flooded eyes.

The boy stood, frowning in thought.

'Look here!' he cried suddenly. 'There's hundreds of minnows in Arley Brook. I'll go and get you some on Saturday. How's that? I say, give me that fish. I'll go and put it back for you. You keep cave.'

She looked round for 'Cavey'. Perhaps it was a dog? Perhaps it was his lesson books? She was still looking for 'Cavey', when George reappeared on the path. Snatching up his books, and, surprisingly, her hand, he hurried up the leafy path.

'I say, I've got to sprint. I'm going to be late. You know, when you've got a scholarship, you've never got to be late. You always must be there to shout 'sum to your name. 'Course, me being at the end of the alphabet gives me a bit more time. But, you see, if you're late, it means an impot, and impots lead to getting your scholarship taken away. You've never got to have a lark, or anything like that. It's rotten. I say, cheer up about that fish. You've got to remember that it's a lot happier in the pool.'

Anne smiled with stiff and salty lips.

'Oh, yes,' she said, 'I never thought of that.'

'And I'll get you another on Saturday.' He was all big-brotherly kindliness and cheer. 'Where 'ull I bring it to you to?'

'Our house is Merlewood, Barden Road,' said Anne, her tongue loosed. 'And I know you. You sit in church with Mildred Yates, and your name's George Yates.'

'Well!' George Yates looked at her in amazement. 'Fancy you knowing all that about me, and I knew nothing about you. What's your name?'

'Anne Pritchard, and my brothers go to your school.'

'Not Pritchard G and Pritchard P?' he asked.

Anne nodded delightedly. It was nice to establish connections with this boy.

But George Yates's face went dark. He looked sullen.

'Don't you like them?' Anne peered up at him in alarm.

'Oh, they're all right, I suppose,' he assented. 'But I say, about this fish. I'll put it behind your garden gate, when it goes dark. That'll be best. I mean – save a lot of bother that way. They'll only come round asking a lot of rotten questions, and I'd have to kick them perhaps, and ten to one I'd get my scholarship taken away. Not that *I'd* mind. Jolly relief it 'ud be for me. But it's Mother – she's so set on it. Crikey! There's the first bell! I must sprint. 'Bye, and cheer up! Fish in jar behind garden gate on Saturday night. 'Bye!'

He was off, in his ridiculous striped cap, with his hair sticking up in a stiff stubble round it.

Anne felt warm and comforted. George Yates was kind. He was the nicest boy in the world. She had had an adventure and another was to come. A fish behind the gate on Saturday night! On her dusty slippers, she sped like the wind up the hill to school. Miss Kate had already put out her slate with a long division sum on it. Anne was soon involved in lessons, but her mind kept flying back to the precious secret of the encounter with George Yates in the Park.

CHAPTER FOUR

§ 1

Olive Pritchard was annoyed. She had been comfortably settled with a book by the drawing room fire, revelling in the fact that her husband was at the office and her children at school, when who should come in but Aunt Orchard, smelling of piety and cleaned gloves. And no sooner was Aunt Orchard settled, with her bonnet strings undone, to a long, disapproving account of how Vera Bowden was leading far too gay a life in Birmingham with a motor car, and dancing and – actually – horse racing, than another ring came at the front door bell, and Emily Barnes almost pushed into the room another visitor:

'Mrs James Yates.'

Olive Pritchard stared. To what, her eyebrows asked, was she indebted for this visit.

Mrs Yates, fluttering with feathers, and smelling, in her turn of skunk furs (everybody smelt of something today, thought Olive Pritchard testily) – Mrs Yates advanced, holding out her tightly-gloved hand.

'I hope I am not intruding, Mrs Pritchard, but my Mildred and your Anne are such friends, and Mr Yates thought I might call to discuss a little matter Mr Yates and myself have in mind.'

She paused, still in the air, so to speak, and waiting for Mrs Pritchard's approval to come down.

Olive Pritchard murmured and moved a chair forward. She was furious with the woman.

So was Emily Barnes. Tea to be got, and her in the middle of ironing, and of course, no cake! People always came calling when there was no cake.

'Oh, that's Emily's good girl!' she called out to Anne, dawdling in from school with Mildred Yates at her heels. 'You've saved my face. Just run to Miss Slater's for a jam sandwich. There's your friend's ma in the drawing room.'

'Oh, Mildred, your mother's here,' cried Anne. 'Fancy that!'

The two children stood looking at each other as if some sort of a miracle had happened.

'Now, go on for that jam sandwich,' urged Emily.

They sped away, bouncing in their rubber pumps like very light balls over the white flags, to Miss Slater's shop smelling of hot bread and spice. They came sedately back, Anne holding the jam sandwich, swathed in tissue paper, carefully on her upturned palms. She felt suddenly solemn with happiness. The grey November sky pressed down on the roofs; everything was sharp and clear in outline. People were buttoned up in their coats, calling out to each other that it was blowing up cold. In the kitchen, Emily Barnes clattered the

cups, got out the best teaspoons, swore at the blunt bread-
knife. In the drawing room was Olive Pritchard, an unwilling
hostess, Aunt Orchard eyeing the silks and prosperity of Mrs
Yates with disapproval, and Mrs Yates talking, talking as if she
would never stop. She had come to say, it appeared, that
she did not approve of the school up the hill.

'So old-fashioned, Mrs Pritchard, and offering none of the
accomplishments. No elocution, no dancing, no music. Mr
Yates and I are at our wits' end. We don't want to send Mildred
to the High School. You know they have scholarship girls
there, and we don't want Mildred to mix with those sort of
people.'

Heavens! And the woman's husband had been a weaver!

'We felt sure you were feeling the same about Anne.
They're growing into big girls now – nearly ten. And we wondered if you would consider sending her to a boarding school
at Southport – Briarholme – the one Lady Brasher's girls go to.
I don't know anything about it, but if Lady Brasher's girls go to
it, it must be all right.'

You could see she adored saying 'Lady Brasher', and the
prospect of having Mildred at the same school filled her with
delight.

Anne and Mildred edged into the room. Mildred was
crushed against the maternal silks in a passion of love. Over
her curls, the maternal eyes asked Olive Pritchard and Aunt
Orchard if this was not certainly the most adorable child in
the world. They got no response from either.

'I mean,' resumed Mrs Yates, taking her tea from Anne's
careful hand. 'You do want a girl to be able to play a piece on

the piano if she's asked, don't you? And you want her to speak good English. I always try to speak correctly myself, Mrs Pritchard.'

Olive Pritchard wondered where she had heard that Mrs Yates was having elocution lessons. She believed it. The woman managed her mouth consciously, twisting it round her neat false teeth, filled here and there with gold to make them look real.

'And all this at the High School about Euclid and algebra and Latin and science, what's the use of it? That's what I want to know. It's not going to help the girls later, is it?'

'Suppose your girl doesn't get married,' croaked Aunt Orchard. She did not hold with Higher Education for women, but she liked to destroy people's pet hopes, or at least scratch them a little in passing.

'Oh, well. . . .' Mrs Yates didn't like to say, but she looked upon the thing as impossible. Her Mildred, with such eyes, such hair, such skin, and such opportunities. . . .

'Even if she doesn't, Mrs Orchard, she will always be well provided for.' How nice to be able to say that! 'But I want her to be able to mix well, and she can't do that unless she is taught to dance nicely, and speak properly, and play a game of tennis, now can she?'

'I really don't know,' said Olive Pritchard, who could not see why she should be bothered by the woman's snobbery. 'I haven't given these problems my full attention, I'm afraid.'

Anne was drinking it all in. Mrs Yates made the future seem very dull. What about the farm she was going to have with Roger in Canada? What about the travels she was going to do? What about adventure? There didn't seem to be much adventure about dancing and playing the piano when you were asked, and speaking properly. Anne trembled lest she should be condemned to this. But her mother relieved her.

'I don't think my husband would care to send Anne to Southport, Mrs Yates. I really don't know what his plans are.'

'Very well,' said Mrs Yates, rising and seeming to breast, confidently, some social stream. 'I thought it would have been nice for the children to go away together. However, I shall send Mildred's notice next term.'

A greater one than she gave notice at the little school up the hill.

Something began to be wrong. Miss Kate's voice was less loud and the big bones of her face stuck out under the skin. Her eyes burned very bright in their sockets and frightened the children into submission. Miss Janey did not come down from upstairs now, and chaos reigned supreme.

Anne and Mildred wondered and grumbled with the rest. They grumbled because there were no new sewing cards or slate pencils, and because there was to be no Christmas party, with its vivid lemonade and cut-up bath buns.

'It's disgusting,' said Muriel Spencer, the biggest girl, at break in the backyard. 'Rotten little school! I don't know why I'm here. Fancy, slates! There isn't another school in England where they have slates now. And they don't know anything, these old maids. Why, every mistress in the High School has a degree.'

'Sh!' warned Anne, 'Miss Kate's by the kitchen window. I'm sure she's heard.'

'Hecky!' said Muriel Spencer. 'There will be a row!'

But there wasn't. Miss Kate went on in her strange, quiet way.

Anne was uncomfortable. What was it? What was it – in the room? Making itself felt above the squeak of the slate pencils?

One day, when the children came straggling up the hill, the school door was shut. A charwoman appeared from the back, and told them to go away. Miss Kate was ill. Whooping and cavorting, they rushed down the hill again, overjoyed to have a holiday. The school did not open again. Miss Kate died a few days later.

'She died of starvation,' said Mildred. 'Mother cried. She said we could have sent heaps of food – chicken and beef and bread and everything. Isn't it awful?'

Starvation! Miss Kate was dead of it, and Miss Janey was so weak and wrong in the head they had taken her to a Home for Aged Poor.

Anne wondered why starvation should be a thing to hide. Her imagination wrought painfully in her, and in the dark at nights, she saw again Miss Kate's burning eyes staring at the packages the girls had brought for lunch.

There was a gap in Anne's schooling. The old maids' school closed its blistered door for the last time in November, and it was not until after Christmas that Anne was to go to the Convent. It seemed to her that her father had chosen the Convent as a new kind of torture for her.

Aunt Orchard arrived to protest against this going to a Convent. Anne sat on a low stool, and stared from her mother to Aunt Orchard and back again. The name of Maria Monk was mentioned by Aunt Orchard, at which Olive Pritchard laughed. But Anne was filled with gloom and fear.

'It's Roman Catholic,' she said to Mildred, who was very important stitching red names on her underclothes. 'You know, Gunpowder Plot and bloody Mary and things.'

'How awful!' gasped Mildred. She had not much imagination of her own, but could always see when Anne showed her. 'I wouldn't dare to go.'

'It's like being thrown into a dungeon,' said Anne. 'I shan't enjoy Christmas a bit with this coming on me afterwards.'

She had no names to stitch on, or any preparation to make for going to the same school as the Brashers, so she took to scribbling in the boys' old exercise books with a stub of pencil. Things evolved – rhymes – tales. She discovered, almost unawares, a vast entertainment in her own imagination. It added zest to her days. Life took on deeper colours. The friendship with Mildred flourished; it meant walks into the country and secrets and dolls' weddings. But Anne kept her best behaviour for Mildred. Whenever she felt wild, she called for the boy next door, whose name was Roger Maitland. Together they worked off their wicked energy by ringing bells and running away, tapping at windows, tying adjacent doors together.

Oh, the joy of those dark nights when she stole out, evading even Emily Barnes, buttoned up crookedly in her old red coat, with a red tam stuck grotesquely on the top of her rakish curls, and whistled for Roger at the window where he did his home-lessons! The heart-beating fun of fixing a button on a stout pin to a kitchen window, and from a distance pulling at a string to make it tap-tap to frighten a super-stitious maid! Or of ringing a bell to make irate gentlemen beat the gardens for them! What hairbreadth escapes they had, when Anne flew on her lengthening legs and thought wildly as she ran:

'Ooooh, what if Father finds out!'

That put wings on her heels indeed.

CHAPTER FIVE

§ 1

Stiff in a new sailor suit, with a black pinafore and a pair of slippers in a bag, Anne set out for the Convent at eight o'clock on a January morning.

The tramcar was packed with men and women going to work. Most of them were ugly and pale, and looked as if they hadn't slept enough. They swayed helplessly to the car's movement, and their eyes glittered in the electric light. The conductor on the platform drank tea out of a can, and munched bread and bacon. Behind him, things loomed up in the fog and were gone.

'Convent,' called the conductor, and made a sign to Anne.

She extricated herself from her neighbours' pressing hips and, small, pale and timid, she alighted. The car careered on like an illuminated and precipitous caterpillar.

She stood before a door in a high wall that stretched to left and to right as far as she could see. She had a sick feeling and wanted to run away. But she had put her hand to the bell and dare not play her usual game with it. The door swung open. Anne, with beating heart, waited for someone to appear. No one appeared. A blackness of garden waited beyond. Hesitating, she stepped into it, and the door swung to behind her, like magic.

The bulk of the Convent loomed at the end of a long drive. It was punctured here and there by a lighted window. Snow outlined the ledges and roofs. It looked mediæval. Anne shivered. Her body mechanically bore her unwilling spirit to the house-door, and she rang another bell. Bolts were shot back, and into the outer dark was thrust a head bound in black and startling white. Anne was in a panic at the sight of it. But that unaccountable body of hers stood stolidly on the step and said 'Good morning'.

'Are you the new day-boarder?' asked the Sister.

Anne was immensely relieved to find she had an ordinary voice and used ordinary words. She had expected something sepulchral.

She stepped into an atmosphere of incense and beeswax. Walking warily as Agag over floors like glass, she followed the Sister. Saints stood in niches with flowers and red lamps at their feet. Nuns stood about with their hands in their wide sleeves as if they were muffs. They kissed Anne on both cheeks. She was awkward about the business and got her hat knocked off and bumped her nose on their bonnets. She was covered with shame about it.

Then floods of girls came down the corridors. Anne was whirled in among them, taken to class, given a desk. She was conscious of eyes, eyes, eyes on all sides. She felt terribly strange, and as if she were being held up to be laughed at. She buried her head under the lid of her desk and pretended to arrange her few belongings, until the click of the 'signal', a wooden contrivance by which Sister Julie of the Immaculate Conception attracted the attention of her class, brought her out.

The girls rose, Anne a few seconds behind them, said a Hail Mary and sat down again, Anne again a few seconds behind them. The first lesson was Catechism. Anne was completely at a loss. She sat with lowered eyes, listening to strange heavy words: 'Transubstantiation'; 'Extreme Unction'; 'Exposition of the Blessed Sacrament'; 'Holy Sacrifice of the Mass'. What did it all mean?

Again the signal clicked. Another Hail Mary and they were in the English lesson. Sister Julie, standing on a little platform, read Tennyson's 'Oenone'. The gaslight glinted on her round spectacles. Her mouth was almost as round as she turned out the words in an Irish brogue overlaid with gentility.

'My own Ay-own
Beautiful browed Ay-own . . .'

She said 'Ay-own' with great feeling all the way through.

The day dragged its length as if it were hurt somewhere, and could not hurry. Anne suffered agonies of newness. She stood up when she should have sat down, she forgot to end every sentence with 'Sister', she was in a fever to do as the others did, and at the exact time they did it, too, not always a minute behind.

Names were as strange as the catechism at the Convent. 'Juana', 'Gita', 'Delphine', 'Cecelia', 'Theo', 'Marguerite'. And the nuns: 'Sister Frances of the Angels', 'Sister Mary of the Nativity', 'Sister Evangeline of the Seven Sorrows'. Anne murmured them over to herself as they occurred during the day. They were like stories, she thought.

With a black veil on her head, she followed the school into chapel. She was weak with apprehension of not doing the right thing. But she found comfort and escape. It was like a dream of colour: blue of mosaics, gold of candles, scarlet of vestments, white and green of flowers behind a veil of incense. She did not understand a word of the service, but was warmed and heartened by it, and emerged from chapel more capable of meeting the critical eyes.

By horrid contrast came an hour in the great *salle*; where rows of girls on straight chairs, divided by glassy spaces of floor, studied under the hard electric lights, and where, at a raised desk, a patient nun sat and told her beads.

At half-past seven Anne was once more in the dark garden. She looked back at the Convent that had seemed so fearful in the morning.

'It wasn't bad,' she decided. 'Nothing to be afraid of really.'

She felt exhilarated by the discomfort she had gone through. She decided to walk home and spend her carfare on a meat pie. It was hot and the gravy ran down her new coat. She had an exciting sense of having started a new life away from the paternal eye at last.

Seeing on a door a bright bell, labelled 'Press', she obeyed and ran down the dark street with her old glee.

Anne felt important when she came home at nights to her solitary supper set out on a corner of the dining room table by Emily Barnes. She even acquired enough courage to talk to her father occasionally, as he sat reading by the fire.

'It's not an ordinary school, you see,' she explained to him. 'There are Spaniards and Irish and Scotch and French and Germans. And there's an old French priest who speaks so funnily and has hands that go in like dough when you touch them. He calls me "Pu-ure leetle child".' Anne pursed up her mouth to let the sounds out, and continued briskly: 'I thought he meant "pure" like the Virgin Mary. But he doesn't. He means "poor". But we aren't, are we? Well, not very, anyway. P'r'aps it's because I'm not a Catholic. They think that's terrible. Juana Montez said to me today in recreation: 'Do you realise that if you died today, you'd go to hell?'

Anne paused, fork in hand, to stare at the prospect of going to hell. She dismissed it as remote, and chattered on.

'They have a board up for things to pray for. And one of them is "For Protestants and other Heterics". Heterics are people who aren't Catholics,' she explained, perhaps necessarily. 'And there are lines of crosses against that. I think they're all going to pray for me. Now what would happen if I prayed for them to be made Protestants? God wouldn't know what to do with so many prayers sort of criss-crossing. . . .'

'That will do, thank you,' said her father, without looking up from his paper.

'Oh, dear!' said Anne to herself, and was silent.

She was absorbed into her new life; getting up in the dark, riding in the trams, recognising recurrent faces – the woman with a face like a frog, all merged into neck; the man with the thick face, who led, she was sure, a greasy life and liked fat pork with slodgy stuffing; coming home at nights down Penny Street with its pavement all orange peel and paper bags and wisps of straw through which girls trailed their feet and giggled backwards at young men guffawing in groups. There was noise and light and heat in Penny Street, and the smell of chips and fish. But none of it penetrated to the Convent garden, where in the spring evenings, the rooks cawed in the elms and the nuns walked round and round with their hands in their sleeves.

In the school, the strange people sorted themselves and took up their separate strings of life.

There was Sister Margaret, the novice, standing in the corridors.

'Come and talk to me,' she called all the time. 'Do come and talk to me!'

She was like an affectionate young calf, ungainly, with great soft brown eyes. You felt she would suck your fingers if you'd let her.

'Come and talk to me!' Every time you went down the corridor.

When she played with the little ones, she threw the ball about with more abandon than was seemly in a religious. And in a wind, she let her veil blow up and show the brown cropped hair at the back of her neck. The other Sisters always held their veils down with a hand at their waists behind.

'Oh, darling!' she said to you. 'Do come and talk to me!'

In the winter, her fingers were broken with chilblains and she startled you by crying: 'Oh, I am hungry.'

Sometimes, when Anne saw her from afar waiting at the corner to catch someone to talk to, she went round, and up the back stairs, feeling hard and cruel.

And there was Audrey, the head girl, with a cluster of curls like dusky grapes, and the grace of a wild thing. Anne had a secret passion for her, and Audrey, in her turn, had a passion for Sister St Philip, the music mistress. Audrey paled and flushed at Sister St Philip for all to see. She copied her handwriting, and hung about the corridors to open the doors for her. If you went at odd times into Chapel, there Audrey would be, her black veil on her beautiful head, making novenas, saying rosaries, doing mortifications for Sister St Philip's intention. It was a passion that wrung the heart of the school. For Sister St. Philip, walking with the dignity of a queen and the detachment of a saint, ignored Audrey Bush and her hot, earthly misery.

The months went by like a pageant at the Convent: Lent, solemn, with the saints in purple shrouds, and the school eating bread and treacle for tea and mackerel twice a week for dinner, fasting from chocolates and sweet biscuits, to break out into a tremendous gorge on Mid-Lent Sunday, and go back to asceticism again till Easter. Easter, with First Communions and lilies and white tulle, and Anne weeping on a back bench in chapel to be so shut out of the Roman Catholic heaven; May, all flowers and songs for the Blessed Virgin; the richness of June roses for the Sacred Heart.

A year went by thus, and Anne, growing long and lanky and her hair threatening to come out of curl for ever, left the charge of Sister Julie with her 'Houly Mother of God, and what will ye be after saying next?' and moved up to Sister Philomena, with a nose like the Caesar she taught, and a fondness for dressing little dolls.

'If your mother has any little pieces of silk and lace that she doesn't want,' she whispered to Anne, 'I should love to have them, dear child.'

CHAPTER SIX

§ 1

It was summer. Anne, with the awkward legginess of her fifteen years, sat in a sand pew under the green pennon of the Children's Mission. A spectacled young man in a Cambridge blazer arranged his fluttering hymn sheets on the portable harmonium. The morning was lovely. The flat sea curled into unbroken frilled edges on the yellow sands. Two little girls with exquisite limbs crouched in its shallows, looking up at their mother, standing huge, fleshy, squat, in her bathing costume above them.

'A Buddha and two beautiful human worshippers,' thought Anne, pleased with the picture.

Miss Eaves and the Rev Simon Hart turned their backs on it. They were annoyed that the fat lady should choose to bathe under the eyes of their young congregation. Those curves . . . you couldn't get away from them . . . most unseemly.

The service nevertheless began. They sang: 'Pull for the shore, sailor.'

Anne's attention wandered. She could see her mother's hat appear and disappear by the shops along the Front.

'Hope she remembers about the cream cake,' she thought.

She could see her father walking slowly up and down the Promenade, reading a newspaper. She wondered if he felt better. They had come for a month to Port Erin for the sake of his health.

The Children's Mission settled down again into the sand pews and followed the lesson in their halfpenny green gospels. Anne ran sand through her fingers and looked out over the sea. How calm . . . how vast . . . how lovely. . . . She was falling into a dreamy ease, when she became aware of a vague discomfort. Something was demanding her attention. She looked round. It was the eye – the dark, yearning eye of Miss Eaves.

Anne's little green gospel shot up before her face. Behind it she broke into a perspiration.

'It's my turn!' she cried prophetically.

The hour had come. The hour she had feared ever since her father had made her, with Philip, join the CM. She had seen the other girls taken aside, one by one, by Miss Eaves, and the boys, one by one, by the Rev Simon Hart, to have the state of their souls inquired into. And now it was her turn.

The beauty of the morning was gone. She was in a panic.

'What if I get up now and say I'm ill?' she suggested to herself. She felt ill enough. She looked round the edge of the green gospel. Miss Eaves was still looking at her.

'Oh, Lord!' she cried mutely, biting a worried finger. 'She's got an eye like the Ancient Mariner. I shall get up and rush away as soon as the service is over.'

She looked round wildly. Her father was walking up and down on the Promenade to the left, the sea coming in gently, inexorably on the right, and a horrid fate bearing down upon her.

'Oh!' said Anne helplessly. 'Why can't they leave me alone?'

The world seemed full of meddling people. You simply had no peace.

Miss Eaves was adored by the other girls. At picnics, at cricket, they crowded round her and hung on every word she said. In term-time, she was a schoolmistress.

The spectacled young man struck up:

'Oh, that will be
Glory for me.'

Anne stood up with the rest. Now was her time! Now she would escape! Miss Eaves no longer stared. Miss Eaves had moved. Where was she? A gentle pressure on her arm answered her. Miss Eaves was at her side. Miss Eaves had collared her.

The girls and boys stared at her. They knew it was her turn. Some grinned. In twos and threes they ran off. Anne found herself with nothing more companionable than the marks they'd left behind where they had sat.

'Oh,' she thought miserably, tracing patterns on the sand with her foot. 'Fancy having to talk about your soul here.'

People walked up and down the Promenade, bathers

padded down to the sea, children made sand pies at her very feet. It was disgustingly public.

She started like a nervous horse when Miss Eaves laid a hand on her arm.

'My child,' began that lady in a low emotional voice. 'Have you given your heart to Jesus?'

'Yes, I have,' said Anne loudly, as if she were telling a lie and meant to stick to it.

Incredulity and disappointment showed in Miss Eaves's face.

'When?' she faltered.

'Oh, a long time ago,' said Anne, with nonchalance.

'My dear little girl,' said the schoolmistress gravely. Was there, after all, a chance of saving a young soul? 'Your attitude is hardly – shall I say – reverent.'

To her own horror, Anne's chin suddenly gave way, her chest rose on a great heave, she burst into tears.

'Oh, why can't you leave me alone?' she shouted. She wrenched herself from Miss Eaves's gentle hands and, scattering consternation among the holiday makers, fled home.

But there was more to come. Emerging red-eyed and ashamed from her bedroom to go to dinner, she met Philip on the landing. There was something familiar and alarming in his eye.

'Anne,' he said solemnly, 'are you saved?'

'No, I'm not,' she snapped, 'so shut up!'

In future, she would belong, she determined, to the unregenerates among whom Gerald, cheerfully refusing to join in any 'pi stunts', was numbered.

Anne went cheerfully back to school in September, to be chilled immediately by the news that Audrey Bush was going to be a nun. She had returned to the Convent to go to Belgium with Sister Margaret, who was to take the black veil. Audrey went about the familiar corridors serenely; and now at last Sister St Philip took a little notice of her.

Anne had a hard, aching lump in her throat. She had wild notions of imploring Audrey not to be a nun, of seizing somebody and making them stop her.

'She's so young . . . she mustn't be shut up! Oh, think of it . . . shut up for ever! Never to be able to go into the woods, or sit in a field in spring. Don't let her do it! Don't let her . . .'

But she had to choke it down. No one looked at it like that at the Convent. Audrey had a vocation. The exquisite child was dedicated to Our Lord. She was going to take as a nun, it was whispered, the name of Sister St Philip.

The night before she was to leave for Belgium, Anne, from the dark garden, saw her at the lighted window of her room in the Chapel Wing. She was going to bed early to be ready for the long journey on the morrow. In a blue dressing gown she was brushing the hair that was soon to be cut off.

Anne, among the privet bushes, watched her. The lump in her throat broke. Tears came in a hot stream.

'It's wicked – wicked!' she sobbed, plucking at the privet leaves. She felt helpless, irritated, wretched at the inexorableness of other people's fixed ideas.

The light in the window went out. Against the dark square,

a white blur appeared. It was Audrey looking out. She stood a long time, unconscious of Anne crying in the garden below.

In the morning when Anne came to school, Audrey and Sister Margaret were gone.

§ 3

The world of school was the real world to Anne, but she was conscious of stepping in and out of another daily. There, her father still loomed in the foreground, a growing need on him of expatiating on the moral virtues to Anne and Philip. Anne gave him his due; she admitted that all he said was true and sound, but the effect was depressing.

He did not talk to Gerald in this heavy way. For his eldest son he had a smile that was somehow wistful. He loved him, and was afraid of him. He wanted to hold Gerald's affection and interest, and did not know, poor stiff creature, how to do it. He could only yearn over him in secret, and give him what money he asked for, and more.

He had never loved his wife as he loved his son. In his heart of hearts, Henry Pritchard thought women negligible. He had strong puritan ideas of what they ought to be, and as they rarely conformed to them, he thought them wicked or worthless. He thought their arms and legs and necks indecent. The sight of a woman smoking a cigarette made him flush all over his sallow face. He could not consider a woman as an independent being, he could only consider her as a wife, a mother, a sister, a daughter. And considered as such, his wife and his daughter had failed him. Anne had none of the tender filial graces. She seemed to get up and go away from him as soon as she could. And however he forced his ideas upon her, she mutely put them off and developed strange, stubborn ideas of her own.

As for his wife, he knew, and raged impotently, that she ignored him. Her indifference was almost superhuman. From her, Gerald had inherited that aloofness against which his father was helpless. And not only his father. People liked Gerald. People wanted him to like them in return. But no one could be sure that he did. Yet he had a fund of warmth in him. Sometimes when he thought he was alone, Anne heard him talking to Binny, the cat. She listened in amazement.

'Well, my little cat.' Gerald would rub his perfectly-groomed head against Binny's coat. 'My little puss . . . who's a beauty, then? Who is? Well . . . then . . . who likes its friend? Let's rub its chin for it. . . .'

Absolute rubbish he talked, and all in a warm voice Anne never heard him use to any human being.

With her, Gerald was cold and critical. At an early age, he had requested her to drop her habit of kissing him good night. No one must come too near him. He objected to proximity. Anne was painfully conscious that she was not as smart as the girls he knew, and whose photographs lay forgotten in his drawer. It made her awkward with him. On the rare occasions when he expanded and became almost genial, she felt a warm, woollen affection for him. She felt like a humble dog trotting at his heels. It was a feeling that disgusted her, and as she grew older her independence made her put an end to it by some cutting remark or other, at which Gerald raised his eyebrows in faint disdain and retired into silence. And so they reacted to each other in wretched fashion.

With Philip it was different. He would unburden his gloomy soul with the least encouragement, or even without it. He had minute manias, too, over which Anne and Emily Barnes joked in secret. He pretended to be able to tell when a boiled egg was more than twelve hours old, and would go to fetch the egg out of the nest himself so as to ensure its being fresh. He little knew that Emily Barnes ran out before him to pop an egg under a surprised and indignant hen. And in the mornings, another little comedy was often played.

'Is this this morning's milk?' Philip would inquire at breakfast.

'Yes, all this morning's,' Emily would reply cheerfully.

The milkman would suddenly and noisily arrive at the back door, in full view of the breakfast room window.

'I wish you wouldn't lie, Emily,' Philip said sternly.

'Oh, well, y' enjoy it so much more if you think it's this morning's,' said Emily, with a wink offside to Anne, 'so wot's the 'arm? It's my soul as 'ull suffer, anyway, so don't bother yourself, lad.'

But Philip would be furious and sometimes refuse to proceed further with his breakfast.

In the 'home' world, as distinct from the school world, Mildred Yates kept coming home from Southport for holidays, a little more finished each time. She was growing very pretty, and her bright eyes, bright lips, bright teeth gave her an air of extraordinary vitality. She was all flash and colour, all movement and dash; always ready, when asked, to jump up and play the piano, loudly and with great attention to time; ready to recite, with curving wrists and fingers, Irish poems, Cockney dialogues, Scotch ballads, all in perfect English; to dance, rather heavily, the latest dances. She was entirely the perfect product of the school where Lady Brasher's girls went. And yet there was something in her that remained unspoilt. She never lost her faculty of childlike wonder.

'Oh, Anne, look at this daisy! Isn't it perfect? Look at it – every petal tipped with pink. Isn't it wonderful that daisies should move their petals upwards and close at night?'

'Oh, Anne, do look at that tiny little bird in the holly-hocks. . . .'

'Where's your cousin, George?' Anne asked her. It was a long time since she had seen him with books under his arm, his bony wrists hanging out of his frayed cuffs, his eyes red-rimmed from studying.

'Oh, George? George has gone to Cambridge University. He won two scholarships. But' – Mildred lowered her voice – 'I believe it takes Aunt and Uncle all their time to keep him there. They are very poor, you know.'

Anne wondered, with the naïveté of youth, why Mr James Yates couldn't give his brother some of his money.

In this world, too, Vera Bowden burst on the town period-ically in all her beauty and fashion. She came to visit Aunt Orchard, who must, she said, be Kept Warm. She went to church and looked with scorn on Charlie Brookhouse, who had married a quiet little girl and had a son. She stared appraisingly at the growing Anne, and dismissed her as a badly-dressed, leggy creature, with good eyes that she didn't know how to use, and hair she didn't know how to do. Anne thought Vera a miracle of beauty and smartness, and was flattered when she was allowed to listen to accounts of the adoring men in Birmingham. She inadvertently put an end to these confidences. At the end of a description of the passion of a naval man called Stanley, she blurted out, with widened, grey eyes:

'But . . . but . . . I mean . . . you're married.'

Vera looked at her in cold disgust.

'You little idiot,' she said.

She did not discuss her amorous adventures with Anne again.

CHAPTER SEVEN

§ 1

Anne moved on up the school and came to the Senior Class, taught by Sister Mary. By this time her prize essays and English distinctions in the Oxford Locals had brought her considerable favour. Her essays were read in the lower forms, and her fastidious choice of the right word in Latin translations was the subject of conversation in the little room to the left of the front door, where Sister Superior received her French chaplain. In consequence, Anne suffered, at this period, from a slightly swelled head.

Her extreme ignorance of mathematics was even pressed into service to heighten her literary fame.

'Yes, one side of my brain is a blank,' she would say with complacency, implying that the other side was so brilliant that it didn't matter.

She fancied herself as an actress, too, and in the Summer Plays tore passion to tatters for the benefit of priests and nuns and girls, sitting with correctly-folded hands and feet. At least, the nuns and the girls sat like that, but the priests

managed to be delightfully masculine in spite of their cas-
socks, and their careless attitudes were a subject of much
pleasurable conversation in the Convent for days afterwards.

The passion Anne had felt for Audrey Bush was now felt
for her by several of the Juniors. They hung about the
corridors, and goggled at her. One wrote a verse, and lost it –
probably on purpose. It was found and brought to Anne. It
began:

'Oh, noble brow and dearest dark blue eyes . . .'

Anne said, 'What potty rot!' and felt obliged to point out to
the poet, who blushed to the point of perspiration, that her
quantities were wrong. But in secret, she was tremendously
flattered.

On First Fridays, the top of her untidy desk was littered
with holy pictures, inscribed 'To darling Anne, from her ever
loving little Carmen. PPM.' 'From Francesca, with much love.
Say a little prayer for me.' And so on. Names continued exotic
at the Convent, and never lost their charm for Anne.

Mostly, she was pleased to have adorers – 'cracks' they were
called at the Convent; but, at times, she discerned something
faintly sickly in the business, and made them cry by her cold
demeanour.

She was a variable creature at this age. She swung from
extreme dignity and conceit, to the shrieks and giggles and
pranks of a hoyden. She prided herself on being the best
long-jumper in the school. She always took the five steps up
to the Music Room in one bound, landing without a sound

under the very nose of old Sister Clare, who could not stand such shocks. It fell to the lot of this same poor nun, pursuing Anne into the refectory to make her sing a solo, to witness her leap out of the ten-foot window in a panic. Her leaping was put an end to, temporarily, when she tried to jump over a poplar sapling, but inadvertently sat on it and broke it. A bill was sent in to her father, and he was excessively outraged at her lack of decorum.

Although Anne was a power in the school, she had no real friend there. She was separated from real friendship by the fact that she was merely a day-boarder, and more than that, by the fact that she was not a Catholic. She herself was acutely aware of the gulf between herself and the others. At first she had tried to make herself one with them by procuring a coral and silver rosary, by wearing an immense crucifix on the green cord of the Holy Angels, but gradually she gave up the attempt to be included. She knew it was no good; gradually, too, she was influenced by their conviction that Roman Catholics only were heard by God. She said her prayers still, but was very unsure that they were heard.

At times, when she forced herself to think about it, she was utterly bewildered about religion. It was a surprise and relief to her to find that other people were, too. She first realised this from the girl – she was no more – who made her dresses. Letty Cox startled her by saying that she didn't believe Jesus was the actual son of God.

'No more than anyone else is the son of God, I mean,' she said, through the pins she held in her mouth.

Letty Cox was a member of the Workers' Educational Association, and a Fabian and other things that Anne had never heard of before.

'I don't know what to make of it,' said Anne, frowning.

'Neither does anybody else,' said Letty. 'Just turn slowly round till I see if I've got the pleats regular, please.'

'You know . . .' Anne struggled to put her thoughts into words. 'There are other worlds – aren't there?'

'Most probably. Stand straight for one minute, will you?'

'Well, what puzzles me . . . is that Christ can't have gone round to them all – dying to save them all . . .'

Letty passed her pricked hands over Anne's slim body, then shook her head with defiance.

'The God that wants his son to be sacrificed to appease him is no God of mine,' she said.

'Oh!' said Anne, shocked.

She thought about that. Her thoughts focused more intently on religion because she was being prepared for Confirmation by the Rev William Archibald, Aunt Orchard's friend. She plunged into the catechism and doctrine of the Church of England, and laboured with it. At the end of the course, the Vicar took the candidates one by one for a private talk, and Anne, miserably embarrassed, knelt on the drawing room carpet at the Vicarage, with her elbows in the plush of the couch, while the Vicar prayed in a low, hesitant voice. Anne did not hear what he said. She winced at the sight of the soles of his boots, and chattered wildly to herself: 'Oh, I wish it was over. Nobody should make you kneel in a drawing room and be prayed over. They shouldn't do it . . .'

The china clock between the china vases on the mantel-piece ticked the painful minutes away. Because he was ill at ease, the Vicar felt bound to prolong the prayer. At last, he said 'Amen', and Anne, avoiding his eyes, shook his limp hand and stole from the room with shame.

What had Miss Eaves on the seashore, and the Rev. Archibald in his drawing room, to do with God? Not anything. They could not help her.

She went home and closed the door of her room. She knelt by her bed and kept very still, waiting. She wrestled with her mind as if it were some stubborn and resilient obstacle that kept her from the realisation of God.

She heard the household go to bed. Noises died away in the house and in the street. In the stillness Anne struggled to grasp the fact of God. She was conscious of strange unknown forces. The mystery of life, of herself, was borne in on her. Gradually, the tension slackened; a wondering peace came to her.

'Is this . . . God?' she asked.

She was caught up into immensity; she felt a floating-out, a freedom. . . . Gradually, as it had come, the glory receded. She got up from her knees, tired but happy. She felt she had found God for ever.

But the wonder of the moment did not return. She expected a miraculous peace and change of nature to come to her at the laying on of hands by the aged Bishop. But, alas! at the solemn moment, she was chiefly conscious that he had pushed crooked the ridiculous head-dress provided by Aunt Orchard, and remembered uncomfortably how Vera Bowden had burst out laughing when she had seen her dressed for Confirmation.

She went home and took off her white dress. She was discouraged by the way the small, insignificant things pushed in and obscured the big, essential things of life.

§ 2

Anne's schooldays were drawing to an end. She found herself thinking:

'I wonder who'll have my desk. Who'll carry Sister Mary's books when I'm not here? I've been here six years, and now I am leaving.'

She wondered, too, how they would possibly get on without her.

It was borne in on her how she loved everything about the place; from the bulk of the building itself, sitting with its pointed roofs among the elm trees, down to the coiled wax tapers the nuns carried in tobacco tins, so incongruous in their virginal pockets. She loved everything; the fasts, the feasts, the old desks, the shining floors, the pianos, bad and good: old No. 9 with its keyboard like a set of defective teeth, maddening No. 2 with a touch like cotton wool. And the darling nuns, with their childlike gaiety, their sudden human weaknesses, their saintly unselfishness – how she loved them, and how she would hate to leave them.

She went about, remembering and regretting. It was nearly over. She was quite old. Seventeen.

Examination week came with its frets and fevers. Anne sat

for Higher Local, sent in blank mathematic papers, wrote reams on *Hamlet*, and was quite sure she had failed. A great upheaval followed – a grand clearing out. She took her books home in nightly parcels. Her desk was emptied at last. She went the round of the bare classrooms, round the garden. She embraced tenderly her weeping 'cracks', feeling grateful to them for loving her. She wept herself when the Sisters embraced her. Sister Superior talked to her solemnly for quarter of an hour, adjuring her to use her talent for the good of the world, as Dickens had done.

'See how dreadful he made drink appear, dear child. You remember his description of Spontaneous Combustion? Many people must have been saved from drink by the fear of such a terrible thing. Let Dickens be your model, dear child, and may Our Lord and His Blessed Mother guide you.'

Under the significance and the sadness of the closing of the Convent gates behind her, Anne was conscious of an undercurrent of excitement. The prologue was over – now for Life!

CHAPTER EIGHT

§ 1

Anne, wrapped in a pink sheet, sat holding her young neck stiffly while Madame Juliette made short, almost furious, dabs with a comb and hairpins at a strange erection which was Anne's hair being put up for the first time. Anne's eyes, a little startled, followed the operation in the mirror opposite; her cheeks were carnation-pink from the hair-washing. The atmosphere of scent and powder roused in her a longing for beauty, for adornment. She resolved to brush her hair one hundred times every night, and always do her nails when they needed it.

To the right and to the left of her sat Mildred and Mrs Yates. Mildred's hair was already done, and she preened prettily under the maternal eye. Mrs Yates liked to celebrate every event in her daughter's life, and the coiffing of Mildred was assisted at by Madame Juliette as High Priestess, with Anne as attendant, subsequently invited to undergo the same ceremony and to go back to tea afterwards at Whiteholme. The Yateses' house was probably called Whiteholme because the doors and windows were annually repainted white.

'Well, Madame Juliette,' said the fond mother. 'I've lost my baby today. My girlie has gone another step along the way. We shall have them both married before we know where we are.'

Mildred laughed self-consciously at herself in the mirror. But Anne moved a scared glance sideways at the speaker, without turning her head under Madame Juliette's fingers.

'Married?' she said. 'Oh, not yet! Not yet!'

Madame Juliette removed a hairpin as large as a tuning fork from her mouth.

'That's right, Miss Pritchard,' she said, with unexpected fervour. 'Don't you be in any hurry to turn domestic cat. There's more in life than marriage for us women, believe me.'

She went quite red over the mountain of Anne's hair. She wrote chaotic verses which appeared at times side by side with Anne's tales in the *Weekly News*. She believed that each soul had its affinity, and had hers in the shape of a little tailor in the shop downstairs. He was, of course, unhappily married.

Anne looked upwards through the mirror at Madame Juliette. She had been absorbed in having her hair done up, and thinking of Madame Juliette only as the instrument of doing it, and here she was establishing herself as a personality, thrusting herself in on Anne's consciousness. Strange how people were always doing that. Letty Cox, for instance, pinning up her dress and talking about God. Life was full of distinct, separate individuals pushing along in their own ways. Life was something thick, strong, pulsing.

Mrs Yates, bulging over the sides of a fragile chair, made a comfortable movement of her clasped hands on her lap – as if she were gathering closer all she had got. She smiled indulgently. These unmarried women were all alike; pretending they weren't married because they didn't want to be!

'Well, Madame Juliette, I hope my girlie won't get any of those sort of ideas into her head,' she said, smiling at Mildred playfully. 'I am looking forward to seeing her in a nice home of her own, aren't I, pet?'

Madame Juliette, a courageous soul, because it is bad for trade to snort at clients, nevertheless snorted. Anne remembered that she had noticed many times that Mrs Yates roused the indignation of what that lady lumped together and called the 'working classes'.

'A nice home!' said Madame Juliette, and bending low behind Anne's neck made a noise that sounded like 'My God!'

Mrs Yates put an end to the incident, which was growing impertinent, by saying:

'I think your hair will do now, Anne dear. You look very nice. If you will tell me how much you charge, Madame Juliette, I will pay you.'

By the act of paying, she asserted her superiority, and sailed away with the girls, top-heavy little craft indeed with their hats perched insecurely on Madame Juliette's coiffures.

At Whiteholme, tea, the usual Bowford high tea, was waiting for them. Mrs Yates took her place behind the massive silver tea-service and the Crown Derby cups and saucers, and Mildred and Anne sat down on either side of her. James, her husband, went to his place behind a dish of roast chicken and began with small, stiff hands, on one of which was a diamond ring, to carve. His wife watched him as she poured out tea.

She kept her seat with difficulty, and only did it because she knew it was not correct to go and carve herself.

'James, just a little breast for Anne. Now, now . . . you are sending all the best out into the kitchen! Give Milly the oyster. You know she likes it. Don't splash the cloth, dear . . .'

At last everyone was served to her liking, and she was half-way through her sigh of relief, when the dining room door opened abruptly, and a young man walked into the room.

'George!' cried Mildred.

Anne stared. It was a long time since she had seen George Yates. She was embarrassed to remember how the frank smiles of childhood had turned to the self-conscious evasion of eyes, and finally become a blank stare on her part and on his. But she was sure that it was his doing as much as hers.

'Anne dear, do you know my nephew?' asked Mrs Yates. She did not look pleased at the interruption.

Anne half rose. George nodded indifferently in her direction, and she sat down again, covered with confusion.

'Rude thing!' she thought. 'But I wish I hadn't got up . . . I shouldn't have got up . . . I should just have bowed. . . .'

She was humiliated to think she could never do the right thing.

George took a place at the table next to Mildred. Mr Yates, with a repressed sigh, took up the carving knife and fork, and again attacked the chicken under Henrietta's eye.

'And how is Cambridge?' inquired Mr Yates, naming the university with reverence.

'Still there, of course,' said George.

Mr and Mrs Yates exchanged glances.

Anne stole a look at George as he ate. His powerful hooked nose suited his maturer face; his upper lip was still short and scornful, and his lower lip full and turning down a little at the corners. He wore a suit of unfashionable broadcloth. His collar showed a rough edge, and his college tie was faded. He gave an impression of intelligence and a sort of bitter conceit. His crudity set the teeth on edge like a green apple. Yet he made the prosperous Mr Yates look ineffectual and a little silly.

He talked.

'I would have come earlier, but it's washday and I had mangling to do.'

Mrs Yates made a small impatient noise with her tongue.

'That is one of my accomplishments, Miss Pritchard. Are you any good at it?'

'Well . . .' Anne stammered, 'I haven't had much practice yet.'

'Wicked things, mangles, believe me. When ours gets a blanket in its jaws, it refuses either to disgorge or to swallow. It prefers to be dragged bodily round the scullery. Really it's a devil. No, Aunt, I can't mitigate that! It is simply a devil. I have threatened it with castor oil.'

'Come, my boy.' Mr Yates lifted a small, protesting hand. 'This is somewhat fantastic.'

'You're right, Father,' said his wife. 'It is fantastic.'

'And why not?' asked George, with an awkward laugh, and a hitch of his left shoulder in an inelegant shrug. 'But shall I change the subject? Shall I tell you about my shopping? I've been to the Market to buy a pot-posy. Do you know the genus,

Miss Pritchard? It's half a cabbage with a leek and a bunch of thyme and sage secured to it by wire. Its price is tuppence-ha'penny. You put the posy into a pot with a sheep's head and it comes out Scotch Broth.'

He rambled on. Anne was irritated, yet interested. Here was a type of young male she had not met before. She knew the dashing friends of Gerald, and the slow, solid kind of boy who alone could stand Philip, but she had not come across anyone like George Yates. He seemed, in spite of his gibes, to be galled by his own poverty. His conversation annoyed, extremely, his uncle and aunt. The comfortable atmosphere of the Yateses' dining room was disturbed. An awkwardness crept in. Anne was conscious that Madame Juliette's erection on her head had slipped forward. She grew hot at the idea of what she must look like. George Yates seemed to be rudely amused. After tea, she ran upstairs to Mildred's bedroom, pulled out the dozens of hairpins, brushed and combed desperately, twisted her hair up as simply as possible and came down again, still blushing.

'Oh, Anne!' reproached Mrs Yates. 'Why have you taken your hair down? It was so beautifully done. You should have left it, dear. I wanted you and Mildred to take it down very carefully and notice how it had been done, so that you could copy it.'

Anne blushed harder than ever. She didn't know why she had done it. Why should she care what George Yates thought of her appearance?

Mr Yates brought out the card table. He had taken it upon himself to teach the girls how to play Bridge. Under his tuition they became more muddled every time they played. George Yates played with his cousin. He ragged his uncle unmercifully, almost without humour. Mr Yates gradually assumed the appearance of a ruffled hen; his well-brushed strands of hair rose and fluttered; his moustache came unwaxed in his heat and straggled on his cheeks; his round bewildered eyes darted from his cards to his wife for comfort. He was pathetic, and Anne was annoyed with the tormenting George. The evening seemed long, and at half-past nine, Anne thought she would bring it to an end.

'I must really go,' she said.

'Aren't your brothers coming for you?' inquired Mrs Yates hopefully. She thought it would be very nice if Gerald and Mildred *should* . . .

'Oh, no,' said Anne, 'I'm quite used to looking after myself.'

'I'll take Miss Pritchard home,' George volunteered. 'I must be getting back to King Street myself.'

They went out into the spring night together. He hunched his shoulders and took long strides. Anne had difficulty in keeping up with him; but he did not notice. He had the pot-posy wrapped in newspaper under his arm.

'I used to know your brothers,' he remarked. 'Is Gerald still the superior person with a nice taste in ties?'

Anne thought he was impertinent. She began with heat to defend Gerald.

'Don't trouble, really,' he interrupted. 'I know it has to be done for one's family. But we'll take it as read, shall we?'

That seemed to give him an idea. He seized it with relief.

'Do any reading?' he asked.

And then they were fairly launched. They walked, talking like friends, his laugh rising close on Anne's. He loosened up and was natural at last. When he left her, he still strode buoyantly for a time, a reminiscent smile on his lips. But the nearer he came to his home, the more his cheerfulness drained away. He sighed as he opened the front door and went through the sitting room to the kitchen, where his father and mother sat reading.

'Well?' said his mother. 'Been to Uncle James's?'

She always asked him where he had been. She followed him with her eyes as he wandered restlessly about the kitchen, then she put her book aside and set about making the cocoa for supper.

Frances Yates had been a schoolmistress. She was a small, thin woman, with straggling sandy hair, and a raw look about the end of her nose and upper lip. Her pale blue eyes were visionary behind her glasses. She married late, and carried her schoolroom ideals into marriage.

'Plain living and high thinking, William,' she said to her new husband. He thought, quite without resentment, as he looked at her eyes through her spectacles, of water in a glass. 'That must be our ideal.' She had clasped her thin, red hands together; her wrists always protruded a long way from the cuffs of her shirt blouses.

'I'm afraid it is Hobson's choice for us, my dear,' he said. He had a little humour in those days of which clerking year in, year out in a solicitor's office, and a diet of weak cocoa and mutton and buttered teacake had long since drained him. 'Plain living it will be, because we can't afford anything else.'

And plain living it was at No. 6 King Street, one of a long row of dingy brick houses, each with a door and one window, complete with Nottingham lace curtains and aspidistra downstairs, and two windows with Nottingham lace curtains, but minus aspidistra, upstairs.

'I wish, my dear,' said William Yates, sighing, 'I had a better place to bring you to.'

'Oh, William,' said his bride, 'what do externals matter? I myself am heaven or hell. Do you know that quotation, William? It applies to me, dearest. I myself am heaven, and so are you.'

And so, for a time, they were. Especially when the baby arrived. The long agony over, the little schoolmistress lay in the iron bedstead, looking out over the backyards of Bold Street, whispering to herself: 'The gift of a son.' She had paid extra, though they could ill afford it, to have that put in the Births, Marriages and Deaths of the *Bowford Weekly News*:

'To Frances, wife of William Yates, 6 King Street, the gift of a son.'

A gift indeed! A gift to be paid for in sacrifice and denial of self. She saw that, and was inspired by the necessity of it. It was characteristic of her that she did not see her son as he was, a baby needing warmth and cuddling, but as he would be – a man, a great man. How she would teach him! How nobly she would rear him!

It was in this high spirit that she refused James Yates's offer to take George into his mills, when he should be old enough.

'No, James, I thank you very much,' she said, sitting in James's office in a scanty coat and skirt and a black felt hat which was, as usual, too far back on her head. 'I appreciate your offer, but I have other plans for my son. "Plain living and high thinking," James; that is my maxim, you know. I want George to go to a university. I want him to have the best, James. Not the best in the way you understand it, you and Henrietta, but the best in the intellectual sense of the word.' She pushed back a strand of light hair that had fallen over her face, and her nostrils dilated with earnestness and perhaps a little conscious superiority. 'And I feel, if I may say so, that he will not find the best in the atmosphere of a Lancashire cotton mill.'

James, though it might have been expected, was not annoyed. For he was a mild little man, and had, moreover, faint doubts at times that there might be – only might be – something lacking in the life of extreme comfort he lived with Henrietta. Whenever he tried to talk about the doubts to Henrietta, she soon explained them away, or reasoned him out of them. But now he remained looking consideringly at his sister-in-law. He waited, wondering if something were going to express itself in his mind at last, if at last he were going to get at what he felt.

Frances, far away in her dreams, disregarded him. The stirring in James ceased. Whatever it was, it had failed again.

'Well, Frances,' he said, troubled. 'You must please yourself, of course.'

'You have been very kind, James,' she said, rising. 'But I know I am doing the best for my son. I know he will thank me later for my decision today. Oh, James, he is such a clever boy already! I have great hopes of him, James, high hopes. Goodbye.'

When Henrietta heard, she tossed her head.

'She always was a fool,' she said. 'I told you you wouldn't get any thanks, James, and now perhaps you'll believe me. Well, it's all the better for us. We'll keep the place for Milly's husband.'

'Bless me, Henrietta!' gasped James, 'Milly's only ten. By the time she's ready for a husband, there'll be plenty of room for him as well as for George.'

'Never mind about that,' said his wife. 'It's much better to have it clearly understood that Milly's husband is going to follow you. Milly will feel then that the mills are really hers.'

She wanted Mildred to have everything; everything there was to be had, down to the last ounce.

§ 2

Anne closed her bedroom door at half-past ten in the morning, with a sigh of relief. Her household tasks were over. Henry Pritchard repeated daily that a woman's place was at home and that Anne must learn housekeeping. So Anne went round the rooms, dusting the tops of things. After all, nobody under twenty can be expected to dust under a sideboard. She picked up the boys' slippers and folded their pyjamas with indignation.

'Why should I, with a first-class Honours Higher Local Certificate and first in England with English distinction, come down to folding the boys' pyjamas?' she asked Emily Barnes.

'Go on, now,' admonished Emily. 'It doesn't take a minute.'

'It's the principle of the thing,' said Anne, stalking about the bedroom with dignity. 'Why can't the boys fold up their own pyjamas? Just because I am a woman, I have to wait on them. Yet I've got twice as much brain as both of them put together.'

'Yes, love,' said Emily.

Anne was, before Emily, insistent on her brain power. It was only when she was alone in her bedroom, sitting at the yellow oak desk she had bought with a guinea from a story published in the local *Weekly News*, that she felt a poor creature floundering helplessly in a sea of words, a sea of ideas – trackless, unmanageable.

On this April morning, a few days after the tea at the Yateses, she shut her bedroom door with the firm intention of finishing a story begun at midnight. She sat at the inadequate and beloved desk, searching for inspiration in the wallpaper, which was, in colour and pattern, like Edinburgh Rock, ginger flavour. The carpet was red with purple medallions. The room was quite ugly, but Anne loved it because it was hers. In it, as soon as she shut the door, she felt herself. It was a stage for her. There were nights when she stalked the floor, a candle from the pantry in her hand, and was Lady Macbeth in fierce undertones. Nights when, in her nightgown and flowers from last summer's hat, she was Ophelia, weeping at her own madness. Nights when she strove, on the toes of her bedroom slippers, to be a ballet girl. Nights when she was everything, applauded, adored, beautiful, witty, wise; and nights when she was nothing at all, when she sat on the edge of the bed, feeling dull and plain and hopeless, wondering if this life of doing nothing would go on for ever.

Today the wallpaper was barren of inspiration. The window was wide open and tempting. Anne got up and leaned out of it. The air was soft and smelt of buds and grass.

'Emily,' Anne called down to where the busy woman was polishing the brass knob on the front door, 'I would like to go out into the country. Is father coming home to dinner?'

'No, 'e's not. Manchester day today,' said Emily.

'Oh, thank goodness for that! Well, I think I'll go. Can I make sandwiches of anything?'

'Tomatoes, all I can suggest.' Emily rubbed vigorously, her whole body, even her face, engaged on getting the last flash of brightness out of the brass knob. 'I made a few rock buns yesterday, they're in a box in the boot cupboard; I put them out of Philip's way.'

Anne took a red hat from a box hidden under her bed. She put it on, and smiled from under its brim at herself. She really looked rather nice, she thought. It was quite safe to put it on today, since her father was away. He always saw her hats before he would pay for them. But this one she had bought with money from the *Weekly News*. Oh, blessed paper!

She made tomato sandwiches, and took half a dozen secreted rock buns. She put them in a small basket that would come in afterwards for possible primroses. She climbed up between the houses and dropped down the hill on the other side. By the time she had climbed and dropped down another hill, she had left the town as completely behind as if it had never been.

She came to farmyards, and leaned over gates to watch the balls of chicks, throwing out their feet comically as they ran, the yellow ducklings waggling about on parade. She paled at the geese that came squawking at her, but let the leggy calves suck her fingers. She came to three gaunt yews in a field and they cast a spell on her. In the youth and green of spring, they alone were stiff and black like ancient mummies. The knots in their gnarled trunks made grotesque faces, wrinkled by hundreds of years. For a long time Anne stared at them, then shook herself free and climbed through the hedge on to a wide white road. She was happy to be alone and carried on a singing conversation.

'When I am alone on a road, I feel as if it had been made specially for me to walk through the world on. . . .'

The recitative came to an abrupt end. A man had stepped out on to the road she was claiming as hers. He walked towards her. There was something familiar in the hunch of his shoulder and his long stride.

'George Yates!' Anne was seized with a panic. She clapped her hat on her head, and looked round for a way of escape, but the hedge on both sides was thorny and high, and George Yates came on.

'Hello!' he cried. 'Good morning! Imagine meeting you out here!'

They stood awkwardly looking at each other, and away from each other up and down the road.

'Funny how you and I have kept on sort of meeting each other all our lives, isn't it? Just meeting and no more, I mean.' He threw in 'sort of' and 'I mean' after the fashion of youth to disclaim any seriousness.

'Mmm,' said Anne. Then after a pause: 'I'm looking for primroses. Have you seen any?'

'Yes, I have. And where they should be, of course – by the river's brim.'

'The Ribble?'

'Yes, down where I came from. Could I show you?'

'Oh, don't trouble.' She didn't know whether she wanted him to come or not.

Something wistful in his eyes made her give a nod of consent at last, and together they turned down the road to the river.

'I must take off my hat again,' said Anne.

'Let me carry it.' He stuffed his own cap into his pocket, and took possession of the red hat.

'Nice hat,' he remarked. Anne was pleased.

The games of the lambs, the thud, thud of the colt's heels as he ran races by himself in the field, the mad song of the birds, the gurgling of the brooks running, running to the river, the light, high gambols of the puffed clouds – all were contagious of joy. Anne and George drew in exhilaration with the spring air. They laughed at nothing, chattered about nothing, and were as free, as happy, as absurd as the lambs and the clouds.

The wood by the river was starred with primroses. They gathered a basket full, and sat down so that Anne could arrange them with their tender, rucked leaves on moss to keep them damp. George watched her slim fingers busy with the flowers.

'Why is the first of anything so lovely?' asked Anne.

'The last is lovely, too,' he said.

'But sad.'

'So many things are sad. You can stand things when they are sad and beautiful. It's when they're sad and ugly that you can't bear them.'

They were quiet. Sitting in the gloom of the wood, a sense of unreality fell on Anne. It was green and cool and strange. Her spirit seemed to float out of her body, away among the trees, as light as air. She was brought back to earth by George Yates's hand on her arm.

'Where are you?' he said, leaning forward to look into her face. 'Come back! It's lonely. I'm beginning to think you're not a real girl at all, but a fairy.'

'Just wait! Watch me eat,' she threatened. 'Come on. Let's get out into the sun. A wood always makes me creepy. Nicely creepy, but still creepy.' She came nearer and whispered, her eyes wide like a child's. 'You know I feel as if there was Something behind the trees watching, and yet, I feel it's perhaps *Me* – as if I'd got out of myself somehow.'

'Miss Pritchard,' said George Yates with mock severity, 'how old are you?'

'Eighteen.'

'Sure it's not eight?'

'Well, how old are you?'

'Nearly twenty-two – already in the sere and yellow, you see.'

'Well, come on, I'm hungry.'

They sat on a rock in the middle of the river, and ate the tomato sandwiches and Emily's rock buns. George brought a couple of apples from his pockets and carefully peeled one for Anne.

'The other way about this time, you see,' he pointed out.

'Oh, the Adam and Eve business?' said Anne. 'Pooh!'

They walked home in the late afternoon. A slip of a moon hung in the clear green of the sky. They did not talk much. Already the rare faculty of being quiet together was theirs. When they reached the top of the hill above the town, George Yates stopped.

'It won't do for you to be seen with me in town,' he said.

'Oh?' Anne inquired with candid eyes.

'Lord, no! What would the elegant Gerald say if he knew you went about with an impoverished bloke from King Street?'

Anne was annoyed.

'Now you've spoilt it,' she said indignantly, frowning at him. 'It's so silly of you – that. That's a part of you I don't like.'

'I'm sorry,' he said contritely. Then after a pause, he ventured again. 'Could you – do you think?' he hitched his shoulder awkwardly. 'Would you care to repeat this?'

Anne looked down. She was shy, not coy. She considered, fiddling with the primroses.

'Do you think we might? I mean, is it all right?' she asked.

'Depends how you look at it,' said George. 'Your people wouldn't like it, because, as I said, I'm down at heels, and not in your set, and all that. But after all, we're not kids, and we've had a good day and . . . well . . . I've loved it . . . it's . . .'

He stammered into a silence that pleaded as well for him as any words.

'I'll come,' said Anne. 'When?'

His face opened suddenly in a look of frank pleasure. Like that, he was good-looking. They fixed on the following Tuesday. Anne went home with warm feeling in her heart, mixed with a delightful guiltiness. She had been out all day with a man, and nobody knew anything about it!

CHAPTER NINE

§ 1

It was after their third walk together that Anne felt she wanted
to see where George Yates lived. She wanted to walk along the
street and pick out his house from the rest. It might, to a
passer-by, differ not one jot from its neighbours, but to her it
would be unique because he lived in it. And so, at the end of
one April afternoon, when she had finished shopping for
Emily in town, she decided to go and find King Street.

'It would be rather awkward if I met him,' she said to
herself. 'But the chances are ten to one I shan't.'

It is not safe to bank on ten chances. No sooner had she
turned into King Street, and was looking with vivid interest
across the road at No. 6, than George Yates came along with a
loaf of bread under his arm. He had been to the corner shop.

'Good afternoon,' he said. 'Rather off your beat, I think?'

'I've been shopping,' said Anne.

'Did you come to spy out the leanness of the land?' He was
obviously being rude. He sneered with his short upper lip.

'Don't be silly,' said Anne.

But she saw, suddenly, her action through his eyes. He would take it as a piece of vulgar curiosity, or even vulgarer snobbery. Or he might think she was 'running after him', and had come round that way in the hope of seeing him. She blushed miserably.

'Well,' said George Yates, 'have a good look round. I must take the bread in.'

Anne was desperate. He was going back to Cambridge the next day. She couldn't leave him like this.

'Could you – could you walk some of the way home with me?' she stammered, her cheeks a deeper scarlet.

He considered the suggestion with a coldness that enraged her. She was on the verge of crying out: 'All right, don't then, you rude pig!' when he said, 'I'll take the bread in first,' and walked across to No. 6 with the same absurd sneer on his mouth.

They walked through the streets in silence.

'This is awful,' fretted Anne to herself. 'What can I do?'

'Let's go through the Park,' she said aloud.

They turned into the deserted leafy walks. All at once, George Yates began to talk. About Cambridge. About what he and his friends did. How they ragged. What a time they had in May Week, with the bump suppers and the girls and the dances. Anne stared in amazement. He was unmistakably showing off, being waggish, laughingly hinting that he was a bit of a dog with women. It was crude, ridiculous, most dreadfully not right.

'In fact, Miss Pritchard, flirtation is the only amusement a poor devil like me can afford.'

Anne was stung. This man who was beginning to matter to her had only been indulging in a mild form of his cheapest pastime. That was evidently his interpretation of the walks. She was too young and hot to be dignified.

'I hope,' she said, with her chin up, 'you don't consider you've been flirting with me. And if you think you're going to, you'll be wasting your time. I never flirt,' said Anne in her youth, 'and I think a man who can't be merely friendly with women is a despicable creature.'

'All men are despicable, then,' said George Yates, but he shot an anxious glance at her. He had wanted to humiliate her, and now he had succeeded, he was afraid.

She walked like a young queen, her cheeks burning.

'Don't come any further, please,' she said coldly.

'But I must see you out of the Park,' he said. 'It's lonely at this time.'

His voice was flat. He cursed himself. His poverty was a raw wound. It had ached in him throughout his Grammar School days, and made his Cambridge life a misery. He was too poor to join any Varsity clubs; too poor to row, to run, to play golf; too poor to entertain in the smallest way any friends, and so he was careful not to have any. He was voted a 'queer cuss' at Cambridge, and left to himself. And here was this girl laying her fingers on the sore again; he had raved and now he was ashamed.

They walked on.

'I object,' said Anne with icy rudeness, 'to your company.'

They had come to the very spot where, years ago, George had found her crying over the fish in the jar. The trees met over their heads, shutting them away from the world. Suddenly George caught at Anne's hand and pulled her to a standstill.

'Oh, God, I am a fool!' he said.

'You're not. You're not,' said Anne, her rage suddenly gone.

'Yes, I am – an utter damn fool.' He looked so wretched, standing there before her, that she put up her free hand and touched his face.

'No,' she said.

In the dusk of the lane, she was very near to him. He pressed her bare hand against his cheek. He moved it until his lips were in its palm. Anne trembled – waiting. His arms went round her. His lips found hers and closed in a kiss. For one moment, the two young things clung together. Then, shaken, they broke away and walked on in silence. They came to the Park gates; outside, the world was hurrying up and down; the magic hour was over. They stopped by mutual consent.

'It's all right now, isn't it?' asked George, in a low voice.

'Yes, it's all right now,' said Anne, looking up.

He took her hand in both his own and pressed it close. His eyes were dark, but he did not attempt to kiss her again. The first kiss had been too wonderful to bear such close repetition.

'Dear Anne,' he said.

She smiled tenderly, but her eyes were full of tears. It seemed such a long time before she would see him again.

'Goodbye.'

'Goodbye, Anne.'

She drew her hand from its warm prison. When she turned the corner, far away, he was still standing looking after her.

She stole up to her room and closed the door. She stood still with the hand he had kissed pressed against her cheek.

'He loves me,' she said over and over again. 'This is love. I've come to it.'

Strange and wonderful thing; she – Anne – loved and was loved. Life was suddenly suffused with colour. She went to the mirror to look at this girl who was loved. She felt she must look different somehow. Her own eyes, wide and dark, met her. The ashen gold of her hair, making low curves over her ears, shone back mysteriously in the dusk. She considered the oval of her face, the curve of her lips, and wondered if George thought she was pretty.

She wanted to stay in her bedroom and remember. But the business of every day, in the shape of Emily, summoned her to tea.

'You've been a mighty long time,' said Emily, 'coming back with those currant teacakes.'

Anne only smiled. Emily looked at her shrewdly. She saw that something had happened that Anne was not going to tell.

'Eh, well,' said Emily to herself, cutting up the belated teacakes. 'I suppose it had to come.'

But she sighed.

Anne's life was upheaved. She could not settle to anything. She waited with feverish impatience for her first letter from George. It came after an interval she thought altogether too long. It began 'Dear Anne' and ended simply 'George.' It was a letter anybody might have written to anybody else. Anne was profoundly disappointed. She wrote back after the same model, and thereafter received two letters a week. As time went on, she began to wonder if George had ever really kissed her.

She returned to the yellow desk, long neglected. But the atmosphere of the Pritchard household was not favourable to work. Henry Pritchard was ill. He spent hours, sometimes days, in his own room. He came out of it, pale and very tired. To all questions, he obstinately replied that he had indigestion, bad indigestion, but that he could cure it by dieting. Anne suggested a doctor, but Henry Pritchard told her to mind her own business.

'Doctors!' he scoffed. 'I've no faith in them. Look at poor old Carter since he had that operation on his nose. His face twitches incessantly; they cut a nerve. I could quote a dozen cases. Tch! Doctors!'

Aunt Orchard met with the same terseness. She came up to see her nephew at the house when he was not to be found at the office. He managed her affairs for her. She was always altering her will.

'I shan't leave any money to you, Henry, because you won't outlive me. I can see that. Your uncle suffered just the same way. It turned out to be a duodenal ulcer. I shouldn't be at all surprised if you have a duodenal ulcer, Henry.'

'Don't come telling me about duodenal ulcers!' snapped her nephew. 'Old woman's nonsense. I tell you I've got indigestion. I've always had indigestion. It's constitutional with me. Only diet will cure me.'

'Well,' resumed Aunt Orchard, 'I shan't leave you any money anyway. Anne is my god-daughter, but I shan't leave her anything. Because you insisted in putting her into that

Convent in spite of me, and I'm not going to have any of my money getting into Roman Catholic hands. I want you to draw up a will in favour of Gerald. I like Gerald, Henry. He's a very nice boy. He doesn't go to church as often as I should like, but boys will be boys, they say, and perhaps he will return to the fold later.'

Henry Pritchard was glad to draw up a will in favour of his eldest son. He adored him. Sometimes, because he felt so ill, he was emboldened to make a bid for Gerald's company.

'I wish I could stay here tonight, Father,' Gerald would say, bestriding the hearthrug with his long straight legs, his hands smoothing down the fit of his coat over his hips. 'But I simply must see Cooper about that car of his I'm thinking of buying.'

'Of course, my boy.' Henry Pritchard smiled wistfully at his handsome son. 'You go.'

And Gerald, lighting one of his father's best cigars with inimitable grace, would go.

'I don't know how he can,' said Anne fiercely.

'He can do anything,' replied Philip darkly. Philip could believe anything of anybody. The blackest crimes of humanity could not surprise him. It was what he expected.

Aunt Orchard, on one of her tiresome visits, brought the news that Vera Bowden was returning to Bowford to live. She would stay with Aunt Orchard until she and her husband could find a house.

'I haven't seen her for years now,' said Anne. 'Is she as pretty as ever, I wonder?'

'Can't be,' said Gerald. 'She must be thirty-eight, if she's a day. Bound to have gone off.'

Gerald was always slightly contemptuous of age in women.

'Let me remember,' wrote Anne in the very private note-book. 'To dwell on the bald heads, the heave of the stomach, loose necks of middle-aged men. Let me point out their tooth-picking ways, their eructations after food.'

She giggled there, feeling she really was hitting out from the shoulder. But in spite of entries in the private notebook, work at the yellow desk did not progress. Her head propped on her hands, her eyes fixed on the six little pigeon-holes, Anne spent a great deal of her time dreaming.

The summer went on. Henry Pritchard decided not to go farther afield for the annual holiday than Dyke, a village about twenty miles from Bowford. He felt too tired to make a further effort.

They took a cottage set down in the fields a mile from the village. It was pretty and quiet, and had a garden full of roses, and Anne would have been delighted with it, had it not meant that she was leaving Bowford just when George was due home from Cambridge. She thought she would miss seeing him, because, though the boys came and went freely, and Olive Pritchard went into Bowford when she wished, no one could see any reason why Anne should want to go there. So she stayed with Emily and her father at Dyke.

Henry Pritchard sat in the sun with his papers, often falling asleep, often waking to gaze before him, wondering why he had never been able to attach anybody to himself – why his wife, why Gerald should elude him, why Anne should be so self-conscious with him, why Philip hardly ever spoke to him.

Anne slept in a tent in the field adjoining the cottage. Emily had a bed in the tent too, to keep her company. Anne loved the dark and the stars and the wind on her face; and she loved the greyness before dawn, when the ash tree at the bottom of the meadow fluttered its leaves like small, ghostly hands.

§ 2

George Yates sat on the edge of his low iron bed, waiting until everything at No. 6 King Street, should be still. He waited with a dogged patience, that gave no hint of the fever within. He had to see Anne – and soon. Ever since he had come down from Cambridge, he had tried to get away. Now he had decided that the only way to go was in the night, without explanation. He knew his mother too well to risk any.

'She's been pretty bad today,' he thought to himself, his forehead corrugated at the memory of his mother's tongue. How she nagged and fretted! He didn't know how his father stood it. 'But his spirit's gone, poor chap,' mused the son. 'Perhaps he never had much.'

His thoughts went back, slowly, miserably, over the day. His mother had been washing. It always upset her. She washed so inefficiently, wetting the floor in the scullery until her shoes were soaked through, and filling the kitchen with steam and the smell of wet wool. Then in the afternoon, she had her usual headache and groaned over the ironing, until George was driven almost mad with wanting to help her and not being able to. He had ironed the handkerchiefs, slowly, heavily, carefully.

Then his thoughts flew forward with a leap to Anne. His heart beat in heavy thuds at the prospect of seeing her. He smiled at the bare wall opposite, seeing her there with her changing looks, her serious eyes, her mouth and the two little nicks at the corners of it that came when she laughed. He clenched his hands between his knees, and forced himself to wait. Would his mother ever stop fiddling about?

It was well after midnight, when he wrote on a piece of paper: 'Gone tramping in the country for a few days,' and slipped it under their door. Then, picking up his haversack, he cautiously opened his bedroom window, slid down the sloping roof of the outhouse, and dropped into the yard. The night was fine and clear, a night for walking. He set out at a good pace. He had twenty miles to go before morning – before Anne.

All night he walked, smoking his old pipe, eating an occasional apple, and in the dawn he spied a tent pitched at what was, for his object, a safe distance from the cottage to which it obviously belonged. He hoped to get an hour's sleep in it. The grass was drenched with dew in the fields. He made for the tent, but before his hobnailed boot could strike its boarded floor, George Yates backed with a gasp of surprise.

He had found Anne sooner than he expected. She was there, sleeping serenely, her gold hair spread out behind her head like a fan, her lashes making dark, enchanting curves on her cheeks. In the strange, unreal hour of early morning, in the mist and the dew and the greyness, George Yates caught and held something rare, indescribable. Something he never knew again. Beauty was here, that Anne was part of; she was it. Through her he felt it. Holding his breath, he stood and looked at her. Such a passion of tenderness surged in him that his eyes smarted with tears. He wanted to fall on his knees.

'My beautiful . . . beautiful . . .' he whispered.

The sun rose suddenly and strongly over the hill, flooding the tent with light. The occupant of the other bed, of which nothing could be seen but a minute plait of hair tied with a bit of pink wool, stirred. George dropped the tent-flap and slipped away.

Depression followed on his ecstasy. What if Anne should never be his? What if she didn't love him? What if enough bricks and mortar, beds and carpets could never be amassed for her? If he had to die without her, he would never take her to a King Street.

'Oh, damn everything,' he said, and was suddenly conscious of weariness. He ached; his eyes were like stones in his head for lack of sleep. A haystack squatted by the hedgeside, fragrant, inviting. He climbed to the top, and full in the sunshine, stretched himself out and went immediately to sleep.

It was after nine when he awoke. He hurried. He took a flying leap into the cove, towelled briskly, sprinted to the nearest farmhouse, where he had the luck to find a cheerful housewife who gave him a hearty breakfast for ninepence. His depression was gone. He felt buoyant with youth and health, and tremendously excited by his nearness to Anne. He retraced his steps to the cottage and scouted round it, peering through the thorn hedges with caution.

He saw Henry Pritchard come out into the garden with his rugs and pillows.

'Good Lord!' said George under his breath. 'He looks awful. Thin as a rake – and what a colour!'

He saw Emily bustling about, brushing the cobbles with energy. Then out into the sunlight came Anne in a blue dress. She dilly-dallied on the path, smelling at a rose or two, stretching her arms above her head. George, behind the thick hedge, felt his heart beat to bursting point.

'Oh, Anne!' he whispered. 'Come here.'

He tried to compel her to come to him; but she turned into the house and spoke to Emily.

George raged up and down the hedge. How was he going to attract her attention? Lovers' prayers are perhaps answered. She came unromantically to spread tea towels on the hedge to dry. She stood right above him, unconscious of him. Through the thorns he looked at her, and said, very low: 'Anne! Anne!'

She seemed to freeze into stillness. He spoke again.

'Anne! Look over! It's me!'

With dilated eyes and one hand at her throat, she looked over. He saw the blood run up into her cheeks.

'George!' she said.

'Come out!' he begged. 'Get away for the day . . . will you?'

She cast a glance at her father buried in his newspapers at the end of the garden.

'I'll try,' she answered, re-arranging the tea towels. 'I'll come to the end of the meadow, by the ash tree, as soon as I can.'

She ran into the cottage again, her heart beating like a wild thing at her side. Within half an hour, she dropped out of sight of the house into the hollow at the end of the meadow where George waited under the tree.

'However did you get here so early in the morning?' she asked.

'I walked.'

'Walked! Twenty miles! When did you start?'

'About midnight, I think.'

'Why did you walk here in the night?' she asked again. She was amazed to think he had been walking towards her while she slept.

'I wanted to see you,' he said.

'Oh!' Anne drew a long breath.

They stood under the tree, inarticulate. Youth never knows 'what to say.'

'Well,' said George at last. 'How about it? Are we off for the day?'

The tension was loosed.

'Oh, rather!' said Anne. 'I've got sandwiches. Emily is a good thing. She always finds something, and never asks any questions.'

'Good for Emily!' said George. 'Where shall we go? Lead on, and I follow.'

'I found a lovely beech wood yesterday, and d'you know, a little white doe came and ate about in it, and never saw me!'

'How exciting!' he mocked her. 'Let us go in quest of the doe. Hello! I lisped in numbers, for the numbers came. Did you notice?'

'Idiot!'

They were on safe ground there. They rattled absurdly, avoiding silence. But if their hands touched fleetingly, a thrill like flame ran through them both.

It was not until they were deep in the wood that they kissed – once; a close, rare kiss. George held Anne in the hard circle of his arms, and looked into her upturned face as if he could never look enough.

'It's been a long time,' he said.

Anne said 'Yes.' No more. She couldn't talk.

The early morning depression came back to George. He looked out over Anne's head, his mouth bitter, his eyes hard, holding her almost savagely. She put up her arms and drew his head down. She stroked his rough hair. He pressed his face against her; and at that soft, warm contact, some of his misery melted. Anne felt a tenderness almost too poignant to be borne.

Their mood passed. They became wildly happy and absurd. They built a dam across the stream, throwing wet stones to each other, stopping up holes with clay with their red, cold fingers. George's tie dangled into the water, and had to be hung over the bough of a tree to dry. They sat down underneath it, and felt domestic. That tie hanging up to dry seemed to make a home for them. In a silence they were not afraid of now, Anne saw the white doe approaching delicately through the trees. She put a warning finger on her lips and they leaned round the bole of the tree to look.

'It's like a fairy tale,' she whispered. He kissed the back of her neck, and the doe bounded away in fright.

Anne was indignant.

'Never mind,' said George. 'I'll cut a heart on this tree and put 'A' and 'G' inside it. It's the proper thing to do when you're walking out,' he said, carving away.

'Oh,' said Anne, 'are you my young man?'

'I am that,' he said. They talked the pithy Lancashire talk and laughed hugely. The afternoon wore on.

'I must go home to tea,' said Anne. 'Father will wonder where I am. But I'll come out afterwards.'

After a tea consisting of she didn't know what, after vague talk during which she was dimly conscious of her father expatiating on the beauties of nature and the obligation of thankfulness to the Creator, Anne slipped out to meet George.

They stole into the fields. The vivid colours of day were misted into one grey; unreality enwrapped the world as at dawn. Under the quiet trees they held each other close. They spoke very low, with long silences. In the silences, they heard the gentle, monotonous tinkle of water-drops from the dripping moss in the bank.

'Oh, Anne . . . it's wonderful . . . all this.'

'Wonderful.' Her voice was like a sigh, her lips parted, her eyes visionary.

A strange spiritual quality held them both.

'Will it last always . . . this?'

'Don't ask that,' he said, holding her closer.

Their lips were cold in their quiet kisses. . . .

They had four glorious days together; the happiest days of their lives – unspoiled, perfect. It is perhaps as much as anyone can expect. Friday came, the day on which George had decided he must return to King Street. He would go back as he had come, in the night, so as not to waste any time with Anne.

In the afternoon they wandered far from Dyke, hand in hand, careless, happy, in the remote lanes. Anne was in a teasing mood. She screwed his hair into little tight points in a row on the top of his head.

'No – you must let it stay like that!' she protested. 'You can't possibly love me, if you can't do a little thing like that for me. Oh, you do look funny! But you must let it stay like that!'

She pulled his hands down and held them with her own, laughing in his face. He shook himself free, and snatched her up in his arms.

'I'll throw you over the highest tree I can find,' he shouted.

Then, hurriedly, he put her down. A car had appeared suddenly round the bend of the lane and was upon them. Red with embarrassment, they drew aside for it to pass. But it stopped.

'Can you tell me where Green End is?' a woman's voice asked.

'Oh,' said Anne in surprise. 'We live there. . . . Oh, Vera! I didn't know you!'

'I didn't know you either,' said Vera Bowden. 'Funny I should meet you out here.'

The cousins looked at each other.

'Years since I saw you,' said Vera, whose eyes had run all over Anne, noting her dress, shoes, hair, eyes, skin, teeth in the space of ten seconds. Anne only saw that Vera was older, much older.

'Jump in, both of you,' said Vera, 'and show me the way.'

Anne and George looked at each other.

'I think I'd better be getting on,' he said slowly.

'All right, George,' said Anne, as nonchalantly as she could make it. 'Goodbye.'

They shook hands, they who had kissed so closely, and Anne got into the car. George stood aside to let it pass. With a waving of hands, a whir and a grind they were gone. Vera Bowden had appeared from nowhere to take Anne from him in the midst of a kiss. He was left alone, with the taste of dust in his mouth.

CHAPTER TEN

§ 1

Anne sat at the window of Aunt Orchard's front bedroom and looked out at the September aspect of Victoria Street. Elsewhere the afternoon was golden, but here it was yellowish-green. Victoria Street led nowhere, and so its cobbles had an undisturbed, minute green mould which spread over the ancient stone walls and up the trees that hung over from the gardens in a listless way, as if they had been stricken a long time ago. There was a silence in Victoria Street that was almost sinister. There were no children, no cheerful carts; it was a street of old people and obese dogs.

Anne hardly saw the dreary prospect. She thought it a nuisance that Vera Bowden should have asked her to tea on a fine Saturday afternoon, but she had a letter from George in her dress and, when she touched it, it made a small noise like a secret kiss.

Behind her was the concentrated hideousness of Aunt Orchard's front bedroom. The wallpaper was pale green patterned with urns and Prince of Wales feathers, the whole like a nightmare of a freehand drawing set for an examination by the College of Preceptors. On it, Aunt Orchard had hung a collection of uncheerful pictures: a photograph of her husband's grave, a picture of an old woman reading the Bible, called 'Preparing for the Next World', a print of angels bearing a soul to heaven, a portrait of a deceased clergyman and a framed text 'Live that Ye May Die' in red cross-stitch on canvas. Large pieces of glassy, blood-coloured mahogany, like more freehand drawings in solid form, filled the room. The big bed had curtains and a headpiece, stuffed and buttoned, in yellow sateen. In the middle of the bed, fully dressed, lay Vera Bowden, smoking, one leg aerially crossed over the other knee. She was lying down because there was nothing else in the world to do.

'My God,' she said at intervals. 'My good God.'

Anne dreamed on.

'Ya-a-a,' yawned Vera. Her eyes roamed over the yellowing ceiling. Her thoughts roamed everywhere, loosely.

'Just my luck having to come back to this rotten hole,' she grumbled. 'It's all very well for Arthur. He's gone off shooting today, the mean hound. Leaving me all alone with the Aunt. Heavens! When I think of the time I've had – and think of what a damn, slow miserable life I lead now, I could commit suicide. Life's rotten. Men are rotten. They get what they can out of you – good times, fun – then they're off somewhere else for more good times, more fun. Heavens! The times I've given them! The food, the dances, the cars to the races – the money I've spent! That's why we're in this hole now. And is there anybody left, I ask you, who'd come and take me out this damned Saturday afternoon? Damn them all!'

Silence again, while Vera blew spirals of grey smoke into the frowsty distances of the bed-curtains.

'Are you engaged to that boy you were out with?' she asked suddenly.

Anne started and flushed.

'Which boy?' she parried.

'Oh, there are so many, are there?' said Vera. 'Don't be an idiot. That boy you were on such intimate terms with when I came on you with the car. He was handling you pretty thoroughly, I must say.'

Anne winced. She always disliked the words Vera used, but as applied to George, they made her sick.

'Are you engaged to him?' Vera persisted.

'Engaged?' said Anne reluctantly. 'We've not thought about it.'

'Pooh!' Vera disdainfully shook her leg in the air. 'I don't believe you.'

Anne said nothing.

Vera rolled over on her side to get a better view of her cousin.

'Look here,' she said. 'Are you really as green as you pretend to be?'

Anne turned in surprise. 'What do you mean?

'Oh, keep up this God's-little-white-flower pose if you like. But you can't take me in, not after I've seen you at your little games in the lanes, my dear.'

The colour flamed into Anne's face.

'Leave me and my affairs alone, please,' she said angrily. 'It's nothing to do with you.'

'I don't care a damn what you do, my good girl,' said Vera calmly. 'What I object to is this superior purity touch, when you're no better than anyone else – probably worse, because you're a hypocrite.'

Anne stared in alarm and in anger. There was a hard, bitter note in Vera's voice that nothing in the discussion warranted. Anne felt something ugly was coming.

'What's the matter with you?' she asked, puzzled. 'I don't understand . . .'

'Oh, go on,' sneered Vera, lighting another cigarette from the stump between her teeth. 'You and your type – you make me sick. Always so wide-eyed and pi. Think you'll catch the men that way, do you? Well, I'll admit it's jolly clever of you. Men love to think they're the first.'

'What *are* you talking about?' Anne came to the foot of the bed and stared at its occupant.

Vera looked her worst; her cheeks were flushed with little broken veins, her neck sagged and her eyes were haggard. She knew it; she was always conscious of how she looked, and the knowledge made her furious with the cool youth of her cousin. She had a wild desire to scratch her, spoil her, soil her, wreak vengeance on her for her own lost looks, for the good times that were gone, for the fact that Arthur neglected her, that she had to live in this hideous house, that Basil Reade, young Cromer and Bobbie Hebblethwaite no longer wanted her – all this accumulated and burnt her until she shook with nervous rage.

'I suppose you think your affair is so different, so pure, so high and holy and all the rest of it, don't you? And all the time, it's the same thing that's going on in all the dirty little back streets; the same thing – sex, sex, sex! It's not the thing I object to, it's your pretending it's so beautiful. Pah! It'll end the same way, won't it? It'll end the way it ends between the man who pays the woman in Leicester Square to let him go home and sleep with her, won't it?'

Anne's hands gripped the bed. She felt sick, bewildered.

'Vera . . .' she faltered.

'Oh, shut up!' burst out Vera. 'Don't say "I don't understand" to me again – or I shall scream. I suppose you're going to pretend that you don't know about prostitutes now? Were you going to say that? I'd like to take you round some of the places I've been to in Paris. Heavens! I've seen some hot things, but I've never seen anything like that . . .'

Anne put her hands over her ears. She cowered.

'Oh, don't . . . don't talk about it . . . don't. . . .'

'Why shouldn't I talk about it?' demanded Vera, raising herself on her elbows. 'It does you good to hear these things. That's what I mean. That's what I'm getting at. Life *is* like that, and you ought to admit it, you little fool, and not go about with your eyes shut.'

Anne shut her eyes in reality. She could have vomited at the aspect life suddenly presented to her.

'It isn't true about those women, is it?' she faltered.

'True?' Vera sat up to look at the phenomenon who could ask such a question. 'Of course it's true. Go to London and look at them – hundreds, thousands. You don't need to go to London, look at them in this town. . . .'

Anne made an inarticulate sound, half pity, half mortal disgust.

'King Street, here, is full of bad houses,' persisted Vera.

King Street, where George lived! Anne's nausea increased.

'Men are beasts,' said Vera Bowden viciously, revenging herself on Arthur and Basil Reade and young Cromer and Bobbie Hebblethwaite. 'Out and out beasts. I know something about them, I can tell you. They're just dirty beasts.'

'Not all,' protested Anne faintly.

'All,' said Vera firmly. 'My hat, I could open your eyes.'

'Not all,' insisted Anne. 'There are some good men. My father's good. He'd hate anything like that.'

'Your father!' Vera Bowden threw back her head and laughed. '*Your father!* That's funny. That's really funny!'

She threw herself back on the pillows and laughed again.

Anne's voice was cleared of faintness when she spoke; it rang hard.

'What do you mean?'

'Oh, nothing,' said Vera carelessly, rolling over to take another cigarette.

But Anne leaped forward and seized her arm.

'What do you mean? My father's good. D'you hear? Good.'

'How interesting!' Vera lay in Anne's grip and looked up with eyes ugly with meaning.

'What d'you mean?' cried Anne, shaking her. 'Tell me. What d'you mean? Go on! At once!'

'Your father, my child, is no better than the rest.'

'Go on!' said Anne savagely. 'What do you know about my father? You know nothing . . . nothing.'

'I know exactly this, my dear,' drawled Vera, 'and it may be interesting to you. . . . Your father and mother had to be married.'

She shook off the hand that had gone limp on her shoulder and reached for her cigarette.

'If you hadn't been such a little fool,' she said out of the corner of her mouth as she applied the match, 'I should never have told you. But cheer up – it often happens. You don't need to bother about it. What're you doing? I say, you're not going? But you can't go. What will Aunt Orchard think? I say . . .'

'Silly little fool!' she called out pettishly.

The sound of the front door, quietly closed though it was, echoed through the silent house.

'Well, she won't look so damned superior now,' said Vera Bowden.

She thrust her legs beneath the eiderdown and went to sleep.

§ 2

Anne's feet carried her out of the house, down the steps, over the pavement of Victoria Street, up the hill towards home. She was numb; her mind was not working. She said over and over mechanically:

'They had to be married . . . had to be married.'

She reached home. Emily Barnes was just carrying in tea. There was no escape. She sat at the table and ate with stiff lips, bread and butter, even jam. She looked round at her father, thin, pallid, stern, in his place; at her mother sitting indifferently behind the tea-cosy; at Philip, gloomily eating fish-pie; at the blue tea-service; the red paint, the warm gloom of the dining room. Her eyes stared painfully at these things that were the same, and yet so terribly different. From being homely and intimate and simple, they had become sinister. These things had *known*.

Tea was over at last; she went up to her room and sat huddled on the floor by the bed. Dusk hung over her. She sat there a long time. When she moved at last, George's letter crackled in her dress. She pulled it out and looked dully at it. Then, moving carefully because she was stiff, she got up and opened the yellow desk. She wrote:

Dear George,
I can't go on with this any longer. Please don't write any more. I can't explain.
Anne.

She put it in an envelope and went out to post it in the pillar box in the garden wall.

Back in the bedroom, she took George's letters from the yellow desk and tore them up into very small pieces. She wasn't thinking it out, but she meant to herself that she had finished with the thing she had called Love. As her fingers worked, her mind unfroze sufficiently to enable her to feel the shock from which she suffered.

She was very young, younger than her years, and as green as Vera Bowden had dubbed her. Her youth prevented her from seeing beyond the present, provided her with no experience to test the truth of what her cousin had told her. She wondered in a bewildered fashion if she would have believed what Vera had said if she hadn't pushed it home by that last horrible thrust at her parents. It was here, the evil, right at home. She couldn't get away from it.

'How have I been able to go on all these years and not know?' she asked herself. 'Everybody must know . . . how could I not have known?'

She put her head down on her crossed hands and sat very still. The pieces of George's letters lay scattered among her hair.

After a time of which she had made no count, she heard her mother coming upstairs, her father locking the doors. Mechanically she took off her clothes and got into bed.

Somewhere, in the night, a passion of hatred for her father seized her.

'Pretending to be so good . . .' she burst out. 'He's a hypocrite. I hate him.'

She got out of bed and stood at the window. It was dark outside and fresh and still. The houses reared in black masses. What did they hide? The things that Vera had told her pushed in on her mind.

'If only I could ask someone if it's true.'

But she knew she could not. It was a secret she had to keep always.

She crept back to bed, shivering. Restlessly, she turned and turned, lying on her face, on her back, on one side, on the other, wondering if she would ever sleep again. Not a tear came to cool her eyes. She got up at Emily's knock, feeling strangely old, as if she had grown up, with pain, in one night.

She wondered vaguely what she would answer if George wrote back. She wondered unnecessarily. George did not write. By some trick of fate, Anne's letter arrived immediately after the news that he had missed a post in the Indian Woods and Forests on which all his hopes had been set.

'A third-rate schoolmastership for me,' he reflected. 'Jolly sensible of her to turn me down.'

But he was terribly hurt, and as bitter and as secret in his hurt as Anne in hers.

Youth is like that; ridiculous, pitiful youth.

CHAPTER ELEVEN

§ 1

Life went on. The same getting up and going to bed, the same
eating, the same going out and coming in. Morning, afternoon, evening, night. Things that had been set going and
couldn't stop, even though the meaning had gone out of
them.

Anne looked back at the girl she had been, the lucky
stranger who had possessed everything that mattered in this
world: a lover, a friend, and a family life which, though not
overwhelmingly happy, was at least sound and natural; it
made a background; it made the rest possible. It was this very
background, this thing she hadn't noticed, had taken for
granted, that had asserted itself to horrible prominence and
destroyed the rest.

George was gone. Love, as Anne saw it now, was unthink-
able. Her friendship with Mildred Yates was spoilt. With
Anne, friendship without candour was almost impossible. She
could not bear the idea of having anything to hide. When
she went to the Yateses, their prattle about 'nice people' and

the desirability of getting in with them, which before amused her, now made her wince. She spent afternoons of acute unhappiness listening to plans for Mildred's advancement, in which she was expected to share. It was obvious that the Yateses did not know about her parents. She almost wished they did. Mrs Yates was innocently angling for Gerald as son-in-law. Anne worried about it. In spite of Mildred's social ambitions, in which she docilely followed her mother's lead, in spite of her overlay of bright conversation, pieces on the piano, recitations, and a certain hard materialism, Anne loved Mildred because, at heart, she was sincere and simple. Her greatest joy was still a walk in the country with Anne, and tea in a cottage.

These walks became a prolonged agony to Anne, with her secret to keep. Mildred's candour was a reproach to her. Mildred chattered with eager joy about the future, about what she was going to do, what her mother was going to get for her, what her father was going to take her to see, who was beginning to notice her, who might fall in love with her.

'Raymond Dean walked up High Street twice after me on Saturday morning, Anne! But of course, I pretended I didn't notice it. Anne, isn't he nice? So gentlemanly, don't you think?'

What had Anne to do with all this talk? For her, the future held nothing. There was only the present, the slow, heavy present that she could hardly bear. The world was vile; men and women were vile. Everything stank. God was gone. Anne couldn't reconcile her old ideas of God to her new view of life.

'Everything's gone,' she thought heavily. She burnt the notebooks that had held her childish secrets. She had something now too hideous to write down, and since everything hung on it, there would never be any more to record. She could not write. Her own unhappiness was too real to allow the creation of imaginary sorrows, and she had no heart for joys. She was utterly at a loss. Life, like a cross nurse, had slapped her hands away from every thing she had held, and she was left like a child sitting on the floor, blank, bewildered, uncomprehending.

The variability of her own actions and emotions puzzled her. Sometimes she was timid and conciliatory. When Mrs Charles Bramwell called to talk about her maids and her indigestion, Anne sat on a low chair in the drawing room and listened with deference. Once she would have escaped with the cheerful indifference of youth to middle age. But now she harboured an unformed idea that she might thus propitiate Mrs Charles Bramwell, so that she would not find the family canker, or judge it less harshly if she knew of it.

At other times, she faced the world with defiance. She came across a quotation that stiffened her back. 'They say. What say they? Let them say,' she said that over and over again to herself, and it enabled her to behave with extraordinary rudeness to any company in which she found herself.

She began to take a contemptuous view of the people round her. She began to discover in them meannesses and absurdities she had not suspected before. Her lip curled openly at her father's talk. She judged him a hypocrite of the deepest dye. The full tide of bitter feeling was directed to him.

Somehow, it was impossible to feel like that to anyone so indifferent as Olive Pritchard.

And so it went on. Only Emily Barnes knew that something had happened. She made a few tentative advances, but was hurt by the coldness they were met with.

'I'm only a servant, I know,' she said fiercely to herself. 'But goodness me, it's me as brought 'er up. I've felt like I might be 'er own mother, and now she won't tell me what's bothering 'er. I'd better leave and be done with them all. I'd like to know what they'd do without me. Nobody else 'ud put up with them. Like as not it's a man that's upsetting 'er. Drat them all, that's what I say. None of 'em 'ud ever tempt me. I wonder whatever it is. She's not a bit like 'erself – and whatever does she do brooding hour after hour in 'er room? Stone cold, she must be. I think I'll just make 'er a cup of tea. Like as not she'll bite me 'ead off. Well, never mind . . . somebody's got to do something in this 'ouse, and it's generally me.'

But Anne did not bite off her head. Sudden tears came to her eyes, and she pressed her face to Emily's withered cheek.

'Good old Emily,' she said with forced cheerfulness. 'I was just about starved.'

'Well, bless my life,' said the exasperated Emily. 'What do you want to starve for? Come downstairs with you. There's a good fire in the drawing room and only your father 'aving a nap by it. You seem precious fond of your own company nowadays, though for all I can see it's none too lively. Come and sit by the kitchen fire and keep me company. I feel a bit lonely at times, like as if I was getting old or something.'

And so she lured Anne to the fire. She was a great believer

in comfort, was Emily. But when you are young, no material comfort can heal a spiritual dislocation.

§ 2

The winter went on; slow, dark, unhappy months. If George came home for the Christmas vacation, Anne did not see him. She had heard casually from Mildred that he was tutoring in Cambridge until he could find something better to do.

'Aunt Frances was nearly demented when he didn't get a First,' she told Anne. 'She says she knows he's been frittering his time away with girls. Imagine George with girls! Poor boy, he simply doesn't know how to behave in a drawing room. He is so clumsy, and his clothes are too awful.'

Vera Bowden had left Aunt Orchard's roof. She had originally intended to live with the old lady and save expense, but she found she couldn't stand it, she said. So Arthur bought a house in Daybrook Avenue, and there she entertained such of the youth of Bowford as she could attract. Anne avoided her as if she were the plague. Never since that hideous afternoon in Aunt Orchard's front bedroom had she spoken to Vera alone. In their rare meetings, Vera seemed to fluctuate between contempt and propitiation. It was all the same to Anne.

The turn of the year came. The hard clearness went out of the air, out of the silhouettes of the trees; one stranded crocus burst its yellow cup in the Pritchards' sooty garden.

One morning at the end of March, Anne came down to find her mother startled out of her usual indifference.

'Ring up Dr Sefton, Anne,' she said. 'Your father is really ill this morning. His stupid notions about curing himself are killing him.'

She was nearer the truth than she knew. Dr Sefton, after making an examination of his protesting patient, came downstairs with a grave face and shut himself into the drawing room with Olive Pritchard.

Anne, her heart beating fast with apprehension, hung about in the hall, waiting. Her father called from upstairs. She ran up to him.

'Hasn't Sefton gone yet?' he inquired irritably. 'What's his version of this business? He can't tell me anything I don't know. Diet will cure me. I must have plenty of fruit and cold water. Get me a glass of water now, Anne. Oh – that pain is coming on again.'

His pallid hands clutched the bed-coverings, sweat broke out under his closed eyes, his lips went white.

Anne threw herself down by the bed in an agony of pity.

'Oh, Father, what can I do? What can I do?'

'Nothing,' he said, through clenched teeth.

'Shall I call the doctor back?' she begged.

'No. I forbid you to – absolutely. It's going . . . it's going.'

He sank back on the pillows, exhausted.

'That water,' he said, waving her away.

She brought it to him. She heard the front door close, and the departing whirr of the doctor's car. She smoothed the bed-clothes uncertainly. Her father's eyes were still closed, but his face was calm. She stole to the head of the stairs. Below, in the hall, she saw the white, upturned face of her mother.

Slowly, fear making her feet heavy, Anne went down. The cold hand of Olive Pritchard drew her into the drawing room.

'Anne!' she whispered. 'He's not going to live. He's going to die. Soon. Two months at most. They can't operate. He's left it too long. Nothing can be done.'

Anne tried to echo the words. She shivered suddenly. Mother and daughter stared with blank eyes. The cold silence was shattered by the upstairs bell. Anne caught her mother's arm.

'Don't let him know, Mother,' she whispered in terror. 'He thinks he's getting better. We must never let him know.'

'No, no . . . but how can we manage to hide it, Anne?' Olive Pritchard's face was convulsed. 'Oh, what shall I do? What shall I do?'

The bell rang again, impatiently.

'Mother – pull yourself together, quick! He'll see. He'll suspect.'

'I can't . . . not yet.' Olive Pritchard pushed at her daughter with her hands. 'Anne, you go! You run up! You're so brave.'

The bell rang again furiously.

Anne went out into the hall. Standing in the gloomy well of it, she swallowed on a dry throat, and called out:

'I'm coming, Father. Just one minute.'

She pressed her hands against her aching lips, smoothed her eyes to wipe all expression out of them, and went upstairs, whistling silently.

'Now . . .' she said, coming into the full sunlight of the bedroom. 'Here I am. What is it?'

The sick man glared from his pillows.

'Why doesn't your mother come up and tell me what Sefton said? I suppose she thinks it doesn't matter?'

'I don't think,' lied Anne, 'that there is anything really to matter, Father. Mother's going to make some barley water, I think.'

'What did he say? That's what I want to know.'

'I don't really know,' said Anne, gaining time. 'I just heard something about your being able to get up when you want to, and going on just as before.'

'There,' said Henry Pritchard triumphantly. 'Didn't I tell you? I knew I was right. Isn't it strange how I always seem to know?' He looked at his daughter, his nostrils dilated with a confidence that seemed to her utterly pitiful.

She busied herself with the bedclothes.

'Yes, it's wonderful,' she said.

'Now, don't keep pulling at the sheets,' said Henry Pritchard. 'You women – always fussing! They were quite all right before. Pass the paper, please. I'll read a little before I get up. That pain has made me rather tired.'

Anne escaped from the room with relief. She stood on the landing, trying to grasp the dread news. Her father was to die. The terrible thought drove everything else out of her mind. There was no room for hatred now. Only fear and an overwhelming pity. What did it matter now what he had done? He was so soon to take the last, lonely journey.

They went about, Olive Pritchard and Anne and the boys and Emily Barnes, under the shadow, playing their difficult parts. They were all afraid that the calling in of the specialist by Dr Sefton to confirm his verdict that nothing could be done, would betray the truth to the invalid. But to the amazement of his family, and in spite of terrible pain and dire physical warnings, Henry Pritchard remained unsuspicious and unshaken in his confidence.

They were terrible days. There was born in Anne a passion of protection. She hovered over her father untiringly. All her energies were concentrated in one direction – the hiding of the truth from him. Nothing escaped her.

'Did he notice Gerald staring at him so queerly then?' she fretted. 'Why doesn't Mother agree to have a new fireplace in the dining room before the winter? Oh, what's the matter with them all? They're going to let him see! They're going to let him see!'

Her greatest difficulty was with Aunt Orchard, who had been herself to the doctor to find out the truth. Apart from her irritating and, to Anne, heartless anxiety about her monetary affairs, she showed a morbid curiosity in the slow disintegration of her nephew. Although she was seventy years of age, her own death was as remote from her imagination as from that of a child.

When she visited the sick man, Anne took up a strict vigil at her side, watching every look, weighing every word, ready to cover, to twist, to misinterpret. She sighed with relief when she conducted Aunt Orchard from the sickroom to the dining room, where she harrowed the family by her comments.

'Yes, I see a great change, a great change,' she would say. 'Look how his eyes have sunk into his head. And his colour is so bad. . . . He almost looks as if he were dead already!'

She sat down, loosened her bonnet-strings and took a cup of tea from Emily.

'Have you thought about the grave?' she began again. 'It would be nice for him to lie next to his uncle under the yew tree. You'd better get Davis to undertake. He did everything very nicely for your uncle. Lined the coffin with the very best cotton wool. . . .'

'Oh, Aunt!' Anne burst out, 'must you keep on talking like this?'

'Well!' cried the old lady in astonishment. 'Whatever's the matter? These things have to be thought about. I'm your father's aunt, surely I can. . . .'

'Oh, don't,' implored Anne wearily.

'Dear me.' Aunt Orchard tied her bonnet-strings under an aggrieved chin. 'I don't know what things are coming to, I'm sure. I don't know how you can speak to me like that, Anne Pritchard. I always was against you going to that Convent. I suppose that's the way Roman Catholics bring you up to speak to your elders. But let me tell you this, Anne Pritchard, when your father dies, and you find yourself without a penny, don't come to me for help, because you won't get it. Godchild though you are, you've never behaved like one. My umbrella, Emily, please.'

§ 3

On the first day of June, Aunt Orchard arrived at Merlewood about eleven o'clock in the morning. There was no one about to receive her, but that did not distress her. She took off her new black mantle and bonnet in the hall, and from her reticule she took a packet of black-edged notepaper and envelopes, together with a small parcel of sandwiches which she had brought in case no one thought of giving her any food. She carried them into the dining room.

Holding her stiff black dress away from her feet in front, she went upstairs. The sickroom door was open, but not a sound came through it. She put her head round the screen and saw that the family were gathered round the bedside of Henry Pritchard. Anne looked up. Aunt Orchard made motions with her lips.

'How is he?'

Anne shook her head. Her eyes went back to her father.

'Dear, dear me,' motioned Aunt Orchard again.

Then she whispered loudly:

'Where's the ink?'

Anne's glance, seeming to come from a long way off, returned to her aunt.

'Where's the ink?' repeated Aunt Orchard.

Anne came to her and gently pushed her out of the room.

'I want the ink,' said Aunt Orchard, 'to write a few letters. I've had a lot of inquiries.'

'In the desk,' said Anne, turning away.

'Oh, and a pen?' said Aunt Orchard. 'I need a pen – one with a fine nib.'

'In the desk,' said Anne again, and left her.

Aunt Orchard rustled downstairs again. She opened the desk and smiled to find the ink and a new fine nib, and seated herself at the table. She consulted a list of names she had made. She decided to take the first one first. She arranged a sheet of notepaper, moistened the new nib with her tongue before dipping it into the ink, and began in a fine, firm, old-fashioned hand:

'My dear Emma.'

She was about to write one of the 'beautiful letters' for which she was famous among friends and relations.

There was no sound in the waiting house but the scratch of the pen.

She paused. Should she write: 'Is just passing away,' or 'has just passed away?'

She laid down the pen, and picking up the silk skirt in front, went upstairs.

After an interval, she came down again and shut the dining room door. She seated herself with some haste, and picking up the pen, wrote a little faster than before: 'has just passed away.'

CHAPTER TWELVE

§ 1

The sale was over. The people who had come to buy, and the people who had come out of curiosity, had gone away at last. The rooms were empty; except Anne's bedroom, where were collected the few things they had saved out of the general financial wreck. Anne, left alone, went to look at them again; the yellow desk, her books, remnants of childhood such as LT Meade and Mrs Molesworth, *Little Women* and *Good Wives*; *Arabian Nights* and the *Child's Bible*; later additions in Jane Austen, George MacDonald, Kipling, many of which George Yates had saved to buy her; and with these, her mother's green tea-service that used to be spread out in the drawing room cabinet, a rug or two, some tarnished silver.

Anne looked at them dully. They were all that was left of home. She said that to herself, but she didn't feel it. She had no feelings left. She closed the door on them and went down the naked stairs. She stood in the empty hall and listened. The familiar house where she had spent the nineteen years of her life was taking on a sinister quality. The silence thrust itself on her; the corners seemed to hold more than the dusk. Anne seized the basket that held Onions, the black kitten the milkman had given her, and fled out of the door, banging it behind her.

Outside, she paused. She had done it now. She couldn't get back. She had left home for ever. She wished she had stayed longer, said a longer goodbye. But the strangeness of the house seemed to be creeping outwards to reach her where she stood on the asphalt path. She looked back. With its blank, staring windows, it looked like something that had died with its eyes open. She hurried out of the gate. Onions stirred in his basket. She lifted him out and put him against her face to comfort her. He purred in response.

'Darling!' she said in fierce affection for the warm little thing.

Onions planted a small paw on her cheek and looked out upon the world with dreamy, pale-blue eyes. He yawned, showing his tiny pointed teeth and the incredibly perfect roof of his mouth. Ann put him back into the basket and took the road to Aunt Orchard's.

Aunt Orchard had been right on one point. When Henry Prichard died, there was found to be nothing but a few hundred pounds for his wife. On another point Aunt Orchard had been wrong: she had herself offered to take Anne to live with her. She had also taken over Emily Barnes because she could never get a maid to stop with her.

Anne was amazed that a family could be disintegrated so simply. The boys were already installed in rooms, though not together, in Manchester near their work. Olive Pritchard, as soon as the sale was over, had taken the train for Birmingham, to make a long visit to her sister. They had been bound together under one roof all these years, and now they fell apart without a protest from anyone but Anne.

'Isn't there enough money for us to live together somehow?' she asked. 'Can't we go with the boys to Manchester, and you keep house for them, while I work? Oh, Mother, do let's stick together!'

'How could you work?' asked Olive Pritchard. 'What could you do? Besides, I need a change so badly. I don't want to take on any more responsibility. And the boys don't want us. They want to be free. You mustn't be selfish, Anne. It's so kind of Aunt Orchard to take you.'

Anne knew that Aunt Orchard was not taking her out of kindness alone. Aunt Orchard liked to have objects of charity in the house. She liked to talk about what she did for them to the Vicar and her church friends. Anne remembered a poor little unpaid companion who had wept for weeks and then run away.

But Anne admitted to herself that her resistance had been weak. The fight was gone out of her. That was why she found herself on Aunt Orchard's doorstep now.

Aunt Orchard was reading the Bible, but she put it aside when she saw it was only Anne.

'So you have come, have you?' she asked, raising her oblong yellow-white face.

'Yes, Aunt Orchard.'

Funny, Anne thought, how much conversation is obvious and could be done without.

'I've brought Onions, Aunt. You don't mind, do you?'

'Not if there were any left. Never waste, I say.'

'I mean my kitten. Look, he's rather sweet.'

'I never cared for cats,' said Aunt Orchard, disregarding the ingratiating Onions. 'Take it into the kitchen. It will be something more for Emily Barnes to cry over.'

It was extremely comforting to find Emily preparing tea in the kitchen. Her eyes were fiery red at the rims, and she sniffed continuously. At the sight of Anne, her face crumpled up again uncontrollably.

'Well, to think . . .' she gulped, 'to think we've got to live 'ere.'

'But, Emily,' said Anne, 'you don't need to. You can get another place.'

'What?' cried Emily, jerked out of her weeping. 'Not me. I'm stopping 'ere with you. If you can stick it, I can.'

'Oh, Emily!' Anne threw her arms round the small shoulders and pressed her cheek to Emily's wet face.

Kindness is weakening. Something hard began to break up in Anne's heart. Her breast rose on the heave of a sob.

'Now, come on!' admonished Emily, breaking loose. 'Don't *you* begin. You've been something wonderful up till now. I don't know how they can leave you . . . nay, never mind. . . .' She shook off emotion as a terrier shakes rain. 'But don't begin,' she warned, 'or you'll never stop.'

Anne stood in the alien kitchen, struggling with her tears.

'No,' she said huskily. 'It wouldn't be safe.'

'No, it wouldn't.' Emily gave her nose a firm wipe. 'Eh, she's going to be a rum 'un to live with, is yer aunt. She's been giving me me instructions. There's three sorts of jam in this 'ouse. Ordinary jam for best visitors; jam with a bit of water in for them as is not so best; and water with a bit of jam in for you and me, my dear. Looks cheerful, don't it?'

Emily knew her Anne. The tear storm was averted. Anne laughed.

'Oh, Emily, how killing!'

'Killing's the word,' said Emily grimly. 'But I'll watch her.'

She stumped across to take the kettle off the hob. Anne was amused and comforted to see her coming down on her heels, her toes turning grotesquely up and out. It was Emily's walk when on the rampage.

'And would you believe,' she said, 'there's a Bible in every room – even in the W.'

'Anne!' came a querulous voice from the dining room.

'Oh, bless me life!' exclaimed Emily, throwing down the bread knife in disgust. 'She's done nothing but call at me ever since I came, and when I go it's for some such rubbish as "Is the potatoes boilin, Emily?" "Yes," I says, "they are; fit to bust." And no sooner do I get back to me kitchen than she calls me again and says, "You mustn't let them boil too 'ard, Emily," she says. And me boilin' potatoes for forty years and more.'

'Anne!'

'Eh, a bonny life we're going to 'ave 'ere,' predicted Emily, cutting bread with savagery. 'But go on! Good thing there's two of us.'

Aunt Orchard conducted Anne to the bedroom made hideous to her by that Saturday afternoon with Vera Bowden.

'Oh, Aunt . . .' she stammered on the threshold. 'Must I sleep here?'

'Sleep here?' echoed Aunt Orchard, looking at her niece as if she had lost her senses. 'Why, this is the second-best bedroom!'

'Yes, I know. It's very kind of you to offer it to me. But couldn't you let me have an attic instead? I'd be so much happier.'

'An attic!' Aunt Orchard had a habit of echoing. 'And then people would say I put my niece to sleep in an attic. Dear me, no! When I give you my second-best bedroom, Anne Pritchard, you might at least be grateful for it.'

'I am. I am,' cried Anne. 'But, you see . . .'

'You'll excuse me,' interrupted Aunt Orchard with dignity. 'But that's exactly what I don't. I don't see any reason that warrants a girl without a penny in the world to pick and choose and cavil at the bedroom people she has no claim on are good enough to provide for her.'

'Oh, Aunt, you don't understand. I'll sleep here,' said Anne. 'Don't think I'm not grateful. I am – really, really. I'll always remember that when I had no home, you took me in.'

Aunt Orchard was somewhat mollified.

'It's a very nice bedroom,' she said, bridling over it. She straightened the picture of her husband's grave on the liverish wallpaper, and shook out the bed-curtains, making the corded fringe squirm like a thousand caterpillars.

'And at the front, too,' she added, going to look between the Nottingham lace curtains at the deserted Victoria Street.

'Yes, it is,' agreed Anne, trying to sound cheerful.

127

'Well, take off your things,' said her aunt, moving away. 'Tea will soon be ready. I thought you might do some mending for me afterwards.'

'Certainly,' said Anne, quaking inwardly.

She quaked still more when Aunt Orchard produced a formidable pile of undergarments, things of ribbed wool and striped flannelette, the hideous wear of mid-Victorian times, smelling of time and camphor. Anne conceived a repugnance for them so sudden and so passionate that she could hardly bear to touch them.

'I want you to go through these,' said the old lady. 'They're beginning to wear, but they've done very well.' She purred over them. 'These combinations, now; I've had them for fifty years.'

§ 2

Life at Aunt Orchard's soon proved itself to be a thing of minor discomforts, cumulative and disastrous in their effect. To begin with, Anne's morning bath had to be a hurried and secret affair, not to be indulged in when Aunt Orchard was within hearing of running water. At breakfast, Aunt Orchard would not put enough milk into Anne's tea, and watched to see how much butter Anne put on her toast. The mornings were spent in dusting, about which Aunt Orchard had set little traps with mats and ornaments. She gloated triumphantly and at length when Anne fell into them. Then Anne had to go shopping with the old lady, and suffered agonies of shame at her aunt's querulous and vacillating ways of purchase. In the afternoons, she mended or read aloud out of dull books, sitting in the rooms for which she developed peculiar sensations of dislike. In the dining room she felt like a lonely fish swimming about in an aquarium, so green and gloomy was the light that filtered through the holly bushes outside the windows. In the drawing room, with its white paper, white paint, white rugs, pallid watercolours and faded bamboo tables, she felt like something drained of blood and warmth.

'Tripe,' she said to herself. 'I feel like a piece of tripe.'

Sunday was a dreadful day. Aunt Orchard had Anne and Emily fetching and carrying, running up and down stairs and standing about for a good hour before she was finally ready to go to church. Anne had to accompany her morning and evening. She sat in the front pew, and let her thoughts range. The service meant nothing to her; nothing at all. She was in a fog about religion; but one point was clear to her and that was that the Rev Archibald and his kind, good and well-meaning though they might be, could no more help her than the man in the moon.

'Why should I expect them to help me?' she said to herself. 'It's not fair to them. They are only ordinary.'

'And yet . . .' she said, pursuing her thoughts as the Rev. Archibald fulminated from the pulpit – poor man! he thought he had to be vehement. 'Through it all – all the muddle the churches have made, the figure of Jesus remains – lovely.'

She wanted to believe; but she also wanted to distinguish between truth and legend. She mistrusted emotion in religion; there was so much that appealed by its beauty. The story of the Virgin and the Child, for instance.

Sometimes, in her rare hot bath – Aunt Orchard grudged hot baths, and always came in to look at them before Anne shut the door and say: 'All that good water,' as if she had paid for every drop separately – in her bath, shut away at last from Aunt Orchard, relaxed, happy for the moment, Anne would lift up her voice and sing out: 'Ave . . . Ave Maria!' as she used to sing at the Convent, until Aunt Orchard came rapping at the door.

'Anne Pritchard,' she could call out in a voice strangled with rage. 'I will not have that heathenish nonsense sung in my house. Do you hear? Stop it at once.'

And Anne would stop because Aunt Orchard had a horrible temper. When she got into one of her rages, she would strike out – generally at Emily – with shaking hands, claw at her face and hair, utter strange, sharp sounds, while Emily ducked and dodged, flapping with her apron or kitchen towel as if Aunt Orchard were an infuriated hen. Anne hated these scenes, which were all too frequent.

And so the weeks went on without other events than these. Anne felt completely cut off from the world. No newspaper came to the house; no visitor except the Vicar and a few fellow-parishioners. Very rarely was Anne permitted to go to the Yateses to tea. The summer climbed to its height. On a certain memorable day in August, Aunt Orchard was deeply involved in preparation for the entertainment of the Vicar to supper. Although she was incredibly mean behind the scenes, she spread a lavish table for visitors, and before a 'do' as Emily called it, the kitchen was a pandemonium for days.

On this particular morning, Aunt Orchard stormed at

Emily, following her from cellar to scullery, from scullery to kitchen, from kitchen to cellar again. Emily, who was never one to refrain, stormed back with interest. Anne, deafened and fatigued, dodged between them, trying to get on with the duties assigned to her.

'I tell you, I've never touched yer bloomin' cheese grater. Yer can't remember where you've put a blamed thing. I wish to goodness you'd get out of here and let me get on.'

'Out of my own kitchen! I've never, in all my life, been spoken to as you speak to me, Emily Barnes. I won't have it. I'll give you notice.'

'Nay, you won't,' jeered Emily. 'You'd never get anybody else to stop with you. And I'm only stoppin', let me tell you, to keep an eye on that child. You'd send her crazed if I warn't 'ere to watch you. Go on with you now, and read yer Bible, and let me get something done for them parsons. Where's the fowl? Bless me life! Where's the domned bird got to? I put it on the table.'

'I've got it,' said Aunt Orchard with dignity. 'I don't like the look of it. Anne, I want you to take it back to Tomlinson's and change it.'

'But I've changed it once, Aunt,' protested Anne.

'You can change it again,' said her aunt. 'Good gracious me, I am one of Tomlinson's best customers. If they don't please me, I shall leave them.'

'Upon my life,' commented Emily, hands on hips. 'The poor beggars pay for your custom.'

Anne, with the bird in a basket, threaded the hot August streets towards Tomlinson's.

'I'm not going to stand it,' she said fiercely. 'I'd rather starve.'

Then her preoccupation with herself was shattered. There was a sudden rush of newsboys into the streets. One dreadful word was thrown about like a ball.

Anne caught it, and stood still.

'War . . . war . . . war . . .'

Mrs Charles Bramwell came up, looking startled.

'It can't be true,' she insisted. 'It simply can't be true.'

But it was. Everybody was wildly excited, not grasping the horror of it.

'It will be over in three months,' predicted the Vicar, as he demolished the thrice-changed fowl from Tomlinson's, and the curate agreed.

CHAPTER THIRTEEN

There was bewilderment and confusion in Bowford. The eager young men had disappeared from the streets. In the homes there was anxiety and fear, though the terrible days when the gallant Lancashire lads died in their hundreds in Gallipoli were not yet. Lady Brasher's house was turned into a VAD hospital and the first wounded, mostly Belgians, were coming through.

Gerald and Philip had been over to collect some things stored at Aunt Orchard's. Anne was awed by the real beauty of Gerald as a Lieutenant in the Blanks, a swagger regiment which took some getting into. Philip looked and felt a poor thing beside him. He was only a private, and it was just his luck that his uniform shouldn't even fit. He was gloomy and expected to be killed instantly.

'Though I don't care,' he said darkly.

They went away together; Philip was going back to Salisbury Plain; Gerald was on the next draft for the Front. There was a dreadful moment at the station when they said goodbye. Anne dared not cry. She felt Gerald would not like it. She stood with a twisted, aching face and told him how beautifully his buttons shone. Gerald got into a first-class carriage, Philip into a third.

'Sorry, old man,' said Gerald, 'but you know the regulation.'

'It's all part of the beastly state of the world,' said Philip.

Anne waved them away, her difficult control terribly shaken by the wet faces of the women round her; wives, mothers, sisters, sweethearts, who, like animals, would have hidden themselves when they were hurt, but were compelled to stand out on the crude, cruel railway station and expose their inmost souls.

The back of the train disappeared round the bend. Anne dropped her arm and walked out of the station. She felt suddenly and terribly alone. The well-known streets looked strange. All her family was gone, and only she was left to walk in them. She thought of her father.

'How unhappy he would have been today,' she thought.

At the beginning of Victoria Street, she turned back and went to the cemetery. She sat on the narrow coping of her father's grave and wondered why she had come. Her half-thought had been to comfort him for Gerald's going. But he was beyond comfort, she remembered, plucking at the sparse grass.

The place seemed full of death. Now and again a leaf fluttered down with a last sigh to strew the quiet graves.

'What a mess life is,' said Anne. 'What a mess . . . what a mess . . . I can't understand anything . . .'

She stretched her hands on her knee.

'Some day, these hands will be dead. I shan't be able to

move them.' She curled and uncurled her fingers while she could. 'Oh, what's life *for*?' she burst out. 'What did all these people lying here do with their lives? What did my father live for? He made us; but what do we do? The boys have gone to fight other boys – and I just run about and darn for Aunt Orchard.'

The futility of it all crept into her mind like the dank mist that began to steal among the tombstones of the cemetery. Cold and hopeless, she sat on and on. It was not until the old gatekeeper appeared on his evening round that she roused herself and went home.

A day or two later, Mildred called to say she was going to join the local VAD.

'Anne, do join,' she begged. 'We must do our bit, and besides, it will be fun.'

'I wish I could,' said Anne, pausing in her task of sponging the seven aspidistras Aunt Orchard kept in the porch. 'But I shall have to ask Aunt Orchard.'

'Go and ask her now. Quick! She simply can't say no.'

Aunt Orchard was going through her bonnets in the box-room. Anne flew upstairs to her, rattling the stair-rods in her haste. In a few moments she came slowly down.

'I can't,' she said, taking up the sponge again.

'Oh, Anne!' cried Mildred, her bright eyes brighter with sudden tears for her friend's disappointment. 'It's too bad.'

'She says she didn't take me to live with her so that I could go gadding out all the time,' said Anne.

Then she had an idea.

'Is it paid?' she asked eagerly.

'Oh, no.' Mildred's voice was quite shocked. 'They're all ladies.'

For a time, there was nothing but the sound of water being squeezed out of the penny sponge and the squeak of wiped leaves.

'Oh, well . . .' said Anne at last. 'I'll get out somehow, I'll do my bit too.'

She unfolded the big, brilliant plans of youth, and dazzled herself into silence. She was startled out of her rapt contemplation of the visions she saw among the aspidistra groves by a name.

'George . . .' Mildred was saying.

Anne's heart gave a painful leap.

'George has got a commission from the OTC in the Loyal North Lancashires. Has Philip gone yet?'

'He's going next week,' said Anne, her heart still beating too fast. 'Mother's coming up to see him and then she's coming on here.'

'How nice for you to have your mother again,' sympathised Mildred.

'I hope she'll stay a long time,' said Anne wistfully.

But her hopes were not realised. Olive Pritchard stayed long enough to see her friends, and wash out and iron the nightgowns, bedjackets and boudoir caps she needed for sitting up in other people's beds, and eating other people's breakfasts. She loved being a guest, but not in Aunt Orchard's house.

'Those combinations! No, I couldn't. My nerves would be in

rags, and who could mend those?' she asked Anne. 'I'll go and stay with Laura in St. Annes.'

And so with all her little contrivances for comfort neatly packed, she drifted off again.

It was just before Christmas that Anne heard George was going to the Front.

'Already,' she said in conventional surprise to Mildred, but her heart sank in despair. He was going to the Front, and she could not even say goodbye, or wish him luck.

'He's coming home on leave on Tuesday until Friday. Aunt Frances is terribly upset. You would really think she was mad if you heard her, Anne. She wants to know if this is what's she's starved herself and him for – to be killed by Germans? I don't really know what she means. Starved? I'm sure they've never starved. They've never been short of food, I'm sure.' Mildred was obtuse and indignant. 'It's awful to hear her. Poor Uncle sits and listens until she's tired out, and then goes off for long walks by himself. I go to see them sometimes, but Aunt Frances seems to hate us, because we haven't got a boy to be killed.'

Anne saw George on Friday afternoon. Turning the corner of Manchester Road, she found him coming towards her. Her heart beat to suffocation, the voice with which she was going to speak to him died in her throat. She could not manage herself. She raised her eyes, but lowered them before the hardness of his.

It was pitiful that this Anne, paralysed by a storm of emotion, should present to George Yates nothing more than the spectacle of a girl embarrassed by meeting the man she had jilted because he was poor and had no prospects.

And so they passed each other.

Anne went wearily back to tea. It was a relief to find that Aunt Orchard was out.

'She's gone to visit them Belgiums,' said Emily gleefully. 'Come on into the kitchen and have your tea with me, love. You do look a poor, peaky little thing lately. Sit you down in that rocking chair by the fire, and shall it be Welsh rarebit or poached egg? There's a rind of cheese I've been 'iding for days 'ud just make a nice taste.'

The rocking chair was comforting, the savoury cheese-toast was comforting, the hot tea – but most of all Emily Barnes was comforting. She was the sort of woman – to be found from queens to kitchenmaids – whose mere presence makes a home.

'Emily,' said Anne, 'why didn't you get married?'

'Well,' said Emily reminiscently, both hands round her tea-cup, 'I never seed nobody I liked as well as meself.'

'But . . .' she resumed, with emphasis, 'I've 'ad me chances. There was once a young fellow after me, when you was a little girl, quite the gentleman, at least 'e wore a 'ard 'at; but there were something foreign-like about 'im – sorter dark yeller complexion. Course, it might 'uv been kidney or liver, I don't know – but it looked foreign to me. And I wouldn't take up with a foreigner for all as I could see. I always thinks they'd be up with a knife if you crossed 'em.'

She took an audible sip of tea and put her cup down.

'Nay,' she resumed, crossing her arms on the table. 'If I can see you nicely married and settled somewheres where I can come and do a bit of charrin' for you, I'll get meself a little house nearby, and what with keeping it tidy and going to the pictures I shan't bother about calling the Queen me aunt. But I'll see you settled first.'

'No, Emily . . .' protested Anne. 'Don't bother about me.'

'It's not bothering,' contradicted Emily, pouring out another cup of strong tea. 'Bless me life, I wouldn't leave that cat in this 'ouse with that old woman.'

Onions knew he was being talked about. He leaped with delicate deliberation on to Emily's knee, and surveyed the table inquiringly.

'I wish we could get out,' cried Anne. 'I wish I could get some work and earn enough money for us to go into rooms.'

'Well, isn't there anything?' inquired Emily, putting on the earnest face that consultation of Anne's affairs demanded.

'I've looked everywhere,' said Anne dejectedly. 'When I go out for Aunt Orchard, I rush into the Free Library and look through the "Wanteds"; there are plenty, but they all need shorthand and typing or experience or something.'

'And that reminds me,' said Emily. 'Get down, Onions! I saw a bit in the *Weekly News* what you used to write in. Now, where is it? Oh, here it is. See that top bit: "Technical School". You read that.'

Anne read, but her dejection increased.

'Of course it's just the thing. "Intensive course in short-hand, typewriting, bookkeeping, and office routine – thirty shillings." It's just what I need, Emily. But they might as well ask for thirty thousand pounds as thirty shillings. I've got one and sevenpence ha'penny in the world, and I don't suppose I'll ever even be able to make it up to one and eight. You know

I can't make a penny now that the *Weekly News* isn't taking any outside contributions because of the War.'

'No,' said Emily Barnes, walking with the cups into the scullery. 'But I've got the money.'

'Don't talk rubbish, Emily. I'm not going to take your money.'

'Of course,' said Emily, 'I know I'm only a servant . . .'

Anne flew at her.

'Don't be an idiot, Emily,' she cried. 'A servant's a good thing to be. Can't you see how much better it is to be a servant than to be me? I've got to live with Aunt Orchard because I can't keep myself. Oh, Emily, don't be silly about yourself! You're my best friend. You're all that's left.'

'Well then.' Emily's chin gave a little, as it did in moments of emotion. 'You just let me give you thirty shillings, as friend to friend. Why, I lent the girl next door two pounds to run away with, and I never seen her since. But I've got 'er box, though there's nothing in it but some letters from a man, very nice they are too, I will admit. So why make a bother about taking thirty shillings from me?'

'Oh, Emily, you're too good for words. If you'll lend it me, I'd soon be able to pay it back when I get a job, and see! It says, "This Course is being instituted to provide clerks for the many vacancies in Municipal Offices and others." So I'd perhaps get a job as soon as I'm through.'

She danced about the kitchen like a mad thing, while Onions looked on in dignified surprise.

'Sh . . .' warned Emily, snatching up the incriminating cheese grater. 'I 'eard the front door.'

Anne came to a dead stop.

'Emily,' she faltered, 'suppose she won't let me go? I mean suppose she won't let me stop here until I've finished the Course. It says five weeks.'

Emily looked fierce.

'If that domned creature doesn't let you go I'll . . . I'll . . .' She looked round in vain for a threat terrible enough. 'Eh, by gum, but I don't know what I'll do,' she finished.

'I'll go and ask her now,' said Anne. 'It's best to get it over.'

'Take my bonnet upstairs,' Aunt Orchard greeted her. 'I'm worn out with those Belgians. They're always clamouring for something. The man says he's cold in that suit of your uncle's; he wants underwear now.'

'Oh, Aunt!' burst out Anne, 'give him those combinations of yours.' Her face was radiant at the thought of getting rid of a form of torture as terrible surely as any devised by a classical hell.

'I shall do no such thing.' Aunt Orchard was exceedingly indignant at the insult put upon her intimate garments. 'The very idea! My good combinations that have worn so well! The sooner you learn a little thriftiness the better, Anne Pritchard. Remember, you won't have me to provide for you all your life.'

'That's just what I want to talk to you about,' said Anne.

Eager, young, she stood, turning Aunt Orchard's best bonnet in her hands, and made her request.

The old woman was angry.

'You ungrateful girl!' she gasped. 'Oh, you ungrateful girl! After I've taken you in when you hadn't a penny . . . and now you go . . .'

She was incoherent with rage.

'But what am I going to *do*?' cried Anne. 'I must be able to keep myself. Have I got to keep being taken in by someone all my life? I'm not going to do it, I tell you. I *will* keep myself. I'll go and be a maid, if you don't let me take this Course.'

'And then what'll your friends say?' shouted Emily from the kitchen. 'A nice tale that'll make in the parish.'

Aunt Orchard stood under the incandescent light, looking round helplessly.

'I tell you I will,' Anne said again.

''Appen we'll apply at the Vicarage,' shouted Emily, and guffawed mercilessly.

Aunt Orchard crumpled up on a chair.

'Do as you like,' she muttered.

Anne relented.

'I'll do the mending at nights,' she promised. 'And the aspidistras at dinner times, and I'll pay you back some day, and thank you very much.'

She flew to the yellow desk to write an application for admission to the Intensive Commercial Course.

CHAPTER FOURTEEN

§ 1

'Now is the time for every good man to come to the help of his party. Now is the time for every good man to come to the help of his party. Now is the time for every good man to come to the help of his party.'

Anne, eyes tightly closed, feeling for the keys with her slim fingers, spelling mentally, tapped it out on the Underwood. Three times.

'There.' She unscrewed her eyes and leaned forward to look.

'Mpe od yjr yo,r gpt rbrtu hppf ,sm yp vp,r yp yjr sof pg jod styu zMpe od yjr yo,r gpt rhrtu hppf ,sm yp vp,r yp yjr sof pg jod ⅜styu Mpe od yjr yo,r gpt rbrtu hppf ,sm yp vp,r yp yjr sof pg jod ½stty.'

'Oh, Lord,' she groaned.

Vast disappointment filled her. She sagged back on her chair. It seemed a dreadful thing not to be able to deal with time and the good man and the party. Her eyes wandered dejectedly.

In her half of the hot room, typewriters clicked in rows, some with enviable speed, others tentatively and slow. In the other half of the room, Mr William Wood dictated for shorthand. Across the click-click, she heard scattered words: 'Partitler; chotlate; tittle; giddle.'

She smiled to herself, remembering how she used to get that transcription wrong until she grasped that he meant: 'Particular; chocolate; tickle; giggle.'

Mr William Wood gave no one any reason to wonder why he had not joined the army. C_3 was written large on him. He bulged in the wrong places, and was pale and flabby as a plant grown in a cellar. He smelt sick.

The poor man was in a state of mental perspiration from the beginning of a 'Commercial Course' to the end, and when one was over, he had, without interval, to start on another. He felt it would kill him. Some girls were so stupid they almost drove him mad; some were so clever that they frightened him. Some were so well-bred that he daren't correct them; some so pretty that he didn't want to.

When he took them round to the Municipal Offices to inspect office methods at first hand, he looked like nothing so much as a fat white maggot borne along by chattering birds. Anne liked the hard-working harassed little man; but she wished he would wash.

She pulled herself together for another onslaught on the Underwood. She moored the little finger of her left hand to A, and the little finger of her right hand to colon and semicolon, shut her eyes tightly, and began again.

'Now is the time for every good man . . .'

There was a pause in the rattle of machines, and a 'pittle' died on the air. Anne, fingers poised, opened her eyes.

By the side of Mr William Wood, suddenly dwarfed by contrast, stood a man glowering at the commercial class through horn-rimmed glasses.

'Got a girl?' he inquired abruptly. 'Burton's called up this morning.'

Mr Wood waved to his class to proceed, and withdrew to talk sideways out of his mouth to the new-comer.

The class was in a flutter. Heads bobbed and ducked over typewriters, fingers struck wildly at the keys. Some girls giggled nervously, others frowned importantly, in case they should be chosen.

'Who is it?' whispered Anne to a girl with a hare lip at which she always tried not to look.

'Dr Soames, the Medical Officer,' the girl whispered back.

Dr Soames, William Wood trotting in his wake, walked up and down at the end of the room, his hand set fanwise to his lean waist at each side.

'He goes in there, instead of out,' noticed Anne.

The light from the high windows struck his hair and made a splash of colour out of it; for Dr Soames's hair was red – a dark, rusty red.

Anne remembered her father's saying that all redheads were queer.

'He's queer enough,' she thought. 'His face looks as if it had been hacked out of wood by somebody who couldn't carve. Three, two, one – that's how his face is,' meaning the three deep lines between the eyes that kept him out of the army, the two on his upper lip, and the one wedge out of the middle of his chin.

Dr Soames wheeled suddenly and stared at the class.

'That one,' he said, and bore down on her.

'What about coming into my office?' he said to her.

She was very much taken aback, and looked up at him with fluttering eyelids.

'I need a secretary. Not allowed to offer more than a pound a week.'

'But I'm not trained,' said Anne.

'I'll train you.' The big man dismissed her objection. 'I prefer to train my own people. Well, how about coming to my office and looking it over?'

'When?' asked Anne.

'Now.'

She stood up, feeling bewildered.

'It's a good job, Miss Pritchard,' whispered William Wood, following her as she went to get her hat. 'About the best that's come in yet. The MOH, you know. . . .' He spoke with awe. 'But, my word, he's a worker. If he drives you too hard, come back, Miss Pritchard, and I'll see what I can do elsewhere. I'm sorry you're going before you've finished the course.'

'Yes, and I'd just got "Now is the time for every good man to come to the help of his party" right for the first time,' she said, half-regretfully, though she was elated and dazzled by the thought of a 'job'; magic word to unemancipated femininity; the abracadabra, the open sesame!

She walked through the Bowford streets with Dr Soames, feeling embarrassed and excited. Her skirt kept flying open at the side as she walked revealing her slim left leg. She was worried about it, and hoped it wouldn't prejudice the MOH against her.

At the Municipal Offices, councillors, clerks, messenger boys, mothers with children were going in and coming out. Dr Soames rushed her through the big, echoing, dingy place and finally came to anchor in his own room.

'Well?' he asked, swivelling himself about in his revolving chair.

'Oh, I'd like to come,' said Anne. 'But can I do the work; that's what I'm not sure about.'

'You're too modest,' said Soames. 'Wood told me about you. Higher Local Honours, Matriculation and all that. I want you to do my letters, card index and file my notices and cases and so on. I'll show you how. And later on, I want you to take the minutes at Committee. Well, shall we say nine o'clock tomorrow morning?'

It was done as quickly as that. Anne, slightly breathless, walked out of the office secretary to the MOH on the princely salary of one pound a week.

It is one of the properties of youth to be for ever building out of its imagination innumerable palaces wherein to dwell, and to accept them later for the little mud huts they turn out to be. Anne went to the Health Office in a state of mind approaching reverence.

New, earnest, weighted with a sense of the immense importance of the wooden index boxes that smelt like dried beans left too long in soak, she filed and docketed. With the tip of her little red tongue earnestly protruded, she took down letters and tapped them out carefully on her machine. She went on errands through the echoing corridors, interviewed dusty, fusty undersized clerks – all the sweeping tide of war had left behind – and moved young, vital, bright-haired against the hard background of pitch pine, dirty windows, ledgers, letterpresses, ink and india rubbers.

When the MOH rang, she always had to get a small swallow down before opening his door. She would meet his eyes over the edge of the roll-top desk that faced her as she went in. She would advance, notebook in hand, trying to look the complete secretary, but never being able to disguise her air of being a little girl who had strayed in from somewhere and lost herself. The MOH would flick out the flap at the side of his desk for her to rest her notebook on, and begin with horrid rapidity to dictate.

Anne's pencil flew in a panic. She wrote the names of the diseases in full, and guessed the rest. As she wrote, the MOH tilted himself backwards and forwards in his chair, brandished the big round ruler, snatched a pencil to get out figures with incredible speed, alluded without reference to events of months past, with names, numbers, minute particulars all complete. It seemed to Anne that he never forgot anything. His efficiency startled her. In the pauses of dictation she stole glances at him.

Richard Charles Evelyn Dayborn Soames was a strange mixture. He did innumerable kindnesses to the poor among whom he worked, to the soldiers he tended at the hospital in his spare time. But he undid half of them by his terseness and his complete indifference to the small amenities that oil the wheels of life. It was, and he knew it and did not care, this unaccommodating manner of his that found him, with brilliant degrees and real efficiency, no more than Medical Officer of Health for Bowford, with its population of 200,000, at the age of thirty-eight.

Anne was attracted by this very manner. She confessed to herself that she liked people who were different. When she became efficient enough to follow him into committee, he seemed unique indeed.

She watched him as he sat at the top of the long, leather-topped table, next to the Chairman, Councillor Blackledge, whose waxed moustache and prominent little stomach was repeated, almost without variation, round the board in the other members of the committee. Most of them wore dickies and ties drawn through rings, and watch-chains with fobs. They scorned an aitch and began a motion with: 'Well, A'hm a plain Lancashire man meself. . . .'

They were stubborn. They thought they knew everything. But they were no match for the MOH. He hustled them; he worried them. Like a picador at a bull fight, he stuck them with his small, stinging, verbal darts, until, heavily, they gave in and let him do as he liked. They got up and went away, grumbling, in their fawn raincoats and their little billycock hats, and Anne gleefully recorded their defeat.

The office gods crumbled one by one from the pedestals whereon the green recruit to the world of men's work had set them. She saw Wilkinson for the finicking, detail-obsessed little man he was, and objected to his clipping his nails with a patent pocket arrangement, and making the bits jump all over the desk. She knew that Dexter spent half his time smoking surreptitiously in the cellar; that Berridge slipped out to get a drink; that the most anyone ever saw of Emmett was the back of his head with huge flaps of ears, as he observed the life of Bowford from the window overlooking the Market Square. They were probably not bad in their limited way, but they were mere men, and Anne was getting used to men, was taking them in her everyday stride. Only the MOH remained on a peak.

The going to the office had made a great difference in her life. She was extremely happy to have something to do. Inaction in Bowford at that time was intolerable. Every day brought its own evil; news of the horrors on the far away Front; news of intimate tragedies pushed right home by the losses, day after day, of its own young men; men who, as babies, had played in the Corporation Park, as schoolboys had filled Bowford Grammar School, as young men peopled Bowford offices. None of these familiar places would see them any more. There was Lady Brasher's eldest son gone, and both Bramwell boys. Roger Maitland, who used to live next door, was blinded. Anne could not bear to remember his eyes on those wild nights – brimful of badness they had been, and now they were blank. She wrung her hands and wept for him.

Gerald had been wounded once and was back with his regiment. Philip bore a charmed life, and went through the blood and mud and vermin of the trenches without grumbling any more than usual. George Yates was still safe. Anne thought about him at nights. Once she took up her pen to write to him, but put it down again. There was simply nothing she could say. How explain the storm that had swept her? How say that now she was beginning to accept, inevitably, many things that she had shuddered at? Or say that in the face of this blood and death, the fact that your mother and father had to be married did not matter any more? No, there was nothing to be done. She closed the yellow desk. She was a strangely final creature.

§ 2

On the 28th February, the last day of Anne's first month as a business woman, an atmosphere of restless expectancy permeated the Health Office. The door of the general office opened incessantly on faces that inquired with raised eyebrows: 'Bee not come yet?' Dexter, Berridge, Emmett, Thomson, Coward, even Wilkinson, the head clerk, drifted in and out, making jokes about beam-ends and pawn-shops. Butt, the office boy, said continuously through his adenoids: 'Eh, bud I wish he'd cub.' About 5.30 the office sent up a sigh of relief. Bee, pallid and red-haired, had been sighted by Emmett crossing the Market Square with black bag and ledger. Butt rushed to hold open the swing-door for the welcome visitant. There was not a more popular man in Bowford than Bee, of the Borough Treasurer's Department, and no man exerted himself less to merit it. He was peculiarly silent; made no response at all to the hail of jokes that greeted him. He caught sight of Anne at her typewriter, and thereafter in the intervals of sorting envelopes, kept his light eyes – eyes like a hen's, thought Anne, with a little bright buttony pupil and almost white rims – in an unwinking stare on this unusual addition to the Health Office Staff.

The news of his arrival had gone round like lightning. Strange creatures, unseen at any other time, came up out of the bowels of the earth, scrambled down from the garrets, burst out of unsuspected cubbyholes, drawn by the magnet of Pay. They took their precious narrow envelopes, licked their stamps, signed receipts with the office pen that had a nib made like a pointing hand with a frilled cuff – you wrote with the first finger – glanced with curiosity, resentment, admiration at Anne according to their kind, and scuttled back to their burrows.

Envelopes were distributed in order of amount. Anne's was next to the last, next to Butt's. For a long time, Bee had held it in his hand so as to be ready to give it to her when her turn came. He handed it to her at last, dipped the pointing hand into the ink, and proffered it to her to sign the receipt. Anne thanked him, and was disconcerted by the sudden revelation of a set of enormous false teeth, complete with gums, in Bee's answering smile.

Six o'clock had struck before she received her precious packet. She flew with it to her cloakroom, rammed her hat over her excited eyes, buttoned up her coat, and sped home to Emily Barnes. Emily would be waiting to share her triumph.

'It's mine! It's mine!' she sang to herself. 'I *made* it.'

Aunt Orchard was, mercifully, at a Vicarage Tea. Anne hullaballoed about the place, dancing from the pallid drawing room, to the plushy dining room, with Emily Barnes, remonstrant but indulgent, behind. Onions took refuge in the back garden and sat on the sooty lawn with his back to the house. The envelope was magical indeed. It held not only four pound notes and some odd silver, but independence, hope, new sanity, something that changed Anne's point of view. She felt a sudden unlocking and a letting in of air on her old unhappiness.

After tea, taken comfortably with Emily by the kitchen fire, she sat, with Onions sagging at ease on her knee, and reviewed the past months from her new standpoint. She found, almost with surprise, that she was talking to Emily.

'Emily,' she was saying, 'you've been with our family for years. Is it true that my father and mother had to get married?'

It was out as calmly as that. But her heart began to beat suffocatingly. Emily, taken utterly aback, dropped her mending, her mouth fell open.

'Well,' she gasped, 'well . . . I never did 'ear of such a thing. Whatever . . .'

'My cousin said so,' said Anne, pressing her hand to her side, her eyes wide on Emily.

'What cousin?'

'Vera Bowden.'

'Oh, the liar!' burst out Emily, her face knotted and crimson, 'the wicked liar! The disgustiness of it. . . . I never 'eard of such a trick.'

'Emily . . .' Anne laid a shaking hand on Emily's knee. 'Are you going to say it isn't true?'

'True! It's the domndest lie as ever I 'eard,' cried Emily. 'And the wickedest part about it is as it's 'er father and mother as 'ad to be married. Yes, it is. I remember all about it. 'Er mother was not so good as 'im, and your father's family was against it. She were a bad lot; died of drink in a 'ome when that cousin of yours was a little girl. Well, of all the wicked things . . . for 'er to put 'er own parents' sin on to yours! Whyever didn't you tell me about it before?'

'I couldn't,' said Anne. 'Talking about it . . . well, I couldn't somehow.'

'And your father dying, and you thinking that about 'im,' said Emily reproachfully.

'I didn't. I didn't think about it then. I'm so glad I didn't. But I'll go and see Vera Bowden tomorrow.' Anne's eyes hardened, she set her teeth. 'I'll tell her what she did to me, and how she made me suffer and lose . . . such a lot. . . .'

Tears came into her eyes. She dashed them away.

'I'll not cry today. I should be a fool, Emily. Because, d'you know, I think I'm happier today than I've ever been in my life. I used to be very happy once. . . .' She left a gap and filled it by thoughts of George. 'But by contrast with what I've gone through, this is the best, Emily, the glorious best.'

But Emily was still absorbed in horror at Anne's disclosure.

'Eh, to think . . .' she said, over and over again, 'that anybody could be so spiteful. . . . And your poor father . . . and 'im such a saint in 'is way, not but what 'e wasn't a bit trying, but still 'e's dead . . .'

The next day, Saturday, Anne, who had to give an account of her goings and comings, received Aunt Orchard's grudging permission to go to her cousin's house.

The Manchester road was full of people; bulky mothers with string bags and perambulators making their difficult way to the market, tramcars full of the fathers off to the football match at Spenwood, children straggling up to the Corporation Park with bottles of Spanish juice or ginger beer, cold cheer on a February day. Their object was to draw the old woman at the lodge gates, by throwing stones into the Fountain. When she emerged, they would run in delicious terror.

'She's a witch! Eh, she's a witch!' . . . they told each other and made the babies cry dismally.

Anne hardly saw anybody. She was rehearsing what she was going to say. Nothing sounded adequate. She could never put into words the destruction that Vera Bowden had worked in her life.

'Why did she do it? Why did she do it?' she asked herself continually. She was bewildered. It was so needlessly cruel. She found it hard, being young, to grasp the fact that anyone could want to hurt for the mere sake of hurting.

She turned out of the crowded main road, and entered the open elegant avenues leading to Vera's house. She rang the bell, without having come to any conclusion as to what to say.

Yes, said the fancy maid, Mrs Bowden was at home.

Anne followed her through the hall, white-painted and pink-carpeted, into a room where the cosy note was dreadfully overdone in cushions, and cabbage rose chintz, and artificial carnations, scented, in silver epergnes. On a couch before the hot fire, surrounded by magazines and picture papers, lay Vera Bowden. She raised herself languidly as the door opened and flopped back among the cushions when she saw who it was.

Her eyes were dull, and her mouth, over-rouged, sagged pettishly.

'Oh, it's you, is it?' she said ungraciously.

Anne advanced.

'Move those books and sit down,' said Vera. 'Isn't Saturday a damnable day? I used always to have such a good time on Saturday, motoring to Blackpool for dinner and dancing or a theatre, but now Arthur's always off shooting or something. At least he says he is, but I don't believe him.'

Anne regarded the heated, frowsy picture Vera Bowden made among the cabbage roses and the black satin cushions. She found her rather dreadful.

'Oh damn!' burst out Vera, 'I'm so *bored*.' She turned her head sideways and plucked at the chintz. A tear rolled slowly out of the corner of her eye and made a crooked path through the powder on her cheek.

'Oh, Anne,' whispered Vera Bowden, her face still averted. 'What shall I *do*? I'm so bored.'

Anne was taken aback by this appeal. She stood gazing at her cousin's heaved hip, her feelings a mixture of exasperation, contempt, and a youthful desire to help, where no help could be given.

'You could work at something,' she suggested diffidently.

'I can't. I might start all right, but I'd give it up sooner or later. I can't stick to anything.'

'You could if you wanted to.'

'I can't want to,' said Vera, still plucking at the chintz. 'It isn't in me. Oh, I lead a hell of a life!'

Anne, watching her cousin's tears gather and roll slowly, was annoyed to find herself giving way to a sense of pity. She fought against it.

'It's her own fault. She's brought herself to it.'

She reminded herself of what she had come to say. But at the mere thought of it, her heart began to beat with that terrible suffocating rapidity. The idea of opening up the subject again appalled her. Suppose Vera sat up and insisted that it was true, that Emily Barnes didn't know what she was talking about, that she, Vera, had evidence that it was true. Suppose she started again with her filthy tales, slamming everybody. Anne felt unequal to it. The old nausea overcame her. She couldn't bring out her new assurance into this atmosphere. Far better take it away with her, untouched.

'Coward!' she called herself. But, coward or not, it had to be.

Vera Bowden jumped up from the couch, scattering papers, chocolates, powder puff and lipstick.

'What a fool I am!' she cried, rushing up to the mirror over the mantelpiece. 'I've ruined my eyes, and Freddie Farrar said he might pop in after the match. I must go and bathe my eyes. I think I'll lie down with boracic pads on them. That's the best thing. Oh, I have made a damned mess of myself. Why did you let me weep? Did you come for anything special?'

With reluctance Anne lied.

'No.'

'Oh, well,' said Vera, determined to get rid of her young cousin before Freddie Farrar could arrive. 'D'you mind if I go and see to my face now? Goodbye. Give my love to Aunt Orchard, the old bitch. Wish she'd die and let us see a bit of that money.'

Anne escaped into the fresh, cold air with relief.

She didn't know what to think of herself. Had she been cowardly, or had she been wise? She walked with her head down, wondering.

CHAPTER FIFTEEN

§ 1

Anne sat by the window in the dining room that was like an aquarium. She sat on the rocking chair that had no arms; a thing that would spitefully tip you out sideways or backwards or forwards, but the only chair that could be drawn up close enough to the window to catch the last light of the winter afternoon. Anne needed all the light she could get for the mending of Aunt Orchard's underclothes; the unescapable things that had given out without fail every week of the eighteen months Anne had lived with their wearer.

Anne had her usual feeling that she was sitting far down under water.

'"Sabrina fair, listen where thou art sitting
Beneath the glassy, cool, translucent wave . . ."'

she said to herself, and repeated: 'cool, translucent.'

'Lovely,' she said, and took another piece of natural-coloured wool.

'"With silver braids of lilies knitting
The loose train of thy amber-dropping hair."'

Her hands fell into her lap. She looked out into the dim, greenish silence of Victoria Street beyond the dank garden, and back over her shoulder at the room full of shadows, where Aunt Orchard slept in her chair by the fire.

'There must be beauty somewhere,' said Anne to herself.

Aunt Orchard stirred. Anne remembered her mending and bent her head to it again.

What a day it had been! Emily was still at it in the kitchen. Anne could hear her opening and shutting the oven door, moving pots and pans, trudging backwards and forwards over the tiled floor. Aunt Orchard, exhausted, had dropped into her chair and fallen abruptly to sleep. And all because the Vicar was bringing the visitant preacher, the Rev Canon Verity, to supper after service tomorrow night. To Aunt Orchard, this was a triumph, a feather in her cap indeed. It emphasized her position as the most important member of St Jude's congregation, as the friend of the Vicar. She impressed it upon Anne that it was a very great honour indeed to entertain the Rev Canon Verity to supper.

She had provided more cold chickens, hams, tongues, salads, creams, jellies, fruit pies, than a whole Chapter could have demolished at one sitting, together with a host of side dishes such as potted beef, lemon cheese, Eccles cakes and so on, in case the reverend gentleman might fancy one of them. And on the table there was a 'shopping list', written out in Aunt Orchard's fine pointed hand, of all the things Anne was to fetch from the town when the light failed.

Anne's thoughts flew with her needle. She blessed the work that took her away from the house during the week. What an escape work was!

'How easy things are for men!' she thought. 'They can always get away from these houses. I could never have stood Aunt Orchard without the Health Office to go to.'

She thought with satisfaction how her position in the house had eased since she had been able to hand over fifteen shillings a week out of her salary, now twenty-five shillings, and make up what she considered the deficiency in mending and aspidistra washing and putting up with Aunt Orchard generally. The bread of dependence had been very bitter. It might have been different if she had been able to like Aunt Orchard. But that she could not do. She had been taught, in her convent, that there was something likeable in everybody. She had searched conscientiously for it in Aunt Orchard at first, but had given it up long ago now. Aunt Orchard's show of piety and outward generosity were repulsive to Anne, who knew all her little tricks and secret meannesses, her vanities incredible in an old woman, and her terrible sudden rages. There was, besides, some sinister quality in the old woman that acted on Anne disastrously. Something that made her not like to be alone with her, not like to pass her on the dim stairs, made her lock her bedroom door at night. She had done that ever since the night she had awakened in cold terror to find the old woman leaning over her, candle in hand, her dull eyes gleaming through the wisps of old hair that obscured her face. At the scream Anne raised, Emily Barnes came scrambling down from her attic.

'Whatever are you doing?' she cried indignantly, seizing Aunt Orchard's arm. 'Frightening the poor child out of her wits?'

'She is very silly,' said Aunt Orchard, stalking away. 'I only wanted to see how she would look when she was dead.'

There was no fathoming her, as Emily said. Anne wondered if she was mad, but Emily pointed out that nothing could be cleverer than the way she kept up the appearance of being the gentlest, most pious lady in the world. She held the respect of the whole parish of St Jude, and no one in it would have believed a word against her.

It was getting too dark to sew. Anne's hands fell into her lap. Her thoughts turned to Richard Soames. She liked to think of him.

'I feel so alive when he's there,' she said. 'I feel galvanised into energy. And he is a dear, funny thing. That poor blushing youth wouldn't know what to make of him yesterday when he turned into the general office, instead of into the vestibule. 'This is the better exit, I think. You'd have to go through the window that way, you see.'

She laughed silently in the darkening room. His ways were a delight to her. And she found something tremendously appealing about the hole in the thumb of his glove. It seemed to her a pathetic, almost unbearable thing, that he should be going about with a hole in the thumb of his glove.

'I wish I dare mend it,' she said, hotness enveloping her at the daring of the thought.

Suddenly the silence of the house was shattered by a peal at the front door bell. Aunt Orchard did not stir in her chair by the fire, but Anne heard Emily's footsteps as she went to answer it. There was a muffled sound of voices, of someone being admitted to the drawing room, and Emily came into the dining room.

'We'se have to wake her,' she said, her white apron alone showing in the firelight. 'Eh, and would you believe? Yon bloomin' orange cream 'as gone and curdled.'

'What?' cried Anne, who realised the magnitude of the catastrophe.

'That bloomin' orange cream,' repeated Emily, ''as gone and curdled.'

There was a strange rasping sound from the chair by the fire. Anne and Emily drew near in alarm.

'Did you say, Emily Barnes, that the orange cream had curdled?'

Aunt Orchard raised herself with difficulty out of her chair and stood peering at Emily's white apron.

'I did, cos it 'as,' said Emily stoutly.

Aunt Orchard made an inarticulate sound and raised her shaking hands above her head.

'Good 'eavens!' cried Emily. 'She's off in one of 'er rages!'

The old woman was on her, scuffling, clawing. Emily beat her off, protesting loudly.

''Ere, leave me alone, will you? GET OFF, y'orrible old woman! Stop it, t'isn't yuman the way you carry on!'

'Oh, Aunt . . .' begged Anne, pulling her from behind. 'Don't do that, don't!'

'Get out of my house!' shrieked Aunt Orchard, pursuing Emily. 'Get out of my house, you wasteful, thieving creature! Get out . . . come here! Let me get hold of you! Just let me get my hands on you. . . .'

Emily burst out into the lighted hall. Aunt Orchard, with a leap of incredible agility, burst out after her, and got her clawing fingers in her hair. Emily let off a shriek that would have awakened the dead – and then there was a silence as complete as if a hand had been clapped simultaneously over each mouth. On the threshold of the drawing room stood the Vicar and Canon Verity, staring as if their eyes would drop out of their reverend heads.

Aunt Orchard's fingers dropped from her victim's hair. Falteringly she wiped her slavering mouth.

'Dear, dear me,' said the Vicar. 'This is most unfortunate.'

He did not know what to say. He was utterly taken aback at the sight of Aunt Orchard.

The hall was full of the pantings, perhaps exaggerated, of the dishevelled Emily. She was not at all sorry that Aunt Orchard had revealed herself at last.

'I beg your pardon,' stammered the Vicar, 'I do truly beg your pardon for intruding at – er – such a time.' He might have been making the scene himself the way he felt about it. 'Has anything happened?' He did not want to seem to inquire, yet felt an explanation would be welcome, after all he had said to the Canon about the delightful Mrs Orchard.

'It's because the orange cream for tomorrow's supper 'as gone and curdled,' said Emily.

'It's this woman who upsets me.' Aunt Orchard spoke at last in a voice of stifled rage.

'Y'upset yerself,' said Emily sharply.

The Vicar blinked as if he expected blows to fall.

'Perhaps we'd better go, sir,' he said. 'Some other time when Mrs Orchard is less – er – occupied. . . . We only called to say that Canon Verity finds he must return home directly after service tomorrow and cannot therefore accept your hospitality. Thank you very much – er – all the same. Thank you, thank you – er – excuse me.'

He engineered the Canon almost protectingly past Aunt Orchard, and tiptoed behind him to the door. Anne so far recovered from her awkwardness to hold the door for them.

'You must excuse her,' she said. 'She's old.'

'Oh, of course,' said the Vicar, putting on his shovel hat. He was shocked that she should think he would fail in his Christian duty. 'But it's best to go now, I think. Best to go. Good night. Good night, Mrs Orchard. Good night.'

The black backs of the clergy disappeared through the door.

Aunt Orchard stood as if turned to stone until the clang of the gate reached her. Then she came to life with a wail:

'He never introduced the Canon to me. He never introduced the Canon to me. He never introduced the Canon to me.' They had to put her to bed.

§ 2

It was no use going to town with the shopping list now, so Anne escaped with relief to the Yateses' house. They

165

welcomed her heartily. Mrs James Yates had been rather shocked when Anne went to the Health Office, but when Gwendolin Brasher went into a bank, and other girls from 'the best families' trooped to the desk and the typewriter, Mrs Yates was reassured. The only difference she made to Anne was to tell her, now, how very much she paid for everything.

'Isn't it dreadful?' she would say. 'Six guineas for a set of crêpe de chine underclothes for Mildred? Six guineas!'

She was secretly overjoyed about it.

Mr James Yates was not a 'profiteer' by any means, but his mills were unaffected by the war. He prospered accordingly.

His wife prospered, too. She joined the bandaging classes, the VAD practices at Lady Brasher's, the Soldiers' and Sailors' Families Association, the War Pensions committee – anything that was organised, Mrs James Yates was there to be found. She was indefatigable and extremely useful. She glowed with satisfaction to know that she was serving her country and, incidentally, mixing with the best people in Bowford. Yes, there was no doubt about it, Mrs James Yates was 'in' with 'everybody' at last, and Mildred was having opportunities that she would otherwise never have had.

Happy satisfaction with her lot in life shone in Mrs Yates as she sat by the fire on this winter evening, knitting a woollen khaki helmet.

Her eyes beamed as they rested on her husband. Mr James Yates gave off minute and shining reflections from all points; from the patent-leather pumps he wore as house shoes, from his eyeglasses, from his polished bald head, from his small rosy face. He looked as if he had just been spring cleaned. He was glancing quickly through his *Times* so that he could get on to his *Daily Mail* with a clear conscience.

Mrs Yates's eyes, when they turned to Mildred, became wonderfully tender. Her daughter! How beautiful the child was, how bright, how taking! Who could help loving her? She trembled to think of the man who would surely come soon and take her away. But of course it was ridiculous to think like that about it. Mildred must marry, and marry well. It was her natural right. How proud her mother would be! She had a vision of Mildred in a palatial house, such as, well, Amherst Lodge, on Lower Avenue, with a butler in the hall, and a nurse upstairs in the nursery with the children, and herself taking a few friends to tea and showing them over the house. Or was it perhaps not the thing to show people over the house? Her needles clicked busily. She would have liked to ask Anne.

'Anne looks so distinguished,' she said many a time to Mildred. 'I don't know how she does it, in those old clothes.'

'Oh, she's so thin,' said Mildred. 'It's easy to be elegant when you're thin; besides, she has such pretty hands and feet.'

'Anyway, she isn't half so pretty as my pet,' said her mother fondly.

'Oh, you're prejudiced, Mums.'

Mrs Yates took Anne in her comfortable survey. Anne sat on a low stool by the fire and spread the admired hands to the warmth. Mrs Yates's heart yearned over her. No father, and a mother who was no mother at all – always away spending the only bit of money there had been left. Anne looked wistful. As a matter of fact, she was thinking what a difference a good fire, bright lights, and plenty of cushions made to your feelings.

'Anne dear,' said Mrs Yates, 'do you think Gerald would like this woollen helmet?'

'I should think so,' said Anne. 'It's very kind of you. Isn't it funny, I can never imagine Gerald wearing anything like that or getting all dirty and messed up. I try, but I simply can't. He used to be so immaculate at home, poor boy. I used to envy his beautiful mauve silk vests and – things.'

She had been going to say 'pants', but Mr Yates looked up nervously from his *Daily Mail*.

'Well, I'll hurry with it,' said Mrs Yates, 'and you must give me his address. Mildred might make some of her nice toffee, and I'll put a cake and some cigarettes in and make a little parcel of it.'

Anne's thanks were interrupted by a ring at the front door.

'Now who can that be?' asked Mrs Yates, consulting her husband.

Suddenly Anne's heart set up a painful clamour.

'What if it should be George?' she cried to herself.

It was not George but his mother.

The Yateses betrayed their surprise at the visit. 'Nothing wrong?' asked Mr Yates, whipping off his eyeglasses. 'Nothing wrong, I hope, Frances?'

'No, nothing is wrong, for a change,' said his sister-in-law. Her thin, shrill voice made her hearers wince involuntarily. Anne wondered if George had ever got used to it.

Frances Yates, wearing a skimpy serge costume, with a sudden incongruous flounce at the waist, and a black felt hat, sat down and looked round the comfortable room as if it were a person and she could affront it.

'William is well, I hope?' said Mrs Yates, her eyes inquiring of her husband the reason of this visit.

'As well as usual,' returned the visitor, 'which isn't saying much.'

A constrained silence fell on the company. Anne regarded the mother of George. It seemed incredible that she should be the mother of anybody.

'Her lips are so thin they look as if they'd hurt when she kissed a baby. But perhaps she didn't kiss George. . . .'

'How is George?' broke in Mildred. Her parents had not dared to ask. These were days when one did not dare to ask for news from the Front.

'He's not killed – yet,' said George's mother, compressing her lips into a straight line. She had a nervous toss of the head which recurred at distressingly frequent intervals and jerked the poor felt hat still further back on her head. She looked as if she were trying ineffectually to keep it on by raising her eyebrows.

Suddenly the thin cheeks of Frances Yates flushed and she cried out in a triumphant voice:

'He's been made a Captain, and what's more he's got an MC.'

'Well done, well done!' 'That's splendid!' 'Oh, Aunt Frances, how lovely!'

Frances Yates broke through the buzz of voices.

'Yes, I'm proud of him. I'm proud.' Her nostrils dilated and her eyes flashed behind her glinting glasses. With one brown kid-gloved hand clasping the wrist of the other, one shoulder pushed high, she fell into gazing at the fire. The comfortable Yateses stirred uneasily, but she was unconscious of them. Gradually her rapt gaze faded, and was replaced by a stare of such fear that Anne involuntarily put out her hand. She knew what George's mother was seeing in the fire.

Then a nervous toss of her head seemed to jerk Frances Yates back into the present.

'I have some photographs of George here,' she said, opening a shabby handbag. She took out some snapshots, and after looking at them again herself, handed them to her brother-in-law.

'There he is with Paul Brasher, Lady Brasher's son . . . they are friends.'

'Really,' cried Mrs Yates, leaning forward with sudden interest to take the photograph from her husband's fingers. 'Really . . . how nice for George to be in the same Company.'

'George is his superior officer now.' Frances Yates found a satisfaction she had never expected to feel in the material success of her son.

Mrs James looked as if that could hardly be . . . George to be superior in any way to Lady Brasher's son.

The photographs came round to Anne.

Her fingers shook as she took them. She hardly knew him, and had to peer into the groups to find him. How changed he was! His old awkwardness quite gone – an erect, gallant figure in faultless uniform.

There was George sitting on his horse as if he had been born to the saddle; George in a 'rag', absurd and gay in a cabbage helmet; George arm in arm with a French girl in a château garden somewhere 'behind'. Her name was written underneath by George: 'Marie Odile'; and she was very pretty. Looking at this photograph, Anne felt suddenly lonely, plain and insignificant. She handed the photographs back to George's mother and smiled and said the right thing about them. But the feeling remained. Cold and heavy she felt, in that warm room. She looked round at the Yateses.

'What have I to do with these people, or they to do with me?' she asked herself.

She felt as isolated as if she were dead. She stood it for another half-hour, struggling, as women will, to put up unnecessarily with surroundings that have become distasteful. Then she said she was tired and would go.

In spite of protests, she got away, leaving Frances Yates boasting about George to her uneasy listeners.

Outside in the cold darkness, Anne walked vaguely. Her thoughts wandered. Everything was all wrong. This terrible war that went on and on. How long yet? People couldn't stand it; they couldn't bear all this and keep sane. George's mother looked quite mad at times, poor thing! Poor, poor thing! Of course, you couldn't like her awfully, but she was pitiful. Everybody was pitiful. Even the Yateses – who were untouched by the war; their little ambitions were pitiful. They wanted to get into the right set, to get Mildred well married. Mrs Yates even confessed that she tried to speak 'with a good accent'. How painfully little it all was!

'And I'm ridiculous too,' said Anne to herself. 'I'm a futile thing doing typing for twenty-five shillings a week, when I might have been at the Front, nursing, working hard, facing death. If I'd been doing something like that, I'd think more of myself. I feel a useless lump. I feel no good to anybody. I'm tired of myself.'

'Good evening, young secretary.' The voice of Richard Soames came with the surprise of a blow to Anne. 'Isn't it rather cold to saunter like that? Are you going home? May I walk with you? The club was stuffy; I came out for air.'

Anne shook herself briskly and set her pace to his. How fast he went! Tip-tap, tip-tip-tap went her heels on the hard, white road. She was caught up into his energy.

'Good stars tonight,' he said. 'Makes me remember something from a lecture in my Cambridge days; something about those faint stars we can just perceive through the telescope, and our being aware of them only as they were thousands of years ago. They don't exist now. That gives you an idea of time and space, doesn't it?'

Anne murmured. She threw back her head and scanned the night sky. How indescribably grand! How vast! Her tiny fretting fell away from her. There was something big about the chief. There must be, to make her feel like this. She gave a sudden exhilarated skip to keep alongside.

'That's right,' said Soames in a warm friendly voice. 'Come along.'

And then an overwhelming thing happened. Anne felt her hand seized in his. She almost gasped. It was as if the Angel Gabriel had leaned out of heaven and taken her hand in his celestial one. She dazedly left it where it was. She ceased to be a whole girl, and was conscious of being only a hand held by –

incredible! – held by Richard Charles Evelyn Dayborn Soames, the Chief, the Medical Officer of Health.

'However am I to go to the office again after this?' she asked herself wildly.

CHAPTER SIXTEEN

§ 1

The next morning, Anne was nervous at the office. She set about cleaning her typewriter as usual, under Butt's scornful eye.

'You don't want to fuss about that machine, Miss Pritchard,' he said, piling up the letter-books in the leisurely fashion of the male. 'Andrews never cleaned it in all the three years he were here.'

'And a nice state it was in,' said Anne, peering into the dusky ribs of the Underwood. 'I'm only just getting it right. But the roll is ruined. It's pitted with commas and full stops. You men, you know, are too heavy on the hand. I wish I could have a new roll, but I don't suppose the Committee would grant us one in wartime.'

'No,' agreed Butt. 'But the Committee 'ull go on having their afternoon tea just the same. Eh, they do do themselves well, these committees. The nice little jaunts they go on at the town's expense! May the Lord make me an Alderman, Amen.'

'Pass me the petrol, will you?' said Anne. 'The a's and e's are all bunged up.'

'Eh, you look after it as if it was a child, Miss Pritchard.'

Butt slid the bottle over the low table. He leaned his already smudged face in his red hands, and breathed audibly as he watched her.

'Morning's coming lighter,' he remarked. 'But I don't find it no easier to get up. It pulled, did bed, this morning. Some day, it'll win, and I shan't be 'ere.'

'I don't suppose anyone will notice,' said Anne.

Butt's retort was cut short by the 'slap, slap, slap' of the swing doors from the street, vigorously pushed.

Butt leaped to attention.

'Chief's here,' he whispered. He liked Anne, and warned her as a pal.

Anne knew, without any warning. The atmosphere of the office was electrified. She was as bad as Butt, opening and shutting drawers without necessity. Only she did it to hide her panic, and he to prove how busy he was.

Soon, she knew, the buzzer would go and she would have to face the man who had held her hand the night before.

'Trring-trr-rring,' went the buzzer in the wall behind her.

'There you are!' said Butt cheerfully. 'Called up.'

Anne hastily collected her pencil and notebook. Taking advantage of Butt's back, she bent down and peered into the strip of glass set into the office mantelpiece so low down that none but a dwarf could have looked at himself with comfort.

'Oh damn,' said Anne to her flushed cheeks.

As she went along the passage to the chief's room she

pressed her notebook against her face to cool it. Outside the closed door, she swallowed on a dry throat and knocked.

'Come in.'

She opened the door, and turned fully round again to close it with meticulous care. When she faced the room again, Soames's eyes were lowered and he was writing busily.

'Good morning,' he said without looking up.

He pulled out the familiar letter flap for her to write on.

'One moment, please.'

All was formal and ordinary. Anne's nervousness drained away as she sat waiting. Her cheeks cooled. She cooled altogether until she even felt a little chilly after her heat. By the time Soames was ready to dictate, Anne was the complete secretary again.

'I think that's all, Miss Pritchard, thank you. You might come back after the Borough Treasurer has been in.'

'Yes,' said Anne. She got up and went away. He had never once looked at her. Everything was as it had been, only more so.

It went on like that for six months. March, April, May, June, July. In August the chief went for a brief holiday, the first he had taken since the war. Anne too had a holiday. A miserable little holiday. As she sat in the sooty back garden doing the mending which Aunt Orchard had piled up like Pelion upon Ossa, the news came to Bowford of the death of Lady Brasher's only remaining son, Paul, and of the gallantry of Major George Yates in bringing in his wounded friend.

Anne's sewing fell into her lap. She looked out over the garden, wondering that out of the agony of Paul the flower of

George's courage should have bloomed . . . wondering why this news should bring desolation to one mother, and pride to the other. Strange, strange life!

'Oh, God . . . no more! no more!' she prayed, and was saddened to think that she no longer was certain that her prayer was heard.

She went back to the office with relief, and on the first morning after her return, as she sat, with her heels on the rung of the chair, taking down the letters, the hand of Richard Soames, tanned from the sun and the sea, came out and covered her left hand, as it rested on the flap of his desk.

Anne's right hand broke into a panic of dots and dashes on her notebook. The chief's voice ceased. Anne's heart beat so loud she thought he would hear it. She moved her right hand to give her heart a surreptitious pressure so that it would be still. She drew a wavering breath and waited.

'Impetigo,' said Soames loudly, as with an effort: '23 cases.'

He took his hand away from hers and leaned his head on it. Anne thought she heard a breath like a sigh, but was not sure. Her hand felt cold without the covering of his warm, strong fingers.

'Impetigo,' she wrote: '23 cases.'

Wilkinson tapped and came into the office.

'Deputy TC to see you, sir.'

Anne got up and slipped away.

'What am I doing?' she asked herself, as she typed and transcribed and erased. 'What on earth am I doing?'

But the office gave her no more time than to ask herself

that. It was not until she went to bed at night in Aunt Orchard's front bedroom that she could examine the position.

And even then she could not 'think straight', as she put it. To her, Richard Soames was more than human. He was wonderful, unique, brilliant – a contrast to all other men – even to George. George was a boy, her contemporary, blown-about, stumbling, uncertain like herself. Soames was a man, mature, assured, wise.

That he should want to hold her hand was to Anne a disturbing but beautiful thing. It was an incident complete in itself. She did not look beyond it. She could not think that this was the beginning of a love affair. You didn't have a love affair with a god. Sleep descended on her before she had decided anything.

The next few days went by in a sort of breathlessness. Richard Soames seemed to be going through a troubled time of his own. He was even shorter and jerkier in his manner than usual; out of joint with the world and with himself.

Meantime, Anne kept her hand safely on her knee, although the notebook wobbled without it.

There came a day when she forgot. Involved in measles, whooping cough, chickenpox, scarlet fever, mumps, she excitedly put up a hand to call a moment's halt. Immediately, Soames had her fingers fast in his.

He held them and looked at her over their tips. For one tense moment they regarded each other.

Then he put her hand back in her lap.

'It's madness,' he said, and swerved away on his chair.

'Isn't it madness?' he demanded, turning a scowling face on her.

Anne was silent, looking down. She still did not know what to say in crucial moments.

'How old are you?' he asked.

'Twenty-one.'

'And I'm thirty-eight,' he said. 'Thirty-eight. Doesn't it sound heavy? I solemnly warn you against me. There's no fool like an old 'un. Remember that.'

'Old!' said Anne, indignant that her god should consider himself liable to any infirmity. 'Thirty-eight's not old. Besides, you'll never be old.'

'My dear little girl, you mustn't encourage me like this.' He smiled quizzically at her.

Anne blushed furiously. She wished herself at the bottom of the sea.

'Shall I notify the Director of Education about that case of sleeping sickness at the William Street School?' she asked.

'So you put me in my place?' said Soames. 'Well, I deserve it. Let us get on by all means. And God grant that I keep my old head.'

But he didn't. In the general relief and exhilaration at the end of the War, he asked Anne to marry him, and Anne, to her own amazement, said 'Yes'.

§ 2

The news was received in varying ways. The office was electrified. Butt was nervous and wondered what he had said about the chief at odd times to Miss Pritchard. Bee, when he came to give Anne her last pay envelope, looked at her with open reproach. He had been fancying her himself. He felt that women were utterly deceitful.

Emily was dumbfounded. She sank her chin on her breast and looked up at Anne aghast.

'Engaged! Well . . . you could knock me down with a feather. You 'ave been quiet about it and no mistake. And to the gentleman at the office . . . that tall, creased-looking gentleman with horn-rimmed spectacles that I saw when I brought your mackintosh that day? 'Im! Well, I never did. . . . And to think as we'll be leaving this godforsaken 'ouse at last. Eh, I shall be thankful, I can tell you. Ever since the vicar come in and see your Aunt in that tantrum, she's been something awful to live with. She 'ates me like poison. Well, I shall love her and leave 'er now. I shan't stop a minute after you've gone. I'se get myself another place or go out charrin'.'

'No, you will not,' said Anne gleefully. 'You're coming with me. I told Dr Soames' – she still called him that – 'about you and how you'd stuck to me, you good old thing, and he says you must come with me and teach me how to housekeep. Now, what d'you think of that?'

Emily reached out for a hard kitchen chair. She sat down, her chin quivering with emotion.

'Well . . . well . . .' She struggled with speech and sniffed violently once or twice. 'He's a good man, whoever he is, and God bless him for this . . .' She finished chokily.

'Oh, he's wonderful,' cried Anne. 'You wait and see.'

Aunt Orchard was affronted at the news. She did not understand why anyone taken into her house should want to leave it. She looked upon the engagement as another manifestation of Anne's ingratitude.

'This is all the thanks I get,' she grumbled.

Soames went, like a lamb to slaughter, to be inspected by Anne's friends the Yateses. The visit was not a success. Anne discovered that Richard was not a social animal.

On arrival, little James Yates, trying not to look too proud, led Soames to his truly magnificent cigar cabinet. He opened the shining shallow drawers one after the other and invited Soames to take his pick.

'There!' he said, standing back. 'Help yourself!'

'Never smoke cigars, thanks,' Soames replied shortly, turning to see where Anne had got to.

James's face fell.

'Never smoke . . .' he echoed blankly. 'Well . . . well . . .'

One after the other, he closed the drawers of the cabinet, and sat flatly down, his hands on his knees. He looked wistfully at his guest.

'Play something, darling,' suggested Mrs Yates brightly.

Mildred played something. Soames was exceedingly restless during the performance and muttered to Anne that it was a damned row.

They fell back on Bridge. Richard took Anne for partner, and to her relief, continuously made her dummy. The little host stared at his hand as if he would bore through it, slowly chose and put down his card, invariably the wrong one, which Richard, playing with a rapidity and a ruthlessness the like of which Mr Yates had never seen before, snapped up with the rest.

The commentary Richard kept up on the play completed the confusion of Mr James Yates. He so far forgot himself as to say 'Eh?' several times, and Henrietta, sitting by him with her knitting, nudged him remindingly.

It was an uncomfortable evening. The Yateses were hopelessly at sea with Soames. Anne was uncomfortable because they were uncomfortable. Soames was obviously waiting for the time to go home, only seeming to find solace in the contemplation of Anne's bright head turning to look at him and turning quickly from him again in a way that gave him, suddenly, a picture of her as a child.

But the visit came to an end at last in coffee and sandwiches and Mrs Yates's best cream cake.

'Well,' said Mrs Yates as the door closed behind Anne and Richard. 'I can't make head or tail of him.'

'Neither can I, Mother,' agreed her husband disconsolately. 'I could hardly catch a word he said, and when I did I was none the wiser. Right over my head, he was. Now, Milly, don't you be bringing a walking encyclopaedia home to frighten your poor old daddy.'

'Don't worry, darling,' said Mildred, flying to kiss the top of his head. 'I don't want anyone like Dr Soames, though Anne thinks he's perfect. She seems perfectly dazzled by him, Mummie. Is it usual?'

'I don't know, dear,' mused Mrs Yates. She couldn't remember ever having been dazzled by her little James, fondly though she loved him. 'But it's a very good match for

Anne. The best she could expect under the circumstances. Think how nice it will be for her to live on Lower Avenue and have a little car. And professional men always have a certain standing, you know. We must look at that side of things and not worry because he isn't the sort of man we would like for our little girl.'

She took up her knitting complacently, thinking that when the time came they would arrange things better.

Meanwhile, Anne and Richard were returning to Aunt Orchard's.

Anne wanted to laugh a little over the visit, but Richard had finished with it. It had been unpleasant, but it was over and that was the end of it for him.

So Anne gave it up, and skipped alongside her striding betrothed.

Her hand was close in his, and in her heart a warm security. She was so happy to be happy. They went at a good round pace through the wind and the dark. There was no stopping for kisses. Only at Aunt Orchard's door, did Richard take her in his arms and murmur huskily:

'Good night, bless you . . . my little one.' With that he thrust her inside the door abruptly.

She stood in the dim hall and listened to his hurried retreating steps.

'Isn't he dear and funny? Must make faces and rush away because he's said a bit of love to me.'

CHAPTER SEVENTEEN

§ 1

THE dawn was showing faintly at the window. Anne lay in the vast bed where, many a night, she had with terror heard mice climb among the upholsteries. Aunt Orchard's funereal pictures began to show on the walls. Anne talked disjointedly to herself.

'Thank heaven I shan't sleep in this room again. Ugly things hurt. My house is lovely.'

She made a picture of its clear rooms, white walls, black paint, carpets of deep blue, of grey, of green, and of the views from the long windows over fields and woods under a wide sky.

'Think of living there . . . Think! Think!'

She cuddled her feet in ecstasy. Then she sobered.

'I'm going to be married today. It's my wedding day.'

She thought of George. She let her thoughts run out cool and clear at last.

'Think about him,' she told herself. 'Think your last.'

Let him go. He belonged to a past that could never have

been reconstructed. It couldn't come back – that poignant sweetness of first love; the freshness, the purity of feeling. She – she was changed. She lay under the yellow sateen curtains and remembered how, in this room, Vera Bowden had changed her.

'And yet it was bound to come,' she said. 'I couldn't have gone on in ignorance for ever. But I wish I could have got to know about that sort of thing another way. . . but I've got over it. I've got over it, so it doesn't matter now.'

She did not know that there was in her still a profound mistrust, an avoidance. She did not think it out sufficiently far to realise that because George was associated with the very height of this subsided but still present sore, that she had thrust him aside and turned with relief to Richard who represented to her an entirely different set of emotions.

'This is the right way to go into marriage,' she told herself soberly. 'I don't expect romance – glamour. I love Richard without it.'

The feeling she had for Richard was so comforting: something she could sink back in. Oh, blessed peacefulness and rest in loving Richard! It was the most exquisite feeling she had ever had.

The sun rose in his strength and shone on the ottoman where Anne's bridal clothes were laid ready. Demure and virginal they were. Anne had, as yet, no subtlety.

The wheezy grandfather clock in the hall struck seven. The door opened quietly and Emily Barnes, her hair in 'crimpers', appeared with a cup of tea.

'I knew as you'd be awake,' she whispered. 'It's nervous

work gettin' married, I'se be bound. 'Ow d'you feel?' She leaned her wrinkled rosy face over the recumbent Anne.

'Oh, all right,' smiled Anne. 'It doesn't seem to be me somehow.'

'Well,' said Emily, 'thank God you've got a good man. Eh, isn't 'e lovely? Isn't 'e a treat? The way 'e carries them buckets about for me.' She twinkled with tears and grimaces. 'And 'im such a gentleman. It does that old bezom of your Aunt good to see 'im. I bet she'd never seen such a gentleman before. And no nonsense about 'im. No playin' up and panderin'. Are you sure 'e doesn't mind me comin' to live with you?'

'He's jolly pleased about it, of course,' Anne assured her.

'Well, I'll do me best, I'm sure,' said Emily. 'Only I 'ardly feel up to that grand 'ouse. What d'you think of one of them pie dish frills sorter caps for afternoons? 'Ow'd I suit it?' She cocked her little head and looked anxiously at Anne.

'Oh, be blowed to frilled caps,' cried the bride. 'You just wear what you want to, Emily, and don't feel you have to dress up for us.'

'Nay, I'm not going to disgrace you,' said Emily firmly. 'But I'se 'ave to go and be taking your mother's tea, and Gerald 'll 'ave to be stirring 'isself. The hours it takes 'im to get 'imself dressed! I see 'e's got green silk pyjamas this time, and a dressing-gown like nothing I ever seen. Wild beaseses chasing theirselves from back to front; things like large vermin of some sort. Deary me!'

She vanished.

Anne, sipping her tea, wished fervently that she could get married to Richard without anyone looking on. It seemed almost indecent to be looked at. She had refused, in spite of Aunt Orchard and her mother, to wear white satin and a veil.

'No, I couldn't. It's no good worrying me. It's me being married, so I'll please myself how it's done.'

Richard was vastly relieved that she felt as she did. They took out a special licence and chose a remote church almost in the country. Aunt Orchard was tearful about what people would say.

'They'll say I wouldn't give my niece a proper wedding,' she wailed. 'And what will the Vicar think of us not having it at his church?'

Ever since the day the Vicar had caught her with her hands in Emily's hair, she had wondered what the Vicar thought. She was a broken woman, was Aunt Orchard. The only thing she had set a value upon was gone: the Vicar's good opinion.

Anne bathed, dressed and had breakfast with Emily before the others came down. The house was given over to bustle. Aunt Orchard took as much pains with her toilette as if she had been the bride. She misplaced her bonnet, her mantle, her gloves, her shoes, her umbrella, her prayer book. She fussed about the wineglasses, the sandwiches, the cake, until Emily became violent and distraught. Gerald was seriously annoyed because the water wasn't hot, and because his shoes were not polished to his liking. Olive Pritchard was worried about her dress, asking Anne:

'Do you think I was wise to get grey? Don't you think it's rather cold for me? Will you lend me your new mauve scarf to brighten it up?'

'It's packed,' said Anne.

'Well, just unpack it. I'll send it on later.'

Anne was rather glad that Philip had not been able to get the day off; there would have been one more to fuss and finick and spoil the day that should have been solely for Richard and for her.

At last, the taxis, and the church where Richard waited, restless, impatient. There were murmurs of words. A handing about of Anne's hand from Gerald to parson, from parson to Richard. Anne felt inanimate, like a parcel being passed round. When she turned from the altar, she saw the faces of her relations as in a dream; Gerald's bored expression – he did not like relations *en masse*; her mother with her usual serene not-thereness; Aunt Orchard's purring cat-face; Mrs Yates's fussy smiles; Mildred's large-eyed tearfulness; and Emily Barnes with a crumpled-up face, like a piece of soft damp tissue paper, to kiss.

Anne was conscious of signing her name for the last time, of Richard not behaving at all like a bridegroom, saying 'damn' at the confetti, rushing Anne to the car, leaping in, banging the door, flying with her to the train.

Anne, still in a trance, sat back in her corner.

'I'm married,' she told herself, fingering the hard ring under her glove. 'I'm married, and that's my husband.'

'You beautiful little thing!' said Soames fervently. 'Isn't getting married a damnable business?'

Two days later, she waited in the hotel lounge for Richard to come out with her. She sat buried in a luxurious armchair, acutely conscious of the fact that the Hall Porter was looking at her. She felt oppressed by his scrutiny, and a growing desire to escape from it, from all scrutiny, even from Richard's, a desire to be alone came upon her. She stood up and hesitated. Unless she went out now, Richard would come for her. She went to the door, which the Hall Porter swung open for her, watching her go through with approval.

'D'you know what she puts me in mind of?' he said to the Boots. 'A racehorse! Something delicate and proud, and yet free in the way she steps out. See what I mean?'

The Boots was used to the Hall Porter's similes and love of words, so he merely nodded and looked after Anne himself.

Outside the hotel, Anne stood looking round on all sides; behind her was the limitless sea, the downs to the right and left, the white road in front – all bald, offering no shield to anyone wanting to be alone. Panic seized her. Richard might emerge from the hotel at any moment. She began to run along the road away from the sea, up one hill, down the other side, and up another hill until she came into sight of a wood. It promised refuge and she ran for it, looking backwards in apprehension lest anyone should come now and cut her off from it. She climbed the low wall and went deep into the wood; her hurrying ceased. She took off her hat and breathed a sigh of relief. She wandered between the trees, the faint light filtering downwards made a ghostly thing of her in her pale dress, of a stuff so thin that it flowed over her limbs like water. She came to a standstill before a tree, and picked idly at the grey lichen with her fingers. She felt intensely lonely and in need of reassurance.

She picked and picked at the lichen, periodically blinded by the tears that welled up into her eyes, rounded and fell and were succeeded by more.

'It's all right, really,' she said aloud to herself.

'Richard's so good . . . so good.'

'It will be all right,' she said again.

The tears dried on her cheeks, making them stiff. She scrubbed at them with her handkerchief, and laughed at herself.

'Of course, it's all right. I am an idiot.'

She looked at the diamond watch Richard had given her and exclaimed at the time.

'More than an hour! What will Richard think?'

She felt a little apprehensive as if she were going to be late at the office. She snatched up her hat and ran through the trees, bumping against a bole here and there in her haste. She ran down the hot white road, hung over with pink valerian, up the hill and down again into full view of the sea, and there at the jut of the rocks was Richard bending over the pools, his red head aflame in the sun. She ran to him. He was watching a crab and did not look up.

'This fellow's annoyed. Hear him spit?' he said, as if she had been standing by him from the beginning. 'Look at him backing away with those nippers stretched to annihilate me. He has got a temper . . . unpleasant chap to live with.'

Anne bent over to watch, until the crab insinuated himself into a crevice, whence he blew infuriated but uninteresting bubbles.

Richard moved to another pool.

'You'd think there was nothing in this pool, wouldn't you?' he said.

Anne peered closely into the emerald round.

'I can't see anything.'

'Just watch.' Richard dropped in a dead limpet.

Ravening shrimps appeared like small grey shadows from every cranny. Anne exclaimed like a child at them.

'They aren't missing anything, are they?' said Richard. 'Thought I'd lost you.'

His abruptness startled her. She blushed suddenly, then slipped her hand into his wet one.

'No,' she said, 'I'm here.'

He pressed her hand closely. A sudden warmth filled her heart, lightening, reassuring her.

'Oh, Richard!' she cried, leaping from the rock to the hard yellow sand. 'It's a glorious day! Let's run! I'll race you to the lighthouse.'

She was off like something blown by the wind. Richard followed soberly. The sight of her with her thin dress blown against her young body, her slim, swift legs, her bright flung-back head, gave him a strange, fierce pang. He frowned and folded his lips, pressing it down. He was smiling when he reached her.

'I shall have to buy some apples.'

'Oh, Atalanta!' said Anne. She took a schoolgirlish pleasure in placing references.

Together they climbed the hill to the hotel. Anne put her hand into her husband's as they walked, and he in his turn was reassured.

'Funny little hand,' he remarked. 'It seems to go to nothing when I grasp it.'

She wriggled it out of his as they reached the hotel.

'Who daren't be seen holding her husband's hand?' he teased.

'No one must know we're on our honeymoon,' she reminded him.

'You can be quite sure that no one is under any delusion about that,' he said. 'As if anything so young as you could have been married more than five minutes. In fact, I'm ashamed to be seen with you! And when you're in your bathing suit, I tremble in case I should be arrested for abduction.'

Anne smiled at him. Lovely to be loved like this; lovely to be so considered.

She walked through the hotel lounge and knew that everybody was looking at her. She saw herself in a long mirror and smiled. By Richard's side, she went up the wide staircase, trailing her hand on the cool balustrade.

It was very nice to stay in such a luxurious place; it was very nice to have a bath in your own bathroom, all white marble and silver fittings and at least six kinds of shower; it was very nice to spend a long time over dressing and have Richard brushing your hair clumsily and tenderly; nice to have delicious food served by deft waiters, to walk on the terrace in the moonlight, with the sea hush-hushing far below, nice to go back to your room and find your nightgown laid out elegantly on the bed; after the years at Aunt Orchard's it was more than nice; it was a kind of material heaven. Then why – why did something in her remain aloof and wistful? She was angry with it, tried to persuade it, to jostle it into taking part. But it would not; it stood off.

§ 3

Anne's honeymoon was over when George Yates, out in the Sudan for the cotton magnate, Sir Peter Brasher, saw in the *Bowford Weekly News*, sent by his mother, the announcement of the marriage.

'Soames – Pritchard. On the 29th July at St. Mary's Church, Bar Lane, Richard Charles Evelyn Dayborn Soames, MD, to Anne, only daughter of the late Henry Pritchard, Esq and Mrs Pritchard, formerly of Merlewood, Bowford.'

George Yates made no dramatic start. He read it quietly, then read it again. He smiled a little bitterly.

'And yet I got on, as Aunt Henrietta would say, . . . after all.'

He fell into retrospection, holding the news-sheet that had wandered so far from its press. He remembered Anne as she had been that summer morning so long ago. So long ago it seemed, with such crowded years in between then and now, that the memory had almost the calm, remote beauty of a dream.

He tried to remember himself as he was then, and did it with difficulty.

'A raw young fool!' he called himself. 'To think how damnably ashamed I was to wear Uncle James's little boots at

193

the Grammar School. God! I couldn't see beyond those boots. It was always the same; something like boots keeping me miserable. I should have gone after Anne – asked why – done something. I believe I felt like a shambling tramp. And the devil of it is, if I hadn't been so ashamed of it myself, no one would have noticed it. What an ass I was!'

He contrasted his present self. Power, money, the glory of his war record were still so new to him that he hugged them to him with an infinite secret satisfaction. And he meant, with all his strength, to carry through this cotton inquiry successfully for Sir Peter Brasher, to whose gratitude he owed his job.

His thoughts drifted from Anne, to himself, and on to his mother.

'Poor mother,' he thought, half-smiling, tapping his boot with his riding whip.

His mother had opposed the offer of Sir Peter to take George in his dead son's place.

'When you were a child,' she cried with passion, 'I refused the same offer from your uncle, and now you're a man, you go and choose what I refused. Oh, George, it means money and worldly prosperity, but it's not what I planned for you.'

'What did you want, then?'

'I wanted you to be something great in the intellectual sense of the word, George. I thought you might be a scientist – like Sir Oliver Lodge. I pictured you. Or a Fellow of your College. Or at least a schoolmaster.'

George threw back his head and laughed at that.

'A schoolmaster! Come, Mother . . . look at them! They may be little tin gods all right in their own classrooms, but look at the poor, ineffectual figures they cut in real life! Of all the miserable, footling little jobs, you couldn't have chosen a worse!'

He straightened his broad shoulders and looked down his hooked nose at her. A Major, a DSO, turning schoolmaster! It was ludicrous.

'Oh, George!' said his little mother, standing below him and writhing with earnestness. 'There are consolations in the intellectual life you cannot dream of. I have missed them; I've let myself be defeated by washing and ironing and cooking and making ends meet, but I hoped you would be happier and find them and keep them.'

Her nose went suddenly red, and tears filled her light eyes.

'Never mind, Mother,' said George. 'All that's over now, and you can go back to your books and get a maid to look after you. You must feed Dad up a bit. He looks terribly down in the mouth.'

'Your father, George,' said Frances, shaking her head, 'has no spirit.'

She was disappointed in them both. In spite of the fact that George put them into a new house and maintained them in comfort, she remained disappointed in them both.

CHAPTER EIGHTEEN

§ 1

It was Anne's first 'At Home' day. She sat in a red frock behind the silver tea-service set out on a low table over a Venetian lace cloth. She loved this tea-service, once Richard's mother's, and when she was overwhelmed with a sense of being quite lost in her own drawing room, she comforted herself by saying to herself: 'This is a lovely tea-service. Imagine my having a tea-service like this.'

She smiled shyly round on her callers. But they did not seem to notice her much. She felt she really ought to have been the centre of attraction, but was relieved that she was not. She kept looking at a bowl of daffodils on the windowsill. They were like a poem. She wanted to say to the women scattered over her drawing room chairs: 'Aren't they – pure and simple?' It seemed strange to her that no one should be struck by their beauty.

She felt she would never be able to join in the conversation. They were talking about going up to 'town'. Anne didn't like the sound of 'town'. She tried silently to see if she could say it.

'I'm going up to town soon.'

No, she was sure she couldn't. 'London' would come out in spite of her. She had a comfortable feeling that Richard always said 'London' too.

Now they were talking about 'kiddies'.

'There's something the matter with me,' said Anne to herself. 'I couldn't call children "kiddies" either.'

She felt very unsmart and surreptitiously stroked the silver teapot.

Nobody could have felt more out of it than the young bride on her 'At Home' day. She could not find a point of contact with anyone.

Her visitors looked very prosperous, sitting with fur coats thrown open to show pearl necklaces and rich dresses. They all looked much the same, the Bowford women. They went to London for their clothes, it is true, but they made a little Bowford shopping centre of the great city. They found out each other's shops, and what one had, the other had to have too. When brown was fashionable, they were all in brown; when black, all in black with white camellias on the left lapel.

'I suppose you're going to the dance on Tuesday, Mrs Soames?'

Anne, dreamily fingering the silver teapot, did not answer. Then, realising the silence, started and blushed.

'Oh, me?' she cried, looking up with her wide, clear eyes. 'No, I don't think so. Richard doesn't dance.'

'Poor child,' they looked. 'You see . . . already.'

Inwardly, they shook their heads over the marriage.

'Everybody says the tickets are going well,' chirruped Mrs Armitage.

'Lady Brasher is such a capable manager,' said Mrs Verey.

When Mrs Verey spoke, everybody listened and agreed. Mrs Armitage sat on a low chair by her side, and looked up at the cold, pale face with the paralysed gaze of a sparrow at a hawk.

'Oh, yes, isn't she, Mrs Verey,' she gushed suddenly. 'You're right, well, of course, you always are, te-he. I think Lady Brasher is a splendid manager, and so kind. Always the same, isn't she, Mrs Verey? You know, only the other day, I was coming home from town with armfuls of parcels, and I met Lady Brasher coming down in a great hurry; walking, you know, not in the Rolls-Royce, and she stopped and said, "Well, you are laden." Just like that. And she said if I was getting tickets for the Hospital Ball, would I get them from her. She *is* sweet.'

Mrs Armitage's pale blue eyes swam in tears at the remembered sweetness of Bowford's only title.

'Lord,' said young Anne to herself. 'I hope I never take to crying in my speech like that.'

'All the same,' resumed Mrs Verey, having received Mrs Armitage's story with complete indifference, 'I think the caterers should be spoken to. The supper was poor last year. The soup was cold, and the salad dressing tasted of raw cornflower. I don't like tinned asparagus, and the wine in the trifle was corked.'

'Wonderful, wonderful,' thought Anne, 'to remember a supper for a year!'

'Oh, yes, and the horse d'ooves . . .' burbled Mrs Armitage, anxious to corroborate Mrs Verey's statement. 'Weren't they wretched?'

'Pardon,' Mrs Verey, collecting all eyes with her own, leaned towards Mrs Armitage, hoping she would say it again.

Mrs Armitage did.

'The horse d'ooves,' repeated the poor little thing brightly, 'weren't they *dreadful?*'

'Ah!' said Mrs Verey, with a cold smile. 'I understand you.'

Little Mrs Armitage blushed miserably. She guessed she had done something wrong, but didn't know what it was. She drank her tea with trembling lips and did not speak again.

Mrs Charles Bramwell ate a good deal of cake, and talked in a loud voice about the lower classes.

'It's no good putting the lower classes into these model dwellings,' she said. 'They're so dirty. They'll turn them into slums in no time. They've no idea, have they, the lower classes?'

Anne winced. She discovered she had been wincing the whole afternoon.

She was glad when they went, leaving cards, and a smell of scent and powder hanging in the air.

Emily Barnes came in to remove ash trays, shake up cushions, open windows, and make comments.

'Eh, well,' she said, picking up a crumb from the blue carpet with forefinger and thumb. 'Give me me own kind, that's all. What a gabble! It fair amazed me. And 'er that was talking about the lower classes being dirty – did you see her combinations?'

'Emily!' cried Anne. 'How could I?'

'Well, I had a look down that grand low dress of 'ers when she bent down to get an extra big lump of sugar. Dingy at the edges – that's what they were,' said Emily grimly. 'And 'er with all the 'ot water in the world. Makes me sick. Eh, these better-end! There is some goings-on among 'em. Wine-drinking every night and never sitting down by their own wife. Always somebody else's. . . . That shows what they are. Well, I'll be going to see to my dinner now that lot's gone. That almond soup you made smells right good.'

Anne drew up a chair for a solitary half-hour before Richard came home.

The dark blue curtains were drawn. The daffodils gleamed palely against them, still and remote. The lamp with its wine-coloured shade diffused a light made for dreams. Anne liked the look of the shut white door. It kept people out. It made a refuge for her.

'I like to be alone,' she said, snuggling into her chair.

She was too much aware of other people when they were there. Aware of their feelings and glances and words. They cut out the view of other things. Anne couldn't feel anything, value anything to the full unless she were alone.

The quiet beauty of her room filled her with joy. After the years at Aunt Orchard's, it was heaven to her.

'Rooms are beautiful,' she thought, 'and things – curtains, a carpet and that wine-coloured shade make you happy. Isn't that strange? I could look and look at them. . . . Richard is good to give me all this. Strange that I should have had nothing such a little while ago, and now I have all this, just because Richard loved me. But I don't think he feels like this about things. I think he's quite indifferent about things. . . .'

She drifted off into idle speculation.

There was a quick step on the garden path, the front door was flung open and shut, hat and gloves went down on the hall table and Richard came in to press a cold cheek against her warm one.

'I've had such a lot of callers,' she began.

'Oh, yes,' said Richard absently, wandering about the room. 'Hullo, these bulbs without water? I thought so. Dry as bones.'

He took the bowls out of the room one by one to soak them. Anne resumed her conversation as he returned.

'I didn't like anybody much, Richard. . . . I couldn't get going somehow . . .'

'Damn!' said Richard. 'I've broken that leaf right off.'

'You know, Richard . . .' mused Anne, 'I wish I was affected. I think affected people must give themselves a lot of pleasure. How nice to think you're looking nice when you twist your mouth about and flutter your eyelids! Don't you think there's a lot to be said for affectation? So unhappy to have no illusions about yourself . . .'

She chattered, kneeling on a chair and calling out over the back of it.

'Poor little Mrs Armitage . . .'

She stopped suddenly. Richard wasn't listening. He wasn't in the least interested in her callers and their idiosyncrasies. She looked at his face, frowning in preoccupation with his precious bulbs. A sudden wave of anger surged over her. She flew to him and seized his shoulders.

'Look at me!' she cried. 'Look at *me* – *me*! I'm nice too, I need notice too. Aren't I as good as a bulb?'

'Yes, yes, my child, but these bulbs are very dry. I'm only giving them a drink. Then I'll be free.'

'Me first, me first,' implored Anne. It was imperative and somehow significant that Richard should make his choice for her now.

'Just one moment,' said Richard. He disappeared with another bowl.

He came back, deposited it on the windowsill, and came to take her on his knee.

'No,' said Anne coldly. 'It's too late.'

The incident seemed tragic to her. But Richard was, within five minutes, cheerfully immersed in his paper.

Anne regarded him with a gaze alternately furious and bewildered.

§ 2

Anne lay in bed and looked into the dark. Outside the wind howled round the house like a wild thing to get in. Gusts of rain beat against the windows.

Anne's mind was restless.

'Richard?'

'Mmm?' an inquiring grunt from Richard.

'D'you think there is a God?'

'Don't know,' murmured Richard, turning over and evidently, by the sound of it, burying his head further into the pillow.

'But, Richard, I feel I've got to know whether I think there is a God. Don't you?'

Richard murmured indistinguishably.

'I'm all in a muddle,' said Anne, raising herself on her elbow. 'I want to know . . .'

Sundry twitching of bedclothes on the part of Richard. She wanted to poke into his mind, and he didn't want his mind poked into.

'What do *you* think, Richard? Tell me.'

'My child.' Richard's voice came with sudden firm loudness. 'If you thought and I thought from now until we die, we'd never get any nearer. It's no use thinking. Specially at this time of night. Go to sleep like a good little thing, and let me go to sleep too. I've had a hard day.'

Anne was quiet. He wouldn't talk about anything that mattered. She had felt he knew everything, could put her straight on everything. It had been merely childish of her. She was driven in on herself again.

In the windy dark, she was tossed about by speculation.

'I'm a poor thing,' she complained. 'I can't grasp anything. Am I any good at all? What am I doing? Just living with Richard and making beds and shopping and reading can't be called doing anything. The days keep going . . . I never get anything done. . . .'

She was appalled at the way the time went.

'Twenty-two already and nothing done. . . .'

It was terrifying the way life went.

Richard was sound asleep. He slept like a child. Anne marvelled at the way he fell asleep and the way he woke up – so easily and suddenly. No intermediate period of going to sleep and waking like hers.

'Why won't he ever talk things out?' she wondered. Would it have been different if she had married George? George and she used to be tremendously speculative together.

'It was because George and I hadn't got anything settled up. Richard's so much older. He's got things arranged.'

But how he had got things arranged, she didn't know, and felt she never would know.

When morning came, Richard leaped out of bed, rushed energetically to his cold bath, shaved, dressed, breakfasted. Anne had to make up arrears of sleep after her wakeful night. He went up to kiss her goodbye.

'I'm going through some schools today,' he said, looking fierce. 'Yesterday, when I went to Coulton Street School, I found a class working with its back to the light. One little chap was sitting with his back all screwed round to get the light on his book; and they'll wonder later why he gets curvature of the spine. I'm going round to see if there's any more of this damfoolery. Bye-bye, I must run.'

He gave her a hasty kiss and left the house. Anne was subdued.

'He gets on with things,' she admitted.

She tried to emulate his energy by springing out of bed and hurrying down to make pie. Richard loved pie.

Anne felt there must be something in the social business. So many people were in it. So many people seemed to enjoy it. She ventured rather diffidently into it. She still had a youthful idea that all these people at Bridge parties, dinners, dances, must be interesting and experienced. She imagined good talk, interplay of character, interesting friendships. She set out with a sense of adventure for her first bridge afternoon at Mrs Charles Bramwell's.

Waiting on the front steps to be admitted, she had a vision of the country she might have walked in this afternoon – the bleached green of winter fields, the trees like fronds of dark, delicate seaweed pressed against the sky, of Arley Brook slipping crystal cold and clear over its stones, bound in ice.

'It would have been lovely,' thought Anne, and then shook herself. 'But I've been wandering about too much alone. Here are people; full of possibilities.'

A maid, shy of her unaccustomed grandeur of plum-colour and white, opened Mrs Bramwell's front door. Another took her upstairs to leave her coat among the furs, the tulle, the scarves, to powder her nose at a dressing table already snowed under with powder, and to take her down again and usher her into Mrs Bramwell's drawing room, where expensively dressed women were chattering and shuffling cards at the green tables.

Mrs Bramwell took Anne to her own table, where Mrs Shutt, an immensely large and jolly lady of somewhat

Rabelaisian humour, sat with Miss Beech, a spinster. The large hats of these ladies made a roof over Anne's head as she sat on a low stool, her chin almost on the table.

'I don't like this,' she said to herself. 'Not at all.'

It was her deal. The cards stuck to her fingers. She turned up the three of diamonds the wrong way to Mrs Bramwell.

'Deal again, please,' said Miss Beech from over her stiff boned collar. She was one to insist on her rights.

'Oh, dear!' Anne scrabbled at the cards. 'I am sorry. I do deal badly. I must have an afternoon dealing round the dining room table.'

'Are you going to the opera this week?' asked Mrs Bramwell to pass the time.

'I don't know,' replied Miss Beech, 'that there is anything I particularly want to see.'

'I want to see *Samson and Delilah*,' said Anne, joining in to show that she could deal and talk at the same time.

'You should say *Samson and Dayleelah* to be correct,' said Miss Beech. 'It's French.'

'Why not 'Songsong' then?' asked Anne. She was merely interested, but Miss Beech thought her pert, and did not answer.

'These young things,' she snorted to herself. 'Just because they are married! As if that gives them any sense: takes away what little they have, I should say.'

She never liked Anne after that, and was savage with her over the cards.

The room grew hotter and hotter. The chocolates were blurred in the silver dishes; the flowers drooped in the silver vases. Anne lost consistently. Women drifted up to her table and drifted away again. They had little conversations with each other about Philip's cold and Baby Margaret's curls or what an idiot of a maid they had at present. Anne could contribute nothing to talk of that sort; she had no children and Emily was perfect.

She could not join in the stories of another trio who made her feel ashamed and ashamed of being ashamed.

Tea came as a welcome break; the usual Bowford Bridge tea; crab sandwiches, egg-and-cress, and sardine. Everybody made quietly for the crab sandwiches, and looked innocent when it was noticed that there were no more. There was chocolate cake, and jam-and-cream sandwich, cake, éclairs, meringues and brandy snap filled with cream.

Anne had a disaster with her brandy-snap. When she bit it, the brittle thing flew in all directions, on to Mrs Shutt's taffeta dress, on to the carpet, into Miss Beech's tea. Anne was drowned in embarrassment.

'Oh, *Lord!*' she groaned. She was hot and wretched.

After tea, back to the little table that she hated, to be penned in again by hats and play more execrable Bridge.

At last, Mrs Bramwell, pleased and mysterious, asked them to add up their cards.

'Anyone under 116?' – that was Anne's number. 'Anyone over 1,700?' – that was Miss Beech's.

Mrs Bramwell handed, amid murmurs of admiration, a beautiful mauve nightgown, silk and sleeveless, to the angular Miss Beech, and to Anne the booby prize, which was, iron-ically, a Bridge-scorer.

'What's the use,' Anne said to herself, 'of having a scorer when you never have anything to score?'

She escaped from the house with relief. The air was like cold water. She drank a long draught. Even looking at the pavement, she was conscious of the stars. They were so bright. She remembered how she used to think they were holes in the floor of heaven, letting through them the light of the other side where God lived.

'No more Bridge drives for me,' said Anne. And ran home to tell Richard why.

CHAPTER NINETEEN

The cold November rain slid down the windows, blurring the aspect of the desolate and blackened garden. Anne sat alone by the fire, struggling with four steel needles and a ball of buff-coloured wool. In ardent desire to do something wifely, she had undertaken the task of knitting a pair of socks for Richard's Christmas present. Her attitude was one of concentrated effort; her legs were twisted round each other; her brows were drawn together in a frown, and occasionally the tip of her tongue appeared along the gleaming edge of her teeth as she pushed the needle through an extra tight stitch. The first finger of her left hand had a small, painful lump in its tip, due to pushing the needle out again. She wondered how long it would be before she could acquire the oiled efficiency of Mrs James Yates's knitting, and sighed as she turned the sock to begin another row.

But, she reflected, knitting, although painful, was comforting. It somehow reassured you. It made you feel like a wife. She wanted to feel like a wife. There were so many days when she didn't feel like one.

She woke in the mornings with eager happiness; she

bathed and dressed and breakfasted; she did a little cooking if she chose – it was all Emily left for her to do; or she went into town to do a little shopping, sitting in the tramcar with the people she had been used to seeing all her life, bowing in the street to more of the same people, and coming home again to lunch with Richard, who was always in a hurry to get back to his work. And somehow, in the interval between breakfast and lunch, the eager happiness had faded away leaving her with a deadly flatness or an overpowering restlessness. She tried to combat these moods by walking with a simulated energy, or by writing feverishly in her old notebooks. These notebooks had nowadays to be locked away. They were her safety valves – and at times they screamed.

But today she had her knitting, and the afternoon had gone before she realised it, and here was Emily bringing in the little lacquer tray with the exquisite green china. She smiled with pleasure at the sight of it.

'Well, and how are you getting on?' inquired Emily, bending down to look at the knitting.

'I've done quite an inch this afternoon,' said Anne. 'But, oh, my finger is sore!'

'Never mind. It'll get 'ardened to it – like everything else,' said Emily. 'You can get used to anything, I always says.'

'That's comforting,' said Anne.

Emily looked sharply at her, but Anne's face betrayed nothing but concentration on her knitting, and Emily wandered to the window, her hands crossed on her apron.

'What a day! It's fairly tem down all day long.'

'It seems to me,' said Anne, 'that the weather has been worse than usual this year. Do you think it has?'

'Nay, it's only because you've 'ad more time to notice it, love. But I always say to myself, I says, "Well, what's fallen today can't fall tomorrow".'

Anne laughed. 'Oh, Emily,' she cried, putting down the sock and stretching her arms wide, 'I wish I could find things like that to say to myself.'

'Go on with you,' said Emily, 'and you so clever. Is your tea right? I must go and be looking to me dinner.' She paused at the door. 'Seems a bit lonely for you, love, in the afternoons. What about your friend Miss Yates? Can't you 'ave 'er up oftener?'

'Oh, she's very busy nowadays,' smiled Anne.

'Courting, I suppose,' said Emily. 'Yes, 'er ma 'ull be wanting to get 'er grandly matched, and 'urrying 'er from place to place to get 'er shown off. Not but what she's a bonny girl enough – but grasp all lose all, I says, and that's what 'er ma seems to be doing. Eh, me dinner – and me gossiping 'ere!'

Anne picked up the sock again, and the room was very quiet.

The socks were done in the week before Christmas, but to Anne's disgust, one sock was, for some unaccountable reason, much larger than the other. She almost wept over them, but there was no time to undo them now, and she did want Richard to know that she had tried to do something for him.

This was to be her first Christmas in her own house. She made a fuss of it. She and Emily set about making plum puddings and Christmas cakes and mincemeat, and wishing and stirring according to traditional formulæ. They were very busy, scorning simplified preparation of ingredients.

'Not one scrap of shoddy shop stuff goes into this mincemeat if I've any say in it,' said Emily, looking fierce. 'And I dare say you think the same, love.'

'Of course I do,' agreed Anne with warmth.

Outside the snow fell thickly and softly day after day, but inside, the kitchen was warm and smelt of spice. Anne and Emily were absorbed in their cooking; Emily beating mixtures in bowls with capable red hands, Anne darting about, cutting up candied peel and cherries, lining cake tins, making fancy shapes on pie-tops. They made totally unnecessary conversations as women will when they are happy.

'Now, Emily,' Anne would say, 'do you think we dare look into the oven again?'

'Eh, no!' Emily was shocked. 'Give it another five minutes, do. You'll 'ave it as sad as a burying if you don't look out.'

'Well, our first Christmas cake mustn't be that,' chattered Anne. 'Oh, Emily, aren't you glad we aren't at Aunt Orchard's this Christmas?'

'My goodness, I should think I am, the old bezom!' Emily beat furiously as if she had Aunt Orchard in the bowl.

'But you know I'm sometimes very sorry for her.' Anne looked out at the white garden for a moment. 'She's such a miserable old thing.'

'That's 'er fault,' said Emily stoutly. 'You don't want to waste no sorrow on such as 'er.'

Anne took to making stars of pastry again.

'We'll send her a cake anyway.'

'Aye, that little 'un as got a bit scorched at one side 'ull do for 'er,' said Emily.

'No, she shall have a good one,' Anne insisted.

'All right, all right! 'ave it your own way. Now what about just peeping into that oven? What d'you think?'

'Yes, I think we might.'

Oven-cloths in hand, they advanced on the oven with as much caution as if it contained a mad dog. With extreme care, Emily, her face screwed up as if some painful physical experience were going on inside her, lifted the handle and slowly opened the door; but no more than quarter of an inch.

'Oh, shut it!' cried Anne, from her kneeling position on the hearthrug. 'Perfect! Perfect!'

With the same extreme care, Emily closed the oven door, and allowed her face to relax. She beamed on Anne.

'Bonny, isn't it? I'll be bound the master's never seen a cake like that before. Eh, when I think of the stuff we've put in! Fair crammed with the best, isn't it? Now, love, you'll soon be able to get your pies in.'

Anne returned to the table.

'Christmas is rather fun, Emily, isn't it?' she said, as she fitted on the tops of the mince tarts, turning her head sideways to admire her handiwork.

'Aye, Christmas is a grand time; specially where there's children in the 'ouse.'

But Anne offered no views on the subject, and Emily had to change it.

When their cooking was done they went down into the wintry town to buy holly and mistletoe in the market, and with

Emily to hold the steps, Anne dressed the house up very gaily. She was so absorbed that she didn't notice how Richard looked at her and smiled as at some secret speculation.

She addressed the Christmas cards, looking again at the discreet wishes from Dr and Mrs RCED Soames. She felt very established. She tied up her Christmas presents in white paper with red ribbons and sprigs of holly; and all preparations being completed, she betook herself to bed to the sound of bells and carols.

'After all,' she said to herself, 'I'm quite happy when I've got something to do.'

She awoke to find Emily bringing in the morning tea. She switched on the amber-shaded lamp and called out: 'Happy Christmas!'

'Same to you,' said Emily in a muffled voice. Christmas was too much for her. 'That scarf – it's beautiful. Oh, it's a lovely thing! And you, sir, that bag . . . well . . .' She made for the door.

'Poor Emily!' said Anne, in explanation to the awakening Richard. 'She always cries when she's happy.'

She leaned from her bed and kissed her husband.

'Happy Christmas, Richard,' she said, and removed herself from his arms to lean over the other side of her bed. She brought up the unequal socks, unwrapped so that their deficiencies could at once be seen, and Richard not deceived into thinking he was getting something better than he actually was. She thrust them into his hands.

'I made them, Richard; but they've come out wrong. D'you see? One's bigger than the other. I am terribly disappointed in them . . . are you?'

Richard held the socks at arm's length and shrieked with laughter. Anne had never seen him burst out like this before. How nice he was with his teeth showing like that, and his eyes all crinkled up! And how he laughed!

She sat up in bed, with her arms round her knees, and laughed too, ruefully.

'Darling,' she said, 'you're rather rude.'

He wiped his eyes.

'Oh, dear . . .' Laughter shook him again.

'I'm only giving them to you now,' explained Anne, 'to show you that I've done them for you. But I'll undo the big one and knit it the right size. They'll be ready for your birthday, I should think.'

Richard threatened to break out again, but Anne made a leap at him.

'Don't you dare to laugh at my knitting!'

She smothered him in his own eiderdown, but he emerged and covered her up with his blankets.

'You are a funny little thing,' he said. 'I adore those socks. I won't have them touched.'

'The tea will be cold,' she said, and hastily applied herself to pouring out.

It was not until Richard put down his empty cup that he said:

'You haven't asked me what my present to you is.'

'Oh, have you got one for me? I was rather hoping you had. I love a present!'

'It's rather bulky. I couldn't exactly put it by your bed. In fact, I shall have to ask you to wait until you're dressed to see it.'

'Oh, Richard, what is it? Do tell me! Tell me!'

But Richard was firm.

'When you're dressed.'

'But surely I don't need to be dressed. Surely I can run down as I am. Goodness me, you should have seen Aunt Orchard wandering about in the mornings!'

'I have no wish to see Aunt Orchard,' said Richard. 'And it is the neighbours I am thinking about. There might be a David among them, and I'm sure Bathsheba never looked half so fetching as you in that blue nightgown. Dear me, I'm getting flowery. Those socks have unhinged me! Come on, if you want to see your present, you must dress.'

He bundled her out of his bed.

She was waiting impatiently for him when he came down.

'Do hurry,' she begged. 'I'm dying to know what it is.'

'Put your coat on,' he commanded.

'Outside? Is it outside? This is getting curiouser and curiouser. Oh, Richard, do tell me. I shall burst.'

'This way.' Richard opened the side door, and she rushed out into the snow.

'Which way now?'

He took her outstretched hand, and ran her to the garage.

'Oh, I say . . . I guess! It's a dog! Is it?'

He opened the doors of the garage and stood aside.

'Enter, Madame!'

Anne stood stock-still on the threshold. In the hitherto empty garage stood a small Fiat, elegant in buff enamel and silver fittings. She turned wide eyes on her husband.

'Is it . . . for me?' she asked incredulously.

'It is.'

After a pause necessary to take this in, she gave a sudden squeal of joy, and clapped her two hands on the radiator.

'Oh!'

Then she whirled on her husband, clasping her arms round his shoulders.

'Richard – you darling!' She pressed her face to his. 'You darling, to have thought of it.'

She hugged him fiercely, and his arms encircled the ardent young body, stretched taut on tiptoe to hug him the better.

'You like it, then?'

She could not see the happiness of his face above her head.

'Like it! I adore it . . . the beauty! Let me look at it. Let me sit in it. Oh, I say, do you think I shall ever be able to drive?'

'Of course, I'll teach you. First lesson today.'

'But she'll get very dirty today,' objected Anne.

'Then you must clean it tomorrow.'

'I can see I'm going to be busy at last.' Anne looked radiant at the prospect. 'Sit in it, Richard – and feel how comfortable it is. What awfully nice cushions! And two horns.' She tried them both and beamed at their noises. 'And a clock and everything. It's quite, quite perfect. Richard, I shall feel very grand driving us in this car. And think of the picnics in the summer! And the weekends we shall have cruising about!'

She climbed out of the car, and turned up her face to him again, but so anxious was she not to lose sight of the car, that his kiss fell on her front teeth.

'That was a wet one,' he complained.

217

Contritely, she hung round his neck.

'You are good to me,' she said.

'There's Emily ringing for us,' she said. 'Come along; bacon and eggs now, and more car afterwards.'

It was a very happy day.

'I never remember such a good day,' said Anne that night. 'But do you think I shall ever manage to change gear properly?'

She went to sleep with her hand still fast in her husband's across the space between their beds. When he found her arm was growing cold, he carefully loosed her fingers and covered her up with lingering tenderness.

CHAPTER TWENTY

§ 1

Anne thought the Fiat had solved all her problems. Strange that the yearnings of the spirit should be appeased by a piece of machinery, but so, for a time, it was. Anne, preoccupied with gears and crossroads and the vagaries of pedestrians and dogs, was a happy creature. The picnics and the cruising weekends she had planned did not quite materialise. Richard was an ardent gardener. The abomination of his life was the 'jobbing gardener', and Anne had only to suggest that they should get a man to cut the hedges, to draw more conversation from Richard than she could hope for on any other topic.

When she suggested that they should start out in the car:

'And just go anywhere, Richard, just follow the road into the Yorkshire dales perhaps – and stay at a little inn where the dressing table will be dressed up in muslin and the looking-glass full of motes like a sunbeam, and the stairs will be covered with white oilcloth – and in front of the windows there'll be a great hill heaving up, with grey rocks sticking out through the grass – you know, that very short grass that grows on limestone – and the roads will be stony and roll under your feet. . . . Could we?'

'My child, I'm afraid we can't.' Richard looked worried through his glasses. '. . . I've had all those rose trees standing since Tuesday. I must get them in. You won't have a single rose if I don't.'

'Couldn't I put them in on Monday?'

'They need very careful planting, and you know you're no gardener. Besides, this isn't the weather for weekending; far too cold. We'll go later when it's warmer. Now, let me get into the garden. Going to help me? Will you come and tell me where you'd like the trees put, then?'

'Later,' said Anne.

She stayed in the room alone to press down the dream of Yorkshire dales very flat so that it would not rise up to trouble her again. She tried to reason herself out of her disappointment, kneeling on the window seat and looking out at Richard, already absorbed in his rose trees, tramping backwards and forwards in heavy, mud-caked boots and an old Trinity blazer. She was disappointed, not so much that the actual weekend was denied her, but that Richard did not want to go.

She would not have persuaded him. The fact that he did not want to go finished the matter. She could derive no pleasure from his unwilling company. The inn might be there, and the hill and the stony road, but as long as she knew that Richard was wishing himself back in the garden, she could take no joy in them – so she might as well stop at home.

'I can't blame him for liking what he likes,' she told herself. 'Or for not liking what I like.'

'He has only Saturday afternoon and Sunday to do what he likes in. I have all day and every day. . . .'

She felt quite reasonable now, and fit to go out into the garden to settle where the rose trees should go. She went out into the spring sunshine, and thought she had never seen anything so enchanting as the bunches of blue squills, sitting at intervals along the borders by the flagged paths.

'They're the bluest things I've ever seen,' she said.

'You like the flowers, I find,' said Richard. 'But you won't work to get them.'

Which was very true, but somehow dampening to the warmth Anne had reasoned herself into. And when she found in a little while that he had forgotten that he had asked her to choose the site for the rose trees, and knew exactly where he wanted to put them, she drifted away again into the house. She wandered in a lost way from room to room. Emily Barnes had gone to the Saturday market; everything seemed very quiet.

She went to the window and called out to Richard:

'I'll just go for a little run by myself.'

'Run along, then,' called Richard. 'Back for tea?'

'Oh, yes.'

It was still an antidote to depression to drive the car. As soon as she was out on the long shining black road, she felt as brisk as could be, and sang happily to the throb of the car. When she had satisfied her need to drive, she turned into a lane, got out and climbed over the low wall into a wood.

Anne felt it more and more difficult as the months went on to be reasonable. She was becoming resentful, and showing it.

Barely a year had gone and here she was asking Richard: 'Why did you marry me?'

Richard looked at her briefly and said nothing. No one could be a greater adept at saying nothing than Richard. She pursued the subject relentlessly, lying back in her chair, her long slim legs stretched out before her, her eyes fixed on him.

'I was happier at the office,' she said.

No answer from Richard.

'I've got nothing to do,' she said. 'D'you hear? I hate being cooped up in this house with nothing to do.'

'Surely there's an easy way out of that difficulty,' said Richard in a conversational way that maddened Anne.

'What?' she cried. 'Tell me. What?'

'Get something to do.'

'But what?' she cried again.

'There are plenty of my committees, for instance, who would be glad of your help.'

'Committees!' Anne was scornful. It is hard to ask for life and be offered committees. 'Futile things. Everybody trying to get into the limelight. A lot of silly little town councillors standing up to propose and second and pass in the usual way. All led by the nose by their party leaders. I've seen too much of committees from the inside. They bore me stiff.'

Richard sighed.

'I'm afraid you're very often bored stiff,' he said.

'You're right. I am. Bored – bored – bored! What are you going to do about it?'

Richard raised his eyebrows.

'I do about it? Surely only you can do anything about it.'

'Oh!' wailed Anne. 'You're so impersonal. You're so detached. I don't seem to belong to you or anybody or anywhere.'

Tears rushed into her eyes.

'For God's sake,' said Richard quietly, 'don't let's have another scene. I can't stand scenes. I shall have to go out of the room.'

'Go out of the room, then,' blazed Anne. 'Go on . . . get out.'

He went.

She lay back in her chair, with two tears stuck upon her cheeks like glass beads. She felt a vulgar, shouting shrew. That's what she was becoming, she thought; a noisy, nagging shrew.

She beat her hands together.

'But oh, God, God! . . . I want . . . I want . . . I don't know what I want, but I ache with wanting. . . .'

Richard himself was undergoing a hardening change. During his engagement he had expanded wonderfully. Anne could not know, because he stubbornly hid it, with what tenderness and gratitude this lonely man had taken her into his heart. He was lonely, be it admitted, because of his idiosyncrasy of character, but he was not the less lonely for that. Anne had come into his life like the sun, like rain on parched land, like all the softening and healing things in one lovely form. To his marriage he had brought all the enchantment she had left out; but it did not take him long, with the acuteness of love, to find that she had left it out.

With a curse at his own damfoolery in thinking she could love him as he loved her, Richard shrank into himself again, and gradually resumed, to her, the odd casual exterior that baffled and annoyed the rest of his acquaintance.

§ 2

With the onset of winter, Anne entered on another phase. A new assurance came to her. She realised, and it came in the nature of a discovery, that she was really very pretty. She looked at her slender body, her hands, her thin arched feet, her face, as if she had never seen them before; she compared them critically with the bodies, the hands and feet and faces of other people, and they came out of the test well, even triumphantly. She had her hair cut short one morning, and came home to lunch looking five years younger, which was very young indeed. Richard glanced anxiously at her many times when she was not looking.

'Give me some money, please,' she said to him. 'I need clothes.'

She bought a great many. Frocks of silver and apple green and red and black frocks, delicate slippers and underclothes fine enough to go through a ring.

The dance fever, which spread through Bowford like an infection, caught her. She danced without Richard. He didn't dance well, and she had a much better time without him. The young, good dancing partners were not then embarrassed by his restless, hovering presence and his incomprehensible, but suspect, remarks.

When the extraordinarily good band that Bowford got down from London for its dances played, a feeling so wild that it scared her invaded Anne. She longed to dance alone, to go swirling and circling out on to the polished floor. She longed to dance alone – in a wind – on grass. Her heart went beating out into wide, solitary spaces like a bird. She was hardly conscious of the arms of some young man, whose brains, Richard said, were in his feet. When she had a bad partner, she was irritated almost to tears. She would circle round and round furiously, a mechanical smile on her lips, her heart black with hatred of the clumsy creature whose blundering feet spoilt the rhythm and her shoes, whose silly knees knocked hers, and whose soft stomach she had to bend backwards, nauseated, to escape. But to dance well, she put up with young men, who, the moment they sat down, became the most vapid creatures in the world. She put up with parties so boring that everyone yawned in the intervals of dancing. She considered the day lost that had not some dancing in it. She saw more of Mildred Yates again, because Mildred had the dance fever too, together with an increasing fever of another kind.

Brian Clayton, she confided to Anne, had twice taken her home from dances. Brian Clayton was a considerable catch. He was 'different' from the ordinary cotton men of Bowford in that he was fastidious in speech and manner, went in summer to Le Touquet and to Pontresina for the winter sports. His clothes were made in Savile Row, and the young men looked to see when he wore string gloves and when he stopped wearing them. He was rather small and slender, extremely well groomed, with fair hair that men denounced as artificially waved. Mildred was flattered by his attentions, and Mrs Yates already went about with a triumphant gleam in her eye.

Anne saw more of Mildred – but at dances there is no time for conversation. It is the men one sees and sits with, one only nods and smiles to girls as they sit with other men. And so Anne went to the Hospital Ball without being prepared in the least for what was to happen there.

She stood in the throng by the door, waiting to be booked for dances. Bowford was still old-fashioned enough to have programmes for its established balls. The women stood in groups, in little blocks of colour, tapping their programmes with their fingers and laughing self-consciously.

'Isn't it horrible, this being looked over?' asked Evelyn Brasher fiercely. 'I feel as if I were a cow at a cattle market. I hate it. I tell myself after every dance that I'll never go through it again.

'I daren't look round,' said Anne, 'in case I should catch a man's eyes, and he should think he has to dance with me after that.'

The black-coated figures of the men threaded their way circumspectly through the brilliant throng of women. When a man stopped at a woman's elbow, she turned and booked dances with outward indifference and inward relief.

Anne's eyes kept an embarrassed limit, and it was not until her programme was almost full, that she lifted her head and took a bold sweep round the room.

At the sight of a man standing apart from the busy groups, the blood left her heart in one painful leap. She went white above her silver frock. That hooked profile was unmistakable. It was George Yates come back; George come somehow to the Hospital Ball.

Her heart beat so heavily that it shook, visibly, the mauve orchid trailing from her left shoulder. He must have felt the strained gaze of her eyes, for he turned and looked directly at her. His face betrayed no surprise. He had the advantage of her, having seen her five seconds after he came into the room. He bowed distantly.

Anne recovered herself sufficiently to bend her head. Then she turned away. She dropped her eyelids over eyes that felt suddenly burning and hard. Her fingers shook as she pretended to scrutinise her programme. She bit her lips to keep them from trembling.

How changed he was! How assured! A man of the world, this George, who had once been poor, bitter, crude. How changed they both were – elegant, prosperous, conventional, grown far away from the young, inexperienced creatures who had held each other fiercely under the stars and loved. The memory of them as they had been hurt her.

Then, resolutely, she choked the memory down. She lifted her head. A little smile of defiance deepened the nicks at the corners of her mouth. She turned, almost with a twirl, on her heel, and deliberately walked towards George Yates where he stood alone by the drapery of green-and-white butter muslin on the staircase.

He watched her come with perfect composure. Only a

little muscle worked in his cheek. He saw the lovely thing Anne had grown into, he saw the slight lovely curve of her waist, and the clean line of her knee, revealed by the sheath of her frock. He saw how she walked superbly with her cropped head well up, and her silver-shod feet set with assurance on the shining floor. She was not any more the little-girl Anne he had known.

'I haven't seen you for years,' said this young woman of the world.

'No. It is years,' he said with equal calmness. 'Have you anything left?'

It was the conventional thing to do. The new George did it. The old George would not have done.

'Only number 16, I'm afraid.'

'May I have it?'

'You may,' said Anne.

With a crash that made Anne start, the red-coated orchestra burst into action, and Anne's first partner came to claim her. She drifted away with him. Over his shoulder, her eyes followed George, dancing very well indeed, with a girl in a flame-coloured frock. The girl smiled up at him, and at George's answering downward smile, Anne swiftly looked away. She looked at Mildred dancing with Brian Clayton. Mildred was radiant in an exquisite pink frock. Every line of her expressed vitality and happiness. She passed close to Anne and nodded her head in George's direction.

'Look who's here!' she said. 'I hadn't time to . . .'

Brian Clayton masterfully danced her away. Over his shoulder Anne saw her happy eyes.

Foxtrot gave way to one-step, one-step to foxtrot; the Hospital Ball went on. There was supper. Anne and her partner sat with Mildred and Brian Clayton. Anne talked feverishly, terribly conscious that George was not a dozen yards away with Evelyn Brasher and her father. As often as she dared, without attracting notice, Anne turned her head and looked at him as he talked seriously with Sir Peter and flashed laughter at Evelyn.

Back again to the ballroom. The music had no effect on Anne now. She hardly heard it. Her thoughts were projected through the evening to the sixteenth dance. How was she to dance with him? What a fool she had been to speak to him!

At the end of the fifteenth, she slipped away to the dressing-room. She ran a comb through her hair, with nervous fingers she pulled out the pieces that curled inwards over her ears and let them spring back again, she powdered carefully, and assumed an expression of bright indifference before the mirror.

She was standing with her fingers pressed to her lips, when the girl in the flame-coloured frock came in to arrange herself. The sight of her steadied Anne. There must have been many girls for George in the last six years.

The band started, and Anne went out to dance with George.

Without a word, he took her hand in his, placed his right hand on her naked back, moved it until he found an anchorage of material, and led her into the dance.

At the touch of his hands, something melted in Anne. Poise, control deserted her. She had a horrible desire to burst into tears. She turned her face into the shadow of his shoulder and struggled with a quivering lip.

'Stop! Stop!' she told herself fiercely. 'What's the matter with me? What a fool I am!'

Above her head, George's face was indifferent. By and by, as they danced mechanically, Anne gained control over herself.

'I shall never dance with him again,' she thought. 'And this is nearly over.'

For distraction, she took to a device she employed at the dentist's. She said the alphabet. It came into a rhyme.

'Ab*C*; def*G*; Hi*J*k; lmno*P*; Qrs; Tu*V*; Wxyz, you see.' Over and over it she went, a fixed smile upon her lips.

She was able to talk quite calmly to him as they sat on the balcony afterwards, and ask him about his years in Egypt.

'How long are you home for?' she asked conversationally.

'I'm home for good now,' he replied.

Anne's hardly acquired poise was rudely shaken.

'He can't stay! He can't!' she protested mutely. 'What am I going to do?'

'Look at that little tree of almond blossom.' She pointed to where it stood among the palms. 'Isn't it an innocent little thing to be at a ball?'

He turned and looked at her involuntarily. She was the same Anne.

CHAPTER TWENTY-ONE

§ 1

Anne awoke. She opened her eyes on a darkened room and realised that she was still very tired. Then the faint gleaming of her silver dress from the chair where she had laid it, reminded her that this was the morning after the Hospital Ball where George – George! – had been. She was stung into full consciousness by that. George was in this town. George was at this moment in the house he had bought for his parents in Sheldon Road. George was near. When she went out into the streets she would see him. At the dances and dinners of Bowford she would see him. Life was entirely changed by the fact that George was in the town.

Restlessly she turned in her bed, and her eyes fell on the bed next to it. Ah, for one wild moment she had forgotten, quite, quite forgotten that she was married! How strange, and how horrible of her to have forgotten Richard!

Richard's bed was empty. He had gone. It must be late, then. Yes, the daylight was piercingly white at the edges of the blinds.

A tentative knock came at the door; a knock that inquired whisperingly if she were awake.

'Come in,' she called, and the little stocky figure of Emily Barnes bearing a tray appeared dimly.

'I thought 'appen you'd be awake by now,' she said. 'Gone half-past nine. Shall I pull the blinds up?'

Anne screwed up her eyes against the sudden light.

Emily, on her way back from the windows, bent to pick up two green silk garments that had slipped from a chair. She held them up and shook her head at them.

'And that's all you wear under your frock! It's a mystery to me why you don't get your death of cold.'

Anne detected a note of disapproval in Emily's tone, and for the first time felt a faint resentment. It was ridiculous of Emily to offer any opinion on the subject of her clothes. She did not answer, but merely moved her pillows behind her head, and sat up for the reception of the tray. When Emily went to the wardrobe and brought out the fleecy pink bed-jacket and wrapped it round her shoulders, she smiled contritely.

'You do look after me,' she said.

'And you need it,' said Emily. 'All this dancing. You'll be worn to a thread.'

'Now, Emily,' expostulated Anne, pouring out her tea. 'How many times have you said to me that you'd rather wear out than rust out?'

'So I would,' said Emily stoutly. 'But with work – not with pleasure.'

'But work is your pleasure,' said Anne. 'Admit it.'

It was Emily's turn to detect something hard in Anne's voice. She was hurt.

'Nay,' she said. 'It's not my place to interfere with you. You must excuse me. I'm only a servant, and I don't know any better. Put it down to me ignorance.'

An emotional disturbance in her nose made her sneeze.

'Don't be donkeyish, Emily,' smiled Anne. 'You're only fishing, you know. I see through you. You want me to say you're gold through and through, and that I couldn't get on without you, and that you've stuck to me through thick and thin. You stuck to me through the thin, Emily, and this is the thick now, and you've still got to stick to me. Go on, now. I've said a lot of nice things. You can cheer up.'

'Well, 'ave yer own way,' said Emily, her face crumpling reluctantly into smiles. 'I never knew such a wheedler. But I must get on with me work.'

Left to herself, Anne's thoughts returned to George. She conjured up a picture of him as he had been last night. How well his face had matured! That high, hooked nose; those brows that lifted slightly at the outward corners, but which were so level and dark above his eyes; the firmness of his upper lip and the slight arrogance of his lower one. How coldly he had looked at her!

'What does he think of me? What does he think of my being married to Richard? Does he remember? Does he remember Dyke, and those four days?'

Abruptly, Anne stopped.

'I've no right to remember,' she told herself sternly.

She still tried to be appropriate; to think the right thoughts.

To drive others away, she decided upon action. She got up and had an ice-cold shower; it was symbolic; but by the time she had dressed and gone, she had relaxed the control and was again wondering about George.

'If only I had a child.'

She wanted an anchorage.

'I feel as if I were just floating about,' she said, 'a queer, unreal floating about. . . . I wish I had three or four children to get up in the mornings and wash and dress and get off to school and cook for and consider.' Her imagination ran on. She gave the children names. Mary, one should be, fair-haired and deliciously solemn, and her sister, Aline – yes, that was a pretty name. She should be rather naughty. And two boys – Paul, perhaps, and George – yes, George. She couldn't help it if George was her favourite name – it was just a coincidence. She couldn't quite imagine the boys. Girls were much more real to her. But their finger marks would be all round the door and the electric light switches, and their boots would kick the skirting boards, and the piano would be thumby. She looked round the room, immaculate in its morning freshness. She stared at the curtains; they hung down so still. She listened – her lips parted. Not a sound. The quiet, the emptiness of it was suddenly intolerable. She got up and fled from it.

She went into the kitchen to Emily.

'I think I shall bake.' It struck her as ridiculous that whenever she wanted to escape from her thoughts, she had to bake or take the car out.

'Come along then,' said Emily, glad of her company. Glad too that Anne should do anything. Emily didn't like the way she sat about in chairs and looked listlessly at nothing.

Anne was soon busy with flour and sugar and butter and eggs.

'If all else fails,' she said to Emily, 'I shall set up a pastry-cook's shop. Wouldn't it be fun?'

'Nay, it's all right when they turn out well,' said Emily. 'But take yesterday, for instance. Could I get the oven 'ot? No, I couldn't, try me domdest, and it was as well, because Onions was inside. Yes, when I opens the door, out 'e falls, gasping like yer aunt's old bellows. I 'ope it'll teach 'im a lesson. 'E's that fond of warmth that it wouldn't be no punishment to that cat to go to 'ell.'

When Richard returned to demolish her cookery with what seemed to her a disrespectful haste, Anne felt steadier on her moral feet and made a few advances.

'I'm afraid I've been out rather a lot lately,' she began.

'You have,' he agreed.

'I'll not leave you so much, if you'd rather I didn't.' She hoped for a word to show he had some need of her.

'Oh, don't bother about me,' said Richard cheerfully. 'Unlike you, I'm never at a loose end, and when the evenings are longer I shall be able to play golf, you know.'

Anne hesitated; then said boldly:

'Don't you mind when I go out to dance with other men? They are quite willing to flirt with me, I find.'

'Let 'em,' said Richard shortly, getting up from the table. 'If you have no objection.'

'Don't you care?' asked Anne. 'Doesn't it matter to you at all what I do?'

Richard unhooked the window into the garden.

'Your attitude, my child,' he said, 'is all wrong. If you want to flirt, you'll flirt. Nothing I can do will rid you of a propensity to flirt. You're a free agent, you know. I can't interfere.'

Anne was nonplussed. This was not the traditional behaviour of husbands. She sat on at the table, her hands fallen among the plates and glasses, staring out into the garden where Richard, the wind flickering at his hair, was examining with careful hands his rock plants.

§ 2

Anne was right in her surmise that she would see George Yates everywhere. On Saturday morning, Mildred Yates made a signal to her from the windows of Fisher's – Bowford's morning coffee house – and Anne went up to find George there too. Mrs Yates had lost no time in pressing him into attendance on her daughter. Major George Yates, DSO, MC, the friend of Sir Peter Brasher and his family, was an asset to be seen about with, and very far removed from the shabby little relation who had shamed her by his haircut and his clothes in the Sunday pew of old.

George stood up with polite indifference as Anne made her way to the table. She, after one startled look, was politely indifferent too. She talked and was amusing in the new way she had acquired to get through Bowford parties; but her coffee remained untouched. She was afraid her hand would belie her if she lifted the cup.

George contributed very little to the talk, but Mildred unconsciously covered all deficiencies. Her mother had brought her up to make conversation. As she chattered, her face was suddenly suffused with colour, and Anne, turning involuntarily to find the cause, saw Brian Clayton following Mrs Yates down the room.

Mrs Yates looked very prosperous in tight beige kid gloves and sable furs. She beamed on them.

'Darling,' she said, 'I told Mr Clayton I thought we'd find you here with George. I've brought him to have a cup of coffee with you. Put it all down to me – at the desk, I mean. No, I'm not staying, thank you, Anne dear. I promised Mr Yates I'd be home early.' She touched Mildred's cheek fondly with her finger, and beamed on them again.

It was so nice to have Mildred in such company in Fisher's. She remembered how she used to sit obscurely in a corner of the same room on other Saturday mornings, when no one even noticed she was there; and now she could bow to almost everyone as she went out.

Brian talked to Mildred in a low voice through his almost closed teeth. She laughed and blushed and was charming. Anne and George were left to themselves. Desperately, Anne tried to talk, but in spite of her, they fell into silence, both gazing out of the window at the High Street, where people hurried up and down, or loitered, or stood about in groups.

George changed his position unostentatiously, and shaded his eyes with his hand so that he could look at her unobserved.

Now that she had forgotten to be conventional, this was the face that he remembered. Although, he reminded himself, so much had happened to her since he had last seen her – her father had died, her home had been broken up, she had lived with her ghastly old aunt for two years, and finally she had married – her face was for the moment the face of the little girl he used to watch in church. As he looked at her, her dreaming expression quickened, her eyes picked out and followed someone in the street. George looked too, and saw a long, lean figure threading its preoccupied way through the High Street.

'Her husband.'

He looked at Anne again, and saw her thought expressed clearly in her eyes. She was wondering whether to get up and run after Richard, or to stay where she was. A faint colour ran up into her cheeks. She turned her eyes away from Richard to George. Their looks met and held – a questioning in them both. Then Anne looked away.

'My coffee's cold,' she said at random. 'I'd like it changed for hot coffee, please.'

CHAPTER TWENTY-TWO

Mr and Mrs James Yates were giving a dinner party, their first, to celebrate the engagement of their daughter to Brian Clayton.

They were on their way together to make their entry once more into the dining room to get the effect the table would have on their guests.

They paused in the hall, to make their minds a blank of remembered splendours.

'Now, James,' said Mrs Yates, and moved forward, a guest in spirit.

James, very neat in his little dress-suit, followed. They gasped, once more, involuntarily, at the blaze of their glass and silver, the whiteness of damask, the coolness of green smilax, the opulence of pink carnations.

'Well, well,' said James, tugging at his moustache, which was like a little polished wad of tobacco-twist, so tightly was it wound and pomaded. 'I think we have excelled ourselves this time. Excelsior! Excelsior! We shan't be able to say that any more, because, my love, we can't improve on this.'

They hung admiringly over the hors d'œuvres, included in

the menu at Brian's suggestion, and standing on the dumb-waiter to be handed round by Minnie.

'A picture,' said Mrs James Yates.

They beamed on the iridescent sardines, the tender green of lettuce cradling pink shrimps, the minute red radishes, the dull green of olives, the gold and white of egg, the tough and briny *filets d'anchois*.

'A masterpiece,' amended James. 'But not by an *old* master.'

He patted his wife's back affectionately. It was a plump back, encased in tight black satin. The ridge of her new corset stuck out round her shoulder blades.

'Mildred and Brian in the middle there, did you say? And where is George to sit?'

Major George Yates, DSO, MC, was to sit between Mrs Richard Soames and Miss Rosaline Budd, the daughter of Bowford's Conservative MP.

'Yes, yes, my dear, well arranged,' said James, nodding over the places. 'So Anne's husband wouldn't come, wouldn't he? Doesn't dine out, doesn't he? Of all the eccentric . . . well, upon my soul, I don't know why that pretty young thing married him. It beats me.'

'He has a good position,' said Mrs Yates, re-arranging the smilax.

'Pooh!' James blew Soames's position into the air. What was it compared with his?

'And he's a gentleman,' insisted his wife. 'Yes, for all he's short with people, you can see he's a gentleman. I mean you can tell he's been to a public school and a university.'

James tugged silently at his moustache. His round eyes looked wistfully at nothing. He had been educated at the Parish Higher Grade himself and they hadn't even worn those striped caps with PHG in yellow on them in his day. He thought that it was rather hard that Henrietta should say such a thing. Perhaps it was because he had only been to the PHG that Soames wouldn't come to his dinners.

A shrill 'Trrr-rrring' at the bell put his speculations to flight.

'Mother! The bell!' he cried and ran over to her like a flustered robin.

'Into the drawing room, James.' Mrs Yates shoo'd him before her.

'Minnie,' she called as she passed the housemaid in the hall, 'your cap is crooked again. Your head must slope.' She felt aggrieved, as if Minnie should have mentioned the slope on her head when she applied for the situation.

She rustled into the drawing room and tried to look as if she had been there for the past hour.

'Oh, it's only George!' She breathed again. 'How are you, dear boy? And how's Mother?'

She kissed her nephew, sliding her hands with pleasure over the immaculate fit of his coat on his shoulders.

'I suppose,' said James Yates, taking up his stand on the hearthrug, and looking up at George with a mixture of diffidence and importance, 'sherry is the correct thing with soup, and – er – hock with the salmon?'

'Oh, I suppose so, sir,' said George. 'Anything's all right nowadays.'

'Are you sure?'

His uncle could hardly believe that anything could be all right. But, he reflected, George knew. George knew. And he was glad he had asked George instead of Brian. He felt nervous with his prospective son-in-law. Had to mind his p's and q's a bit. Would never do to let Henrietta and Milly down. Brian was what James called in his secret thoughts 'a toff'.

George nodded reassuringly as his eyes wandered to a photograph of Anne. Anne there on the table. Anne everywhere; in France; in the Sudan. Through all his other meetings and partings and relations, she had persisted steadily in his thoughts; or perhaps only unconsciously in his feelings.

He turned to find Anne herself, in a red frock, coming into the drawing room behind Mrs Bramwell, a well-fed carp in bronze sequins.

He held Anne's cool hand in his for a second, then Queenie Robinson's pale face loomed up under a fuzz of dark hair for greeting.

'Good evening, Major Yates. Yes, it *is* wet. It makes you reluctant to leave your own fireside, doesn't it? I mean . . . er . . . yes. Have I lost my scarf? No, it's slipped down my dress at the back. No, don't trouble. It's just as warm there. Unless, of course, it gets too warm for me, and then someone might come to the rescue. Good evening, Mr . . .' She nodded sideways, stared vaguely having forgotten the name, and continued: 'Yes, good for the garden, very, very . . . Bramwell' she threw in as an afterthought. 'We have all sorts of things coming up. Mont Aubretia, and some darling little red things, Alopecia, that's the name I think. And plenty of – er – daisies.'

She was so vague and loose, one felt she might come to pieces at any minute. Her dress was vague and loose too. Mr James Yates slid his eyes away from her uneasily, in case her bosom fell out of her gown while he was looking. The fear of that haunted him through the evening.

The guests stood or sat about the drawing room. Mrs Yates smiled a great deal, but her eyes were worried as they consulted the equally worried eyes of Mildred. Brian had not yet come. He was half an hour late, and the dinner was spoiling.

In the kitchen, Bertha, the cook, was basting and rebasting and reviling the young man. Minnie fluttered backwards and forwards from the dining room in a state bordering on imbecility from suspense. She had never waited at table before when company was present, and though she had been made to practise for weeks on the family, she had never been able to feel anything but flustered.

'Oh, my 'evingly Father, but I do wish it was over!' she said to Bertha, nervous tears in her pale eyes. 'Eh, 'eck, but I do wish it was.'

'Put your cap straight, you soft thing, and pull yerself together! If you goes and spoils my dinner with any of yer gormless ways, upon my word if I don't leave. And you won't get another girl to put up with you coming into 'er bed because you're frightened a man 'ull get into your bedroom. Why' – Bertha chuckled robustly – 'you should be like me. I'm always 'opin' a man will get into mine. Eh, these birds! They're going to be dried to tinder. Bad beginning, I say, for Miss Mildred, for all he's such a toff.'

'Oh, 'evingly Father, the bell! The bell!' moaned Minnie.

'Well, answer it, you fool!' snapped Bertha.

Minnie flutteringly admitted Mr Brian Clayton, who after examining minutely and with extreme leisure a small cut on his chin, allowed her to usher him into the drawing room. In the doorway, he put his feet together and bowed to the company with a disarming smile, but with no word of apology. Immediately, Mildred forgot her apprehension, and Mrs Yates her almost sickening anxiety. Talk shot up like a fountain. Minnie made a muffled din in the hall, and the guests moved into the dining room. Mr James Yates was secretly disappointed that no one exclaimed at the sight of the table. It might not have been good manners, but it would have been pleasant.

Minnie handed the hors d'œuvres.

Anne was terribly conscious that she was sitting next to George. He smelt faintly aromatic from the stuff he put on his hair. How smoothly it lay where it once had been stubborn and badly cut! He talked to Miss Rosaline Budd, who had just finished her education in Paris, and whose Parisian air lay strangely on her eighteen English summers.

Behind the chairs of the guests, Minnie was getting agitated. She sent wild looks of inquiry at her mistress. But Mrs Yates sat in regal state at the top of the table and held no communication with maids.

Minnie floundered out with the soup. After a long and ominous pause, during which the host and hostess picked up and dropped three separate topics of conversation, she returned and planted a dish of roasted chickens before her master. A bomb could not have startled him more. He lowered his head and peered through the pink carnations at his wife.

'Mother,' he said in a low appeal.

Mrs Yates spoke in a rapid fierce whisper out of the corner of her mouth to Minnie.

'Take those away! Take those away! Salmon next, stupid.'

Poor Minnie, her hands at her slipping cap, cast a look of nervous anguish at her mistress.

'Cook was out at the back a minute, mum, and I forgot what follered what . . .'

'That will do,' said Mrs Yates with ice in her voice.

With trembling red hands, Minnie lifted the dish of chickens and disappeared.

The guests talked calmly on.

Mrs Yates stole a glance at Brian. Was he? . . . He was laughing with Miss Budd. Only Mildred knew by the slight distension of his nostril that he was annoyed.

Minnie reappeared, pink as the salmon, and breathing audibly.

The chickens returned at their appointed time, and Mr Yates was now in the limelight. He seized the carvers, frowning portentously and pursing his lips until his moustache stuck out under his nose like two little tusks. Henrietta leaned a little sideways, while conversing, so that she could see what James was doing. She had a conviction that she could carve a great deal better herself. She was jerked back into the perpendicular by the sudden appearance of the vegetables on the table before her. So might Lady Macbeth have gazed on the apparition of the dagger that night at Glamis.

In her fierce sideways whisper, she hissed: 'Take them away! *Hand* them!'

Minnie straightened her cap and, emitting a shuddering sigh, took up the vegetables.

In the babble of conversation that rose to hide Minnie's second lapse, George turned his head and said in a low, friendly voice:

'Poor Aunt! Won't she be in a stew about this? And it's so funny, if only we dared laugh.'

'It's not funny for Minnie,' said Anne.

But she felt a sudden happiness, because she and George had come nearer through the incident. The barrier between them had been lowered a little.

It was lowered still more during the evening, as their eyes met in mutual amusement. Queenie Robinson at Bridge was risible indeed.

She sat sideways, her feet entangled in wisps of train, holding her cards for all to see, gazing vaguely round the room, joining occasionally in conversation from other tables.

'Did you really, dear? How tragic for you! My turn, did you say? John dear, you mustn't be cross. After all, Bridge is only a game. Do try to remember that. Shall I put my little Knave on, or not? Oh, no, wait a minute! I'll give you all a shock. Where's my? . . . There!' With triumph, she trumped her partner's trick, amid a chorus of protest.

'I knew . . .' she said, waving their voices away. 'I knew I'd give you a shock. Well, never mind. Get on with your game, children. Let me know when it's my turn.'

Outside, the rain beat against the windows. Mrs Yates drew

the curtains closer, and poked the fire into a brighter blaze. Brian, his good humour restored, held Mildred's little foot tightly between his own under the table, and in the intervals of play, he found a keen delight in making her drop her eyes before the hard, insistent gaze of his.

It was still raining at midnight, when Anne went to get her car out of the garage.

'Anyone coming my way?' she asked. 'Queenie, what about you and John? I can take three. Anyone else?'

'There's me,' said George, a black bulk in the doorway. 'If you don't mind.'

'Of course not,' said Anne.

John and Queenie packed in with her at the front, and George climbed into the dicky. Mr and Mrs Yates stood in the lighted porch to speed their parting guests. Behind them Mildred was trying to impress upon Brian the necessity of seeing people off before shutting themselves up in the deserted drawing room.

'Goodbye . . . thanks so much . . . perfectly delightful . . . 'bye.'

The voices faded away, with something of the significance they have on the stage, when parting is a prelude to something that is going to happen.

'Greasy roads,' said John Robinson, wishing he had the wheel in his own hands. He felt that no one could drive a car but himself.

Anne drove confidently and fast. The arc lamps with their huge rainbow circles in the rain went by as if on the march; the mud sucked and spattered under the tyres. She came to a standstill before the imposing iron gates of the Robinsons' house.

'Goodbye . . . thanks so much. . . . Goodbye . . . 'bye.'

'One moment,' said George, 'do you mind if I come inside?'

He bent himself in half and got in under the hood. They were shut away together in that small space, close, close.

'You go straight home,' said George. 'I'll walk home from there. It's quite near.'

'No,' she protested. 'I'll drive you home.'

'No, thanks. It's stopped raining.'

Anne obediently turned down the hill towards her own house. She was past argument. She felt suddenly tired.

'It's dark here,' said George.

'Yes, the lamps stop halfway down the hill. We're almost in the country here.'

'Rather a bad bit,' commented George again, as the headlights revealed a deep ditch to the left, and to the right a hedge broken by a gate on an upward rise to a field, and a wall looming at the foot of the hill.

'Oh, it's all right when you get used to it,' said Anne. But she registered the fact, subconsciously, that she was going too fast down the hill. She put out a hand to apply the brake more forcibly. There was a snap and a cry simultaneously. She went rigid as the car hurtled downhill towards the wall; she cowered in her seat before disaster – when, by some swift miracle, the car heaved sideways, burst through the rickety gate and came to a lumbering halt in the field. Then, and then only, was Anne conscious of the pain of her hands crushed under George's on the wheel.

'A very near shave,' said George, after a breathless silence.

'The handbrake went,' said Anne, very shaken.

'I heard it,' he said grimly.

'How wonderfully quick you were!' she breathed.

He got out of the car and swiftly examined it.

'Nothing very serious as far as I can see,' he called out. 'Your mudguards are pretty badly bent, and one headlamp's broken.'

He went to the gate.

'The gate's done for. Come and see.'

Anne climbed out of the car.

'Wait a minute,' she said. 'I feel weak at the knees.'

'Do you?' George's voice was tender. He put his hands under her elbows and held her firmly. The moment of danger had marvellously cleared the barrier between them. They were themselves.

'Let's sit on the step of the car for a minute,' he said.

They sat down side by side, Anne leaning slightly against George.

'What a good thing you were with me,' she said. 'I don't know what would have happened if you hadn't been.'

She put out a grateful hand. George gripped it convulsively.

'Don't let's think about that,' he said, in a voice that showed he had thought and shuddered at it.

There was silence except for the sound of the fallen rain running heavily in the dyke.

'However are we going to move the car?' asked Anne wearily.

'Push her out and run her into the garage on low gear, with the foot brakes. Quite easy,' said George.

'Let's do it, then.' Anne stirred.

'I should keep still a little longer,' he advised.

There was silence again.

Several times Anne felt George draw a breath as if he were going to speak but thought better of it. At last he said in a conversational tone:

'Anne, it's all over, years ago, of course, and you're married, and lots of water has passed under my bridges, and all that. Could I – put it down to curiosity, if you like – could I ask you why you gave me up so suddenly? Was there a reason? Was it because I was too poor? Or was it mere caprice? What was it? I didn't question it much then, but I have done since, especially since I came home and saw you again. Why did you do it, Anne? We can talk quite calmly about it now, can't we?'

'I suppose so.' If he could, she must.

'But it's too long to explain,' she said, in a low voice.

'Tell me,' he urged. 'You owe it to me. I have a right to know.'

Falteringly, with difficulty, she told him, raking up painfully Vera Bowden, her terror and disgust. They looked like crumbled skeletons, brought out into the damp night now – all substance gone out of them, so that one could hardly tell what they had been.

'And that was all?' George's voice was thick. 'For a thing like that, you threw me over!'

Anne murmured, her hands moving like the hurt wings of a bird in the night.

'As if I cared a damn about a thing like that . . .'

'It wasn't only that I thought you would have cared about it . . .' she said. 'It was I who was so sickened. I don't know why I was so affected by it. Looking back, I don't know why I was. But you can't understand, you have no sense of proportion when you're young, George.'

She stood up, and George stood near her. A dangerous tenderness invaded him.

'Poor, funny little thing,' he said, putting his face down on her hair.

'Don't. There's Richard, you know.'

'Yes,' said George, his arms falling heavily. 'There's Richard.'

He wanted, urgently, to ask her why she had married Richard. Why – why – why? But he dared not. He had to spare her if she could not say she loved Richard; and he had to spare himself if she could say she loved Richard.

'I can't understand,' was all he dared say.

'Oh, well . . .' Anne's voice was weary. 'It's no use talking.'

She got into the car.

'I can back. Look out for me.'

They drove into the garage, where Richard had left the light on for her. Somehow this thoughtfulness of Richard in leaving the light on for her, after she had been to the party without him, touched her.

'Good night, Anne.' George took her limp hand in his.

'Good night.'

A sense of flat helplessness assailed them both. George stood staring at the bespattered car; then he turned and disappeared into the night. Anne strained her eyes to see the last of him. Nothing was left of him but the sound of his footsteps going away, away – away from her.

CHAPTER TWENTY-THREE

§ 1

Anne and Richard were at lunch. Richard sat at one end of the table, eating biscuits and cheese. By the side of his plate he had a gardening catalogue, over which he pored, occasionally pulling out a pencil from his waistcoat pocket to make marks in the margin.

Anne thought: 'He'll go on gardening whatever happens to me.'

She watched him with hostility, noting the strongly marked lines on his face, the greying of his red hair at the temples, the capable, nervous hands that were so skilful among the delicate rock plants, nipping off here and there, settling them down, dibbling soil around them – hands that used to smooth back Anne's hair from her forehead.

In the silence of the dining room, the crunch of his teeth on the biscuits sounded loud and insistent.

Crunch . . . crunch . . . crunch.

Anne tried not to notice it.

Crunch . . . crunch . . . crunch.

'Oh, stop – stop!' she protested mutely.

Crunch . . . crunch . . . crunch. Pause. Crunch . . . crunch . . . crunch.

She made a sudden movement of desperation, pressing her hand to her cheek. For the imperceptible fraction of a second, Richard suspended his pencil and his breath; but she did not know it.

He began on another biscuit. She clenched her hands under the table until he finished, then he closed the catalogue and went through the window into the garden. When Emily came in to clear away, Anne went into the drawing room to be out of the range of Emily's eye. Emily seemed always to be looking at her, watching her, wondering about her. Anne was irritated by it. She had tried to exorcise the demon that possessed her in these days by reminding herself how staunch Emily had been, how much she owed to her. But the irritation stubbornly persisted.

She went into the drawing room and closed the door, uncomfortably conscious that she had neither looked at nor spoken to Emily.

'Why should I always speak to her – when I don't want to? It gets a nuisance always having to speak. This is my house; why shouldn't I behave exactly as I want to in it?'

She stretched herself out in a long, low chair by the fire and stared across the room through the low windows where, in the March wind, the trees swayed and the hedges shuddered. Her thoughts revolved, like a clockwork toy with a broken spring, round herself and George and Richard.

Richard came in to say goodbye before going back to the office. He did not offer to kiss her, but stood looking at her as she lay in the chair, before he said curtly:

'Goodbye. I shan't be back for dinner tonight; evening meeting. I shall get something in town.'

'Very well.' Anne glanced up at his inscrutable face and dropped her eyes again.

Richard still stood looking at her. She stirred uneasily. She felt that he thought she was a poor creature.

'It's cold with the door open,' she said at random.

Her husband turned on his heel and left her.

'He thinks I'm a poor creature,' she told herself again. 'But I don't care what he thinks. Why should I?'

These questions were futile. She knew it, and was the more irritated. She gave way to the rising tide of exasperation until it engulfed her; it was at this crucial moment that poor Emily put her head round the drawing room door. She hadn't been able to bear Anne's surliness at lunchtime, and had come to see if she could dispel it by her usual charm.

'Would you like a cup of tea?' she asked.

'No, thank you.' Anne did not turn her head, but a frown drew her brows together.

'Your fire's going down,' said Emily. 'I'd better poke it for you.'

'I am quite capable of poking the fire for myself,' said Anne in a voice of ice, 'and I wish to heaven I could have some peace in my own house.'

Emily's lower jaw dropped. She stood with hanging hands staring at Anne, who had never in her life spoken to her like this before. Anne stared coldly back at her from the depths of the chair. A devil possessed her.

'Prying,' said Anne. 'That's what you are doing. Prying.'

'Well, I never!' Emily was incoherent. 'To think . . . as you should think as I'd pry . . . I've only seen as you're upset about something, but I can't help seeing that. You're not a bit like your nateral self . . . and I've been bothered about it . . .'

'Why can't you leave me alone?' asked Anne fiercely, the more fiercely because Emily's red, crumpled face touched her. 'I can't get a place to myself anywhere.'

'Well' – Emily suddenly bristled – 'if that's the way you look at it, it's time I took myself off. For good, too. I'll leave. I'm only a servant, but I don't need to be told my place by one as I've brought up from a baby. I give a month's notice.'

She marched out of the room, poker in hand. Anne made no protest. Her lips were tight. Let her go. She was tired of being under observation. Yet something clamoured within that it was a shameful thing that she had done. She hardened herself against it.

And now that she had thrust Richard and Emily aside, she was free to release a longing that she had been trying to stifle all day – a longing to see George. Just to look at him; not to speak to him – merely to look. It would be enough. If she took the car out for a run, she could come back by the Station Road about five o'clock, and George would certainly be coming from the Manchester train at that time. What was the harm in just looking at him?

This question brought her to a standstill.

'Come now,' she said to herself. 'I know there's harm – but I'm doing it all the same.'

She dressed feverishly, choosing a small hat that turned up in the front. George had once told her that she should always wear a hat turned up in the front.

'I like to see your eyebrows,' he had said.

She pulled her hair out at the sides and sent it curling over the hat brim. Once she had looked in the glass and wondered if she were pretty enough for him. Now she knew that she was.

She took the car out of the garage and drove away, glad, with a hard, cold gladness to leave the house where Emily would be crying in the kitchen. She felt towards her as she used to feel for Sister Margaret, the novice at the Convent, when she tried to waylay you in the corridors and ask you to talk to her when you didn't want to.

She drove at an exhilarating pace along the good Manchester Road; her cheeks glowed in the fresh wind; recklessness rose in her.

'George! George! George!' her heart sang; and she allowed it to.

She turned the car and timed her speed so that she should be in the Station Road exactly as the 5.30 train from Manchester was dispersing its Bowford passengers. There, as she had planned, she saw George Yates coming towards her alone.

She did not mean to stop. She only meant to look at him as she passed, to let her eyes dwell a moment on his face. But he saw her as she came, and stopped abruptly on the edge of the pavement. His eyes were alight, he made a slight gesture that implored her to stop.

She drew up.

'Good afternoon,' she said.

'Good afternoon.'

No more than that, but there was a warm contentment in their voices as if at last something was appeased in them.

Anne's eyes were on her hands at the wheel, and George's eyes were on Anne, so neither of them saw that Richard, on his way to 'get something in town' before his evening meeting, was observing them from the other side of the road. He stood still for a half minute, with people pushing to and from the station past him. He stared at them, and saw how Anne looked up at George – almost with difficulty, as though there was something in her eyes she wished to hide.

Richard Soames turned abruptly away, and forgetting his intention, hurried back the way he had come.

'They give themselves away . . .' he muttered. 'They stand there and give themselves away. . . .'

§ 2

Anne, coming in from the garage that evening, switched on the lights in the drawing room and went to the fire to warm her hands. She still, from time to time, drew long breaths of elation. The Queen Anne mirror over the mantelpiece reflected, unnoticed, a face of defiant joy – a joy got at the expense of something and held in spite of it. There was a darkening of her eyes, a slight distension of nostrils and a curve of lips quite new to this face. For a moment or two, she warmed her hands, smiling down at them. Then gradually the smile faded and she crisped her fingers. Something in the atmosphere of the house had reached her. She remembered that Richard was not coming home, and that Emily was probably crying in the kitchen.

'This is a miserable house,' she sighed. 'A miserable, heavy place to live in. I wish I was free of it. I wish I could rush out and say to George: 'Come on, let's run in this wind on the top of the hills! Let's get blown about! And let me hold your hand again, and let's walk through the night! Do you remember how you once walked to me during the night? But this time, let's walk together!'

She caught sight of her face in the mirror, and stopped.

'I'm mad,' she said. 'Mad. Mad. Mad.'

She picked the turned-up hat from the floor and went slowly upstairs.

'I feel as wild as a Pendle witch,' she said. 'And I must sit by the drawing room fire and eat a poached egg on toast at a little table.'

A poached egg on toast was her standard meal when Richard did not come home. She dreaded the sight of Emily bringing it in. When the time came, she snatched up a book and held it protectingly before her face. From behind it, she looked at Emily. The dignity of Emily's face startled her. Sniffs and tears she had expected, and had hardened herself against them. But this quietness humiliated her. Emily had retired in upon herself and closed the door against Anne.

The wildness drained away, leaving her strangely subdued. But it returned to her sleeping. She came, in the faint dawn, out of a dream so real as to be more vivid than life. She had heard herself call George. She still felt the warm impress of his arms. She awoke fully, and looked with incredulity at her husband.

'I can't sleep with Richard and dream about George,' she said, with tears.

She moved her things, that day, into the room she called the Wood room, because it looked closely on to the wood that began there and clothed the hill to the left of the house.

Richard made no comment.

Emily Barnes suddenly started to spring clean. Her world was crashing about her, but her instinct was to 'leave everything proper'. The house must be gone through. So she washed and scrubbed and polished, her tears falling on the dusters as she rubbed, and her violent sniffs echoing through the emptied rooms. She only cried when Anne was out. Her pride would not let her give way before her. She was startled when the master came into the kitchen and asked her if she was ill.

'Oh, no, sir, I'm quite well,' she replied, turning away to hide her red eyes.

If Anne hadn't told him she was leaving, Emily wasn't going to. For one moment, a hope leaped in her that perhaps after all Anne didn't mean to keep it up to the bitter end.

CHAPTER TWENTY-FOUR

§ 1

Mr and Mrs James Yates were again entertaining. This time to celebrate their daughter's wedding day. The principals had gone away after the ceremony, and the stage seemed strangely empty, although it was full of extras revolving and revolving in the billiard room through the evening and late into the night.

Mr James Yates showed a tendency to drift off into his bedroom and sit on the edge of the bed to stare at the toes of his new patent pumps. Mrs Yates had to retrieve him many times during the evening.

'Come, come, James,' she said. 'It's no good moping here. You must do your duty by your guests. Besides, whatever is there to mope about? Our girlie's made a beautiful marriage and she looked so happy – so happy, James.'

She spoke in such a brisk voice that James had to look twice to notice that the brightness of her eyes was due to unshed tears.

'Yes, Mother,' he said, sliding from the bed and pulling

down his white waistcoat which would peak outwards over his little stomach. 'She looked very happy and so – so lovely. But isn't it nearly time for these people to go home? Though the house will be very quiet when they've gone. It 'ull be very quiet without her.'

He looked piteously at his wife for comfort.

'Now do pull yourself together, James,' said Henrietta, forcing a laugh. 'Why, deary me, you wouldn't have liked our beautiful little girl to have been an old maid, would you now?'

'Oh, no. No.'

'Well, then, there's nothing else for it,' said his wife briskly. 'Either she's got to be an old maid, or she's got to be married, and there it is. We must make the best of it.'

'Yes, but do you think he's . . . all right for her?' He turned his eyes wistfully to her again as she led him out of his refuge.

'James!' Henrietta was really shocked. 'How can you? He's such a gentleman. His manners are perfect, and look at all he can give her – position . . . and . . . and everything. . . . And everybody likes him. I couldn't have found a better husband for my girl if I looked the world over.'

Henrietta was so confident that James was comforted.

'Besides,' she said, shutting the bedroom door firmly behind her, 'she loves him with all her heart.'

'Yes, yes,' agreed James, trailing down the stairs in his wife's wake. 'I suppose it's all right.'

Then his mind flopped back like a piece of worn elastic.

'But if it isn't . . .' he murmured inaudibly. 'It's too late now . . . too late now.'

He passed Anne and George sitting on the stairs.

'Well, well,' he said, with an effort at the proper demeanour of a host. 'Enjoying yourselves? That's right.'

'Just cooling down,' said George.

'The whisky's in the smoking room,' James said. 'Help yourself, my boy.'

He went into the morning room, letting the smile fall from his face. But a boy and girl were there, sitting out, so he put the smile back again and wandered away. He had a look round at everybody dutifully, and when he saw Henrietta busy with Minnie over the refreshments, he stole back to the bedroom.

Anne and George were back in the billiard room, dancing together. And although Anne looked with outward indifference over his shoulder, and George with steadiness over her head, and nobody knew it – his breath came quickly near her ear, and her heart beat heavily at his side, and their fingers were intertwined with such unconscious force that Anne's ached on release. The gramophone played on and on; the dancers' feet went sip-sip on the polished floor; warm, muffled murmurs of conversation rose and fell. The other dancers drifted off two by two until only Anne and George were left in the billiard room. They danced on in silence, terribly conscious of each other. Then Anne moved her head backwards until she could look up at him. At the sight of her tilted face so near his own, George Yates made an inarticulate sound like a groan. Abruptly he laid his cheek on her hair. She broke away, trembling.

'Let's go down,' she said, walking across the floor. She turned at the door, he stood where she had left him. 'You'd better stop the gramophone, perhaps.'

She waited until he stopped it. He came to her, and took her arm above the elbow in a hard grip.

'Anne . . . I want to talk to you – somewhere where we can't be interrupted.'

'There is nowhere where we can't be interrupted,' she said in a low, defensive voice.

'We must make somewhere,' said George irritably.

'How can we?'

'Can't you go out in your car to the river, where we used to go – where we went that first day?'

'Oh!' Anne raised troubled eyes. 'Don't let's start that sort of thing.'

George dropped her arm and walked away from her. Restlessly, he walked to the fireplace and leaned his elbows on the mantelpiece. Then he turned again to her. His eyes were hard and hot and miserable.

'I never wanted to get into this damned mess,' he said.

He went to her again and took both her hands.

'You know what we've come to, don't you?' he said to her. 'Don't you?' he insisted.

Anne looked up.

'Yes,' she said.

A fierce, sweet flame ran through them both.

'Don't bicker about convention, then,' said George. 'I must see you. Tuesday. Shall it be Tuesday? At eight? Will that do?'

It was hideous having to arrange it like this. Anne made a movement of distaste.

'Anne, you must come,' he pleaded. 'I must see you. . . .

I love you, Anne . . . I love you still . . . I love you more than ever. . . .'

His voice began to burn and glow, his hands drew her.

'Stop,' she said, keeping him off. 'I'll come . . . but not this – here.'

She left him and went out to the stairs.

'Come and have an ice, dear,' called Mrs Yates, who was just leaving her bedroom with James in tow. 'Come with me.'

She put a motherly arm round Anne and led her away.

§ 2

It had come to the last day of Emily's miserable month of notice-serving. She climbed late to her room that Anne had made so pretty for her to come to, with apple-green paint and hollyhocks in the chintz.

She drew out from under the bed the Japanese basket-hamper she had always had so little use for. She had never been one for going away. She folded up her going-out dress of magenta cloth and put it at the bottom of the hamper. Then the grey jersey that had been washed and gone all shapes. Then the frilled caps she had put on her head in the afternoons to do credit to Anne. One by one her few belongings; and in the corners the plush box with the glossy photograph of Blackpool tower on the lid, the tin of camphor ice for her chapped hands, the ornament of the fat man with a nodding head that Anne had won once at the Fair. She took the lid and pushed the springy thing down on the hamper. It gave and twisted under her hands. She felt she had not the strength to battle with it. A feeling of such sickness came over her, that she gave up the attempt and sagged back onto the oilclothed floor.

The effort of packing over, her thoughts returned painfully to the groove they had worn in her tired head.

'She's letting me go. I've to go. I didn't keep my place . . . too interfering, that's what I was. If I just 'adn't gone into the drawing room that day . . . if only I 'adn't gone in. . . . I should have kept to my kitchen, in my proper place. There's something she doesn't want me to see. I know that, right enough. And it 'ull be a man at the bottom of all this. It's always a man that makes trouble with us women. There's no peace for us until we're too old to bother with them. Not but what the master isn't a gentleman. But queer in his ways. They're like two poor stones in the 'ouse, the pair of them. Sleeping in separate rooms. Why can't they be warm and comfortable together? She's changed. She's not the girl she was. She's got kind of secret – all wrapped up in herself. She doesn't want me. She doesn't want the master. But what's she going to do? She can't give 'im notice.'

At that unhappy word, Emily remembered herself. Tears welled up into her eyes, her chin quivered uncontrollably.

'I never thought,' she whispered, turning her head from side to side, 'as I'd have to leave 'er unkindly. I allus looked on 'er as a bit of my own. All as I've 'ad . . . all as I've 'ad. . . .'

'I'm nothing but a servant . . . an old woman . . . and where 'ave I to go now?'

The Japanese hamper bulged dangerously beneath the shock of her body.

'Oh, dear . . .' sobbed Emily, 'oh, deary me. . . .'

The door opened reluctantly. Anne stood in it and looked at Emily bowed over the hamper in the electric light, serene in the ceiling.

Anne frowned and her lips were folded straight, but in spite of that her eyes filled with tears, and she fumbled uncertainly with the door handle. Round and round she twisted the loose brass knob.

Emily did not hear.

Anne came slowly across the floor and stood beside the crumpled and desolate figure. She knelt down and put out her hand.

'Emily,' she said, reluctant, embarrassed, ashamed.

At the touch, Emily crouched farther into her own arms. The Japanese hamper almost disappeared beneath her body. Emily was launched on such a sea of woe as she had never charted before. Anne put her arms round her.

'Emily . . . you're not going, are you?'

She forcibly pulled Emily from the basket-hamper.

'Listen, Emily! I'm saying . . . you're not going. D'you hear, Emily? You're not to go. I can't do without you.'

'But I must,' moaned Emily. 'You don't want me 'ere.'

'I was mean,' said Anne humbly. 'I was horrible. But I couldn't help it. I feel all – all wrong, somehow.'

'I know,' sobbed Emily.

'But I don't want you to know.'

'I know you don't.' Poor Emily was fully aware that her fault was to know too much.

'But you're going to stay,' said Anne, kissing the wet,

crumpled cheek. 'You've got to stay, Emily. And forgive me for being so unkind.'

'I'll never pry again,' quavered Emily. 'I'll keep to my kitchen. I'll not know what you don't want me to. Not but what I can't 'elp seeing something's wrong – a blind cat could see that. But I'll not take no notice. I'll try to think on it's nothing to do wi' me. Oh . . . I'll mind my own business, love.'

§ 3

It was Tuesday, and nearing half-past seven in the evening. In the dreaming serenity of the garden, a blackbird sang late, and the light was wonderful on Richard's roses. Anne wandered from the garden to the house, from the house to the garden, waiting, yet dreading, the time to go to meet George in the wood.

Richard was out; playing golf perhaps. Emily was shut resolutely into her kitchen.

Anne's heart beat away the seconds with the clock. She stood with her fingers at her lips, at one window, then at another. She put on her hat and took it off again.

'I can't go,' she said, and sat turning it round and round in her hands.

In her mind, she saw George waiting in the wood. He would wait until the sun went down and the wood grew cold and grey. She saw how he would look through the trees for her. She put on her hat again, and went to get the car out of the garage.

Emily heard her go and clutched her Pansy novelette firmly, reading on.

Anne ran out along the great main road, into the quiet lanes, into a farmyard, where a friendly woman said she could leave the car, and smiled on her comfortably.

'Going to do a bit of courting by the river likely,' she said to her husband.

Anne went over the fields and plunged into the wood. Twigs cracked under her feet. She felt like a thief, like something furtive sneaking about, and she hated it passionately.

'What if he isn't there?' she thought. She had a fleeting hope that he would not be, so that she would be able to run back to the car and go home with a clear mind.

But he was there. They came face to face, she with her hand at her heart and her eyes dilated, and he eager, exulting that he had her alone at last.

They did not speak at once. He put his arms round her and held her very lightly, waiting. He watched her pale face tenderly, half-smiling, because he loved her every look. She did not look at him, but leaned against him, her eyes on the misty reaches of the wood. He put up a hand and took off her hat. He laid his cheek against her hair, and so they stood, silent. The old spell was on them.

'Anne . . .' he said, at last. 'Kiss me.'

She shook her head.

'Why?'

He tried to make her look at him, but she took his hand from under her chin and turned away.

'Anne . . . why?' he urged. 'Tell me.' He moved until his cheek was against hers, and felt the sudden warmth of her skin.

She did not speak.

'Kiss me,' he said again.

'I daren't,' she said, very low.

She felt that if that barrier went, all would go; that she would not be able to stop the flood that swelled in her; that she would drown, drown, drown.

She had forgotten her distaste for getting to George, of sneaking out to meet him, of leaving Richard. She stood trembling in his arms. He trembled too, holding his fierce want in check, forcing himself to wait, though he could hardly bear the waiting, knowing that he must not start her away.

He held her closer, and her heart beat against his hand like a wild thing.

The wood was very still, enwrapped in grey-green dusk.

She turned suddenly to him, lifting up her face.

'I must . . .' she said, 'I must kiss you.'

His eager lips closed on hers; a terrible, fierce ecstasy shook them both; then came a tenderness almost as unbearable.

He hung over her, looking his fill of her face at last, and she looking through half-closed lids at his. Her body was limp in the hard circle of his arm; his free hand caressed her hair, her ears; he wanted to touch, to hold all of her at once.

'My darling . . .' he murmured. 'Darling . . .'

'See!' he said, 'it's here still – this little piece of hair that springs back and makes a curl! They didn't cut it off, then?'

He pulled it out and let it fly back against her cheek and kissed it when it curled up according to its habit.

'It is a darling trick – that,' he said, and did it again.

A faint, happy smile curved Anne's lips. He looked long at her.

'Oh . . .' he broke out. 'You're too lovely – I can't bear it.'

Abruptly, he loosed her. She stood up and shivered suddenly without the warmth of his arms. She came out of the spell sufficiently to ask distressfully:

'George – what are we doing?'

He took her back into his arms.

'Hush!' he said. 'Don't let's think about anything but being together just now.'

'But I must . . .' cried Anne, 'I must think about Richard.'

'Is Richard entitled to it?' asked George. 'He ought never to have married you. He ought never to have married anybody – a detached, cold, scientific fish!'

'No, no,' protested Anne. 'He's nothing like that. . . .'

'Why did you marry him?' George persisted. 'I can't understand that. You never stopped loving me, Anne. Why did you marry him?'

'Why does anyone marry anyone else?' she asked. 'You're not responsible at twenty-two; you're incapable of knowing why you do things; you rush on from one thing to another, blindly, with no idea what you ought to make for.'

'I can't understand why you did it,' said George again.

'Oh, well,' said Anne wearily. 'It's done.'

There was silence. The sleek river flowed on without a sound at their feet.

'I'm going back to the Sudan.' George's voice came abruptly.

'George!'

He looked down into her startled eyes.

'Not alone, Anne. You won't let me go alone, will you?'

She dropped her hands abruptly from his shoulders, and would have withdrawn, but he held her closely.

'Anne, you love me. You know you love me. Come with me, then. It's the only honest thing to do.'

'Ah!' she said. 'If only it were as simple as that.'

'Anne, listen! I love you terribly. The boy's love I had for you was nothing to this. I was a poor, crude boy, full of suspicion – not capable of loving you as I do now. I love you with all my heart and soul. I want you. I know, beyond all doubt, that you are what I want. You complete me, you fill me up. Every want I have, you satisfy.'

He bent his head into her neck, and from that warm contact his voice reached her . . . 'Come with me, Anne! Come with me. . . .'

'Oh, but Richard . . . Richard!' she cried out above his head.

George stood up.

'Let's look at it squarely,' he said. 'What keeps us apart? You have no children.'

'No,' she said.

'Richard would let you divorce him.'

'Do you think I'd do that? It's horrible that women should get what they want that way. Let them go through their own mud.'

He took her in his arms again.

'Anne . . . Anne . . . here, close as you are to me, you know there's nothing else in life like this. What do their conventions matter? What can stand against this? Come with me! . . . To be together always! Think of it, Anne – think! Think!'

'I can't think,' she said almost fretfully. 'I can't think here with you so close. I must get away by myself to think.'

'Well, go and think. But I warn you, thinking is no good. If it had been, I should have been free of you long ago.'

He held her closer.

'Think as much as you like; but not now. Let's have this little time unspoilt, at any rate. Beloved . . .' His warm lips sought hers. Her head found again the hollow of his shoulder. Sighing, she thrust all else away and gave herself up to the exquisite joy of being where she was.

Gloom enwrapped the wood, and the chill of night crept like a ghost over the ungleaming river. But they were warm and close and unheeding.

Anne stirred at last.

'We must go,' she whispered.

Slowly, with lingering kisses, they emerged from their enchantment. They went across the grey fields with hardly a word and parted.

It was quite dark when Anne reached home. She ran the car almost without a sound into the garage. The long windows of the dining room showed yellow in the night; the curtains had not been drawn. Anne wondered if Richard were in the room; she wanted suddenly to see him from outside, as it were. She tiptoed across the grass to look in.

He sat at the table, his head buried in his hands. It looked as if he had been sitting like that a long time. It struck her that she had never seen Richard idle before. As she looked in at him, he moved his hands. One fell listlessly on to the table, and she saw that his face was tired, lined, sad. Richard was off his guard.

CHAPTER TWENTY-FIVE

§ 1

Anne went on, outwardly, with her normal life. She lived in the house with Richard and Emily; she shopped, she made beds, she went out in the car, she attempted to read. But side by side with this life she lived another – a life that rose in feverish anticipation to one high point – a meeting with George in the wood – and ebbed from this point in unhappy distaste.

'I'm not cut out for an intrigue,' she told herself with something like scorn. 'Why do I do these things if I can't carry them right through? If I will do them, why do I regret them? I ought either to go on and not regret them; or stop and be free of this nagging conscience.'

But she went on. She went on.

Her life was divided into two halves: the life with George and the life with Richard. She would emerge from the ecstasy of a meeting with George, to a painful and acute realisation of Richard. . . . Strange, she mused, that she should understand Richard now better than she had ever done. The affair with

George had thrust him on her consciousness. She saw the new lines on his face, and knew that she had put them there. She heard now his indrawn sigh – which, whenever he was conscious of it, he held and let go noiselessly. She understood his dogged and desperate occupation of his hands and brain. The odd, tortuous workings of Richard's personality were becoming comprehensible to her by this new insight. His fineness and strength hurt her. They hurt her.

'Oh, God . . . what a muddle I am in!' she said over and over again.

George and she met publicly everywhere. Although social life had become an irritation and a bore to them, they went to the usual Bowford affairs so that they could be together. No one seemed to be aware of the surge of their passion under the smooth surface of conventional behaviour. No one saw George's burning eyes on Anne as they dined at the same tables; no one knew that when they danced together, they were caught up into a particular heaven of their own – from which they made mechanical and empty replies to the chatterings of the people outside it.

The snatched kiss, the furtive touch of hands – Anne loved it and she loathed it. What had once been young, clear, happy between these two, was now heavy and hot and furtive.

'I must go with him – or I must stop this. I can't bear it,' she said to herself.

But she went on – driven.

All this waiting, this hand-holding, this shuddering closeness, these terrible kisses, the restlessness, the madness, the cruelty . . . 'I hate it,' she said with tears.

And there was always Richard, quiet, tortured, waiting too. The strain told on Anne.

'How ill the child looks!' Mrs James Yates had time to notice that, even on the triumphant day of Mildred's first At Home.

As Mildred's friend, Anne was helping, although Mildred had a butler and a parlourmaid and her mother and the bridesmaids. She walked about over the deep carpet, handing dark wedges of wedding cake to expensively-dressed women. Mildred, radiantly happy, was enthroned behind a dazzle of silver. Anne had a second of self-pity.

'Why couldn't I have been happy like that? Even if it goes, she will have had something.'

She went on handing cake to new arrivals.

Mrs Yates was at the very summit of her social triumphs; at the summit, though she did not know it. Her bright brown eyes beamed on the company; her be-ringed hands pressed their hands with eager affection. She loved them all; she loved them for being rich; for having pearls and fur coats and limousines and servants; she loved them for coming to see Mildred, who was also rich and had all that they had. She looked round on the luxurious room and consciously loved that too. What a setting for her child! She looked at Mildred and her eyes softened with tears. So lovely . . . and so well married.

'Oh, George, dear boy, how nice of you to look in!' She bustled forward to welcome her nephew. George, above her head, looked swiftly over the guests. Ah, there she was! His heart clamoured Anne, Anne, Anne. She turned and saw him, and the colour ran up into her cheeks. He was here; and soon, she knew, he would arrange to be alone with her, so that he could seize her in his arms and kiss her over and over again. She trembled in anticipation of that.

'Oh, I must – I must think this out. I must decide something,' she said to herself.

She handed him the wedding cake.

§ 2

Mrs James Yates was putting on her hat – the hat she had worn for Mildred's wedding, a black one covered with white ospreys. She smiled in the mirror as she adjusted it. She smiled at her thoughts as well as at the hat, which she considered a beautiful hat and a prosperous-looking one. She was going to slip over to see Mildred for half an hour or so. Mildred's last At Home day had been yesterday, and so many people had called on her and so much had happened, that Mrs Yates felt she must slip over, although unexpected, to discuss things. It was really very nice, she reflected, twiddling her veil to a point under her chin, to have Mildred married and living in such a beautiful house as Green Lodge, looking so lovely and important handing the cups to the butler to pass round. Secretly, Mrs Yates did not care for the butler. He looked contemptuous when he handed the cucumber sandwiches, and Mrs Yates was sure she heard him whistling with unbecoming nonchalance in the hall. His eyebrows were permanently in his hair. But Mrs Yates felt that he was one of the penalties of prosperity, and must be put up with.

'I'm just going to run over to see Milly, James,' said Mrs Yates, putting her head into the drawing room. 'Are you coming with me?'

'Er . . .' James looked over his eyeglasses and thought of the butler. 'N-no, Henrietta . . . I don't think I will this afternoon. Perhaps the child will be popping over later. It's very warm.'

'All right. Goodbye for the present.' She beamed on him, blessing him for her feeling of happiness.

She walked slowly along the warm roads. She smiled round on the world, clasping the wrist of one beige kid-gloved hand with the fingers of the other, her elbows resting on her capacious hips. She sailed along, looking from the undulation of her ospreys as if she were borne by some invisible and balmy breeze denied to less prosperous mortals on this hot day.

She was very happy. Her thoughts were busy with the idea of giving a few little dinner parties, if only that Minnie wouldn't be such a fool at table and would manage to keep her cap straight on her stupid head! Not that the girl was bad. Mrs Yates was quite fond of her, when no company was present. A few little dinner parties . . . She knew quite a lot of people to ask now. And Brian and Mildred were such an asset. And George too. A slight disturbance crossed the surface of Mrs Yates's placid happiness. She wondered why for a moment, and then remembered that Frances had said that George was talking about going abroad again.

'Can't stand the Bowford life.' An echo of George's restlessness reached his aunt.

'How ridiculous!' she said, closing her eyelids at a branch of laburnum hanging over a wall. 'How *wicked*! Not to be able to stand Bowford . . . what could he ask for better than this? People all so kind, and him in such a good position now. . . .'

She came to the small side gate into the Green Lodge garden and paused. She preferred to make her entry by the big gates and the drive, but it was very hot, and Mrs Yates was by no means thin and easy to move about.

She sacrificed effect to comfort and went in by the side gate.

Ah, the beautiful house, the elegance, the wealth it displayed from the outside, the rows of long windows draped with the most delicate net and the most expensive velvet. This was Mildred's house, and through Mildred, she, Henrietta, had a share in it and basked in its atmosphere of elegance.

The door of Green Lodge stood wide open to the summer air. The hall was empty, a space of cool black-and-white marble. Mrs Yates smiled with relief to think she was escaping the butler. She tiptoed across the hall, smiling, expectant, towards the voices she heard on the other side of the half-opened drawing room door.

She was arrested by the sudden raising of Brian's voice; something in its tone made her pause. . . .

'My dear Mildred,' he was saying, 'let us quite understand each other. Your mother is impossible. I utterly refuse to have her here with the Brashers. Your mother, my ridiculous infant, must be kept in the background. . . .'

Her ears straining, her eyes dilated, Mrs James Yates stood in the middle of the chequerboard hall like a discarded pawn.

A rush of blood crimsoned her face; there was no sound of Mildred's voice; no protest; no defence.

Only steps coming in the direction of the hall, indicating the advance of the butler. Very pale now, Mrs Yates turned and went out as silently as she had come in. As unnoticed, she left by the small side gate, retraced her steps along the hot road. Gone now was the proud port and the beneficent beam. The ospreys drooped over her bowed head like weeping willows. Feeling it was a very long way, she got home somehow – home to James, who was watering the garden.

'Come in, James, will you?' she said to him, in such a quiet voice that he dropped the watering can instantly and hurried after her.

They went into the drawing room and shut the door. She told him, twisting the beige kid gloves, what had happened.

He gazed miserably at her, his small feet encased in linen spats wound round the legs of the mahogany chair.

'Oh, James!' she faltered. 'What mistakes we've made! We've brought her up wrong. What's all this?' She waved her gloves over the expensive comfort. 'It can't help us now. Our girl's ashamed of us. Her husband's made her ashamed of her father and mother. It's our fault. We've brought her up to be able to be ashamed of us.'

Tears came slowly into the eyes of James, making them strangely glassy.

'It's not been anything to do with you, James,' said Henrietta. 'It's my fault. It's my fault. I'm to blame.'

A sob raised her ample bosom. Little James stumbled to her and clasped her in his arms.

'Don't say that, Henrietta,' he begged. 'Don't, you've been such a good mother. . . .'

'No – no,' she sobbed into his shoulder, 'always after the wrong things for her; always telling her things weren't good enough for her; and now her husband's told her we're not good enough. We've lost her, James.'

Through their weeping, they became aware of the grind of brakes at the gates.

'Someone's here!' cried Henrietta, jumping up and dabbing at her eyes. 'Oh, dear!'

She hurried to the mirror over the mantelpiece and adjusted her hat, patting and pulling at herself and constricting her lips into a smile.

She hustled James through the French windows to compose himself in the garden, and turned to find Mildred in the doorway, her arms full of roses.

With a difficult effort, Mrs Yates forced herself to be natural.

Mildred embraced her closely.

'Mother,' she said, 'I just had to see you; just to look at you, if it's only for a minute. And see! I picked every single rose I could find in the garden for you.'

Mrs Yates's reply choked in her throat. She smiled tremulously as she held out her hands for the flowers. Over them she looked again at her daughter. The child had certainly been crying. Such a passion of maternal love rose in her heart that she bit her lips to keep from crying it out. Mildred wasn't ashamed of her, then? She didn't think her mother was impossible? She didn't side with her husband? She still loved her poor, foolish mother. . . . The roses shook in the storm of emotion. Mrs Yates turned them round and round agitatedly, pretending to admire and smell at them, using them as a screen for her convulsed face.

'Will you come to dinner on Tuesday with the Brashers, Mother, and Daddy too, of course?' Mildred looked quickly at her mother, and quickly away again. She too was bent on hiding traces of her recent tears.

Mrs Yates was calm enough to speak at last.

'No, dear, I don't think we will. I think Father and I would rather come when you are alone, so that we can be comfortable and quiet.'

'Oh, but, Mother, do come . . .' Mildred burst out, forgetting her red eyes in her amazement.

'No, dear, thank you very much.' Mrs Yates was quite firm.

Mr Yates came through the window. He looked as if he didn't know whether he was permitted still to kiss his daughter. When she flew to hug him, his little downcast face brightened dangerously. He whisked off his glasses, and polished them with his handkerchief.

'It's very warm,' he breathed; 'it's really very warm indeed.'

'Here's Mother refusing to come to dinner with the Brashers on Tuesday,' said Mildred.

'I'm just saying we'd rather go when Milly's alone, James – so that we can have her all to ourselves. That's what I mean, dear.'

'Mother's right, Milly,' said James, breathing heavily on his glasses and rubbing away with his handkerchief. 'We miss you very much, and when we do see you, want to be selfish and have you all to ourselves.'

'You are two naughty things,' complained Mildred. She was very puzzled that their decision should have come so pat on her first quarrel with Brian. She was still terribly sore from that – hurt and bewildered, longing to be comforted by her mother, and yet unable to breathe a word of what had happened. For the first time in her life, Mildred felt apprehensive of the future. Brian had been so cold and hard. . . . He had sneered so uglily; and at her mother. That was unforgivable. Mildred was all at sea.

The Yateses sat on the drawing room chairs and avoided each other's eyes. An awkwardness had fallen upon these three who had always been so happy together. At last Mildred got up to go.

'I shall have more callers today, I suppose.' She sighed. How was she going to sit handing cups of tea to the butler when her heart was heavy?

She went away in her car.

Mrs and Mr Yates came slowly back to the drawing room.

'She's a good girl, Mother,' said James huskily.

'Yes, we haven't spoilt her heart,' said Henrietta, with tearful gravity. 'Only laid up a lot of trouble for her.'

She sighed deeply.

'A lot of trouble,' she said again.

And James, saying nothing, felt its heavy presage.

CHAPTER TWENTY-SIX

Anne was waiting to be alone; waiting to come to a decision this night. They knew, in the house, that one way or another this thing was coming to its climax. Anne's eyes told them, at times unseeing, at times aware of them as never before.

It was a painful meal, that last meal of the day. Anne, pale in her place; Richard opposite, his lips folded in repression, his eyes obstinately lowered; Emily going in and out with dishes, striving desperately to pretend not to notice anything, but darting covert, anxious glances at Anne and Richard.

'Eh, dear me . . .' she whispered to herself, going back to the kitchen. 'Dear, dear me. Oh, Our Father!' she suddenly burst out, 'let it come all right between them two. Oh, Lord, let it come all right between them! I ought to be kneeling down, but I must take the pudding in quick. Please excuse me for that, this once, oh Lord! Amen.'

She went back to the dining room a little comforted. Anne looked up and saw Emily's face transfigured with love. She looked swiftly away again.

Anne had held off her thoughts for so long that she did not know how they were ranged; whether for George or for

Richard. She looked at Richard across the table and wondered if this would be the last meal she would ever have with him. Tears stung her eyes at that; an intolerable desire to cry out to him to help her, to appeal to him in some way, seized her. But she stifled it, and went on eating pudding with stiff lips. The meal got to an end at last.

Emily came in to clear away. Richard and Anne went into the drawing room. Richard sat under the reading lamp, turning over his newspaper. Anne held a book. The clock ticked on the mantelpiece; coal fell softly in the grate.

'Have I sat here long enough?' Anne wondered.

Very quietly, she put down the book. Richard went rigid at her first movement, holding his breath. She got up and went to the door. There she lingered, looking back at him.

'Good night,' she said huskily.

'Good night,' he said to her. He lifted his head and looked at her for what he thought might be the last time.

'Good night,' she said again.

She left him, still looking after her. She left Emily standing about in the kitchen. She went upstairs and shut herself into the Wood room. She sat on the bed, but gradually, as she struggled to think this thing out, she slipped to the floor, clenching her hands on the green eiderdown, digging her fingers into its soft resistance.

From the loved little print, Max's *Anna Brigitta*, holding her kingcups, stared with the unconcern of childhood at Anne, torn with mental stress, under the serene electric lights in the bland ceiling.

'What a muddler I've been . . . muddling through school,

muddling through home, muddling through the office, muddling into marriage, muddling into – what now? No. I won't muddle into this. I'll see it straight. I'll know what I'm doing this time.'

She stared before her, twisting her hands. She was making the effort of her life.

The clock on the table ticked the hours away.

Still she knelt by the bed; tears ran down her cheeks and fell into the puffed folds of the eiderdown; they dried stiff on her cheeks; more fell and dried unheeded. Once she buried her head to stifle the hard sobs that shook her. Then she was calm and still. She got up at last, and went to the old yellow desk.

'I'll write to him . . .' she said. 'It's the best way.'

She shivered in the chill of the night, and drew up a chair. She found some paper in the little pigeon-holes that once held such fascination. She found some paper, and a pen, but she could not begin this letter to George. How could she tell him? She stared before her. The little clock struck two; the house was very still.

She began to write, slowly, forcing the words out of herself, putting down one difficult phrase after another.

'George, I have been thinking about life tonight. I can't make anything of it. I can't make anything of religion; I have no principles of any sort to guide me. I can't see any purpose in my life, or that I matter at all. I can't see *why* I should stay here with Richard rather than go with you. Only one thing I can see clearly, and that is that I must, that I am obliged to be, true to my own self. To go with you and leave Richard feels wrong. Therefore, to me, it is wrong. To other people it could be right; they could go. If I went against my own conviction, I should ruin your life and mine. Why didn't I see this before? Why – why? What a lot of unhappiness it would have saved. But I have been a muddler, George. Looking at myself tonight, I see that I have just been wandering loosely about causing disaster to you and Richard and my own self. If only I could have seen this before . . . but better now than too late.

'Perhaps you won't see anything in this conviction of mine that I can't leave Richard. I don't feel that you will. So you think what our lives would be if we went away together. You would lose your job. Your war record wouldn't save you. Remember Elliott Reade. VC though he was, he was asked to resign from all the Boards he was on. You might get another job; never one as good. People won't have co-respondents – even abroad – in important posts. People would cut us. You couldn't bear it. You like to do well, George. And I love you to like to do well. Think of your mother and father. It would break them completely.

'And what sort of a compensation should I be for all you had lost? I don't know what I should become – drifting about abroad, a drag on you, with no children. If I were divorced, I should have no children. I would never let a child suffer as I did. It was out of all proportion, I know. But you don't reason when you're young; you only suffer.

'Could we ever be happy?

'Oh, we should be happy at times. So happy that I daren't think of it. I daren't think, George – I daren't remember what it is like to kiss you. I have kissed you for the last time. The last time in this life. I can't write any more. Go away – and never see me again. Not till I am old and past this. Go away and work, George. Don't hate me for doing this again. Yes, hate me – if it makes it any easier.'

She bit her swollen lips to keep back the sobs that someone might hear. She thrust, with fingers made clumsy by trembling, the letter into an envelope, stamped it, wrote his name and address. She stood up from the desk. No more thinking now. It was done – must be done, finished. She would go out and post it now, get it beyond recall in the pillar box under the lamp-post.

She opened her door, and looked out into the darkness of the house. Not a sound. She felt her way down the stairs, fumblingly undid the latch and went out into the garden, leaving the door open for her return.

The cool of the night was sweet on her hot eyes. She drew long trembling breaths. She was very tired. The pillar box stood solid and significant under the greenish light of the lamp. She held the letter in her fingers through the gaping slit; held it, then let it fall.

'It's gone,' she said. 'Gone now. Oh, George! George!'

Weeping she had come into his life, and weeping she was to go out of it.

She turned back to the garden, and slowly climbed the path, lost in her tears.

Suddenly she came to a rigid halt. What was that? That strange reiteration – a whispered, strangled sound over and over again.

'God – God – God.' Out of the darkness. 'God – God – God.'

And something dark and twisted against the house wall.

She ran forward.

'Richard!'

The figure against the wall hardened into stillness. There was complete silence. A little wind lifted the leaves with a sigh and passed on.

Anne put out a hand and touched her husband.

'Richard.'

After a pause, he spoke in a voice drained of tone.

'Haven't you gone yet?'

'I'm not going,' she said, very low.

'Not going,' he repeated.

'No,' she said, moving nearer.

They leaned, each in their places, against the wall of the house, motionless.

Richard broke the silence by a strange laugh.

Still they stood there.

'Let's go into the house,' said Anne, at last.

She suppressed a cry at the sight of his face in the light – ravaged, bloody from the rough contact of the wall.

He sank into a chair, and covered his face with his hands. For a long time he stayed like that, while she stood, wrung with pity, above him.

'I can't grasp it,' he said, with the same unsteady laugh. 'I thought you'd gone.'

'No.' She knelt on the floor by him. 'Forgive me,' she said.

Richard lifted his head and smiled with such sudden poignant sweetness that it hurt her intolerably.

'Not a word of that,' he said. 'No forgiving. I'm not fit to have you . . .'

Anne put a hand over his mouth.

'Don't talk like that. What's the good? Let's begin again, differently. But I must have something to do. I've thought about that. I must work. I shall go to your clinics. I shan't like it. I don't like other people's babies in a mass; but I'll do that until I have children of my own.'

Richard smiled tenderly at her. His face was controlled again and quiet.

'That's right. Work's the thing. And you have some of your own to do. It's time those notes and tales were turned to account. Time you began to hack them into shape.'

Anne smiled wearily.

'Is it worth while?' she asked.

'Never ask that about anything,' said Richard earnestly. 'Do it – and you'll find that it is. Now sit here. I'm going to get you something hot.'

She sat by the dead fire. She remembered, against her will, the hours of unhappiness she had spent sitting in this room. Would it be any different now? All ecstasy, colour, fire had gone with George.

As she waited, she became aware of a strangeness – a pit-patter of sound, almost noiseless, yet like singing rain. She turned her tired head towards the windows, listening. From the indistinguishable rustling, there emerged a single note – pure and clear like water.

In spite of herself, Anne got up from her chair.

'A bird singing in the middle of the night?'

She threw back the curtains, and saw with aching eyes the faint radiance of the east.

She turned to her husband, coming back into the room.

'Richard!' she called out. 'It's the dawn!'